The year is A.D. 2806. The interstellar diaspora from Earth has been in progress for nearly seven centuries. The numbers are uncertain, but at least five hundred worlds have been settled, and perhaps well over a thousand. The total human population of the galaxy could be in excess of a trillion. On Earth, the Confederation of Human Worlds still theoretically controls all of those colonies, but the reality is that it can count on its orders being obeyed only as far as the most distant permanent outpost with Earth's system, on Titan. Beyond Saturn, there are two primary interstellar political groupings, the Confederation of Human Worlds (broken away from the organization on Earth with the same name, with its capital on the world known as Union) and the Second Commonwealth, centered on Buckingham. Neither of those political unions is as large or as powerful as they will be in another two centuries, when their diametrically opposed interests finally bring them to the point of war. In the meantime, humans who need military assistance, and do not want the domination of either Confederation or Commonwealth, have only a handful of options. Those who can afford it turn to mercenaries. And the largest source of those is on the world of Dirigent. . . .

Ace Books by Rick Shelley

CAPTAIN

RICK SHELLEY

ACE BOOKS, NEW YORK

This is a work of fiction. Names, characters, places, and incidents are either the product of the author's imagination or are used fictitiously, and any resemblance to actual persons, living or dead, business establishments, events, or locales is entirely coincidental.

CAPTAIN

An Ace Book / published by arrangement with
the author

PRINTING HISTORY
Ace mass-market edition / March 1999

The Penguin Putnam Inc. World Wide Web site address is
http://www.penguinputnam.com

Check out the ACE Science Fiction & Fantasy newsletter
and much more at Club PPI!

ISBN: 0-441-00605-1

ACE®
Ace Books are published
by The Berkley Publishing Group,
a division of Penguin Putnam Inc.,
375 Hudson Street, New York, New York 10014.
ACE and the "A" design are trademarks
belonging to Penguin Putnam Inc.

PRINTED IN THE UNITED STATES OF AMERICA

10 9 8 7 6 5 4 3

Three years earlier, Lon Nolan had not known what a pavane was. Now he was dancing one—if not with the grace of a sixteenth-century European nobleman, at least without tripping over his own feet or stepping on anyone else's. He was not fond of the music; he found it somniferous; but pavanes were routine elements to formal officers' dances in the Dirigent Mercenary Corps, so he had learned the rigid patterns . . . and to suppress the yawns that the music regularly induced. The tunic of his dress white uniform, with its stiff, high collar, helped keep him alert and helped ensure that he kept his back straight and his head high. It was that or have the tabs of his collar bite into his neck.

He had found dancing lessons to be an almost ludicrous sidebar to his service in the DMC. To a greater extent even than in the North American Union on Earth, military officers were expected to be "gentlemen" as well, and the formal recreations imposed by more than a thousand years of military tradition were observed as if they were Holy Writ.

"It's something to get used to," Captain Matt Orlis, Lon's company commander, had told him early in his career. "It can be important to advancement."

"What do obsolete dances and the formal etiquette of a class of people who no longer exist have to do with being a good soldier?" Lon had asked at the time.

Orlis had smiled and shook his head gently. "Tradition. Look at it as similar to the formalized contests we hold in the martial arts. No one gets seriously hurt even though we're using abilities that can be deadly in combat. Or running around a track, going as fast as you can to get back to where you started. When you get right down to it, does that make any more sense?"

"Running is good physical exercise," Lon had said, slightly miffed that running—something he was exceptionally good at—might be compared to effete dances.

"You think dancing isn't exercise?" Orlis had asked with a laugh. "You've seen professional dancers. Have you ever seen people in better physical condition? Except maybe for someone who's just completed our recruit training, that is."

Lon had found the captain's amusement annoying, but he restrained himself. "Seriously," Orlis continued, "sometimes it's not enough to be the best soldier. You have to be good, but you also have to be noticed. That's important to an officer who wants to get ahead." He paused for an instant. "That may be unfortunate, but—so far as I've been able to determine—it's been that way in every army that has left anything more detailed than official histories."

"Sucking up."

"Not really. Call it 'playing the game.' Coming off like a complete toady is self-destructive."

There were a half dozen major balls in the social calendar of the DMC, and lesser affairs about every other week except during the hottest months of summer in Dirigent City. The lesser dances could be safely ignored by junior officers. The major balls could not. Lon counted himself lucky when a contract or training kept him from those. But contracts had been rare for the Corps during the past two years. There was, for the mercenaries of the DMC, an unhealthy epidemic of peace. The only contract for Lon's unit had been three months training a militia that faced no immediate threats. There had been no combat. And, at the rate things were going, it might be a considerable time before a combat contract appeared.

•   •   •

The music ended. Lon bowed to his partner, Angelika Demetrios, daughter of 12th Regiment's executive officer, and smiled. She smiled back.

"I believe I need a breath of fresh air," Angelika said in a timid voice that was as artificial as the pavane.

"It is a bit stuffy in here," Lon replied politely, his smile growing at his own thoughts of the stuffiness of the music.

Angelika took his arm—though they scarcely touched— and let him escort her to the veranda on the eastern facade of Corps Headquarters, which also served as Government House for Dirigent. She was dressed all in white. The dress was of some stiff material that helped to keep her physically separated from anyone else. She wore white gloves. Her only jewelry was a strand of white artificial pearls. Her high-heeled shoes, also white, were (in Lon's down-to-earth view) totally impractical. Even with three-inch heels she was considerably shorter than he, and Lon Nolan was far from being tall.

At one time Lon had been surprised at the number of young women who attended these balls. *Almost a meat market,* he had thought. Senior officers, both currently serving and retired, appeared to parade their daughters and nieces (and occasionally granddaughters), attempting to find husbands for them. Once past his initial consternation, Lon had found himself cynically unsurprised at how often those efforts were successful. Family connections could be helpful to an ambitious junior officer. The grand balls were more, though. They were attended by married officers and their wives, and by those retired officers as well—some of whom had left active service fifty years before Lon was born.

"It's a shame there are no stars out tonight," Angelika said once they were away from the six pairs of double doors that connected the grand ballroom to the veranda. They were almost away from the music as well, but they were not alone. At least a dozen other couples had made the migration.

Lon shrugged stiffly. "At least the rain is holding off,"

he said. *What I'd really like to see is a large moon in the sky, Earth's Moon,* he thought. Dirigent had two insignificant moons of its own, scarcely larger than Deimos and Phobos, the moons of Mars. Dirigent's moons had proper names, Aurora and Vesper, but to most of the men of the DMC, they were Rat and Mouse.

Angelika leaned against the balustrade. Light from the ballroom seemed to make her brown eyes twinkle. Her complexion was as pale as the marble of the veranda. She was not unattractive. "These affairs are so . . . artificial," she complained. Lon was surprised. It was the first sign of individuality he had noted in her. Until then she had seemed interchangeable with a dozen other young women he had escorted to balls of this type. He smiled.

"I noticed," he said.

"People can't really get to know each other. It's 'wear this' and 'do this, that, and the other thing,' just the way people have been doing them for generations. My father had pictures of his grandmother taken at one of these affairs, and this dress might be the exact duplicate of the one she wore."

"It's a pretty dress," Lon said.

"It's like wearing razor wire," Angelika said. "And it makes me itch all over."

Maybe there's hope for you yet, Lon thought. *Maybe there's a real person in there after all* "Sometimes this dress uniform feels as if the collar is going to slice my head straight off."

They laughed together. Lon felt himself relaxing a little. *It would be nice if we could see each other when we could behave and dress like real people instead of figures in a tableau,* he thought. But he had learned enough about Dirigent society to restrain any impulse to suggest that. It would mean approaching her father for permission to see her, and *that* could be seen as tantamount to a declaration of intent to court her seriously . . . two steps short of engagement. Nor did Angelika suggest it.

"You're from Earth, aren't you?" she asked.

"Yes. North America." Lon was no longer surprised

when someone brought that up. His accent was certainly not Dirigentan, and he was not the only Terran in the DMC. "I've been here more than three years, though. This is my home now. I doubt that I'll ever go back." That statement still brought an uncomfortable feeling to his stomach, but he could not deny its truth. Going back to Earth would be . . . problematic.

"I visited Earth once," Angelika said. "Father was a delegate to some official conference and he took Mother and me along. We were there a month, but I didn't get to see much, just a few of the famous sites in Europe. But there were so many *people* everywhere. Sometimes I wanted to scream and just run, find someplace where I could be alone."

"It is crowded," he admitted. "And it can be dangerous, not at all like Dirigent."

"Father told me that Earth has twenty cities, each of which has more people than all of Dirigent."

Lon nodded. "At least twenty. There's both good and bad about that. A lot happens when you put ten or fifteen million people close together, not all of it bad."

They talked for another ten minutes before Angelika suggested that they go back inside. Just before they entered the ballroom, she asked, "Do you miss it? Earth, I mean."

Lon swallowed before he said, "Sometimes."

One day each week, while the men of Lon's two platoons drew fatigue details around the base, Lon's duties took him to Corps headquarters. "Part of the continuing education of a young officer," he had been told. Of late his work had been in the contracts office, going through intelligence reports on worlds where contracts might be in the offing, and studying reports submitted by contract officers. There might come a day when he would be sent out to evaluate a possible contract, even negotiate employment for part of the Corps. And, with business as slack as it had been for the past two years, his duties *might* give him a little advance notice if a contract were due for his men.

That made the reading, the detailed assessments, easier to bear. It also helped that Lon's day was Monday, which gave him that much longer to recover from any excesses of the weekend. There had been fewer of those lately, for a variety of reasons. Janno Belzer had left the Corps, four months after his marriage, taking civilian employment with the Corps that would continue his accrual of time for retirement. And Lon's forays into Camo Town, the section of Dirigent City that existed to serve (and service) soldiers, with Phip Steesen and Dean Ericks, had diminished in frequency. The gap between officer and enlisted man, always present, seemed to weigh more heavily on all of them after many months without a combat contract. Lon found himself more in the company of other officers, and not just on duty.

"I know it's as much make-work as anything," he told Lieutenant Carl Hoper, who commanded Alpha Company's other two platoons. "It's not as if anything I write or think is going to make any difference, but it could be worse." They were eating lunch in the junior officers' cafeteria at Corps Headquarters.

"You never can tell, Lon," Carl said. "Sure, they *hope* that everything's been thought of before one of us gets to it, but there's always a chance that you'll see something, notice something no one else has. Different perspective, that sort of thing. Especially you."

Lon had not been paying a lot of attention to his own talk. Hoper's comment caught him off-guard. "Why especially me?"

"You're from Earth."

"Right next to the bearded lady and the sword swallower?"

Carl laughed. "Different perspective, what I said. You've walked a different road than most of us. Somewhere down the line, don't be surprised if they want you to take a six-month tour in intelligence, for just that reason."

Lon feigned a shiver. "That's not for me. I'd go batty. I'd rather do thirty-mile hikes every day."

"I'm not sure I'd go that far, but I know what you mean. Still, it's something to think of. Not all of that work is stuck in an office here, if you know what you mean. They get to travel. Or so I understand."

"You done a tour with them?" Lon asked.

Carl shook his head. "No more than what you're doing now. I don't have anything . . . special to offer. You do."

"Just because I'm from Earth?"

Carl shrugged.

That's not soldiering, Lon thought. *All I want to do is be a soldier* That had been the mantra that led him to Dirigent in the first place.

Third and fourth platoons of Alpha Company, 2nd Battalion, 7th Regiment, DMC had changed considerably since Lon Nolan had first stood in formation with them. It was not just the departure of Janno Belzer. Men had died. A few, like Platoon Sergeant Ivar Dendrow, had chosen medical retirement rather than continue after rehabilitation. There had been promotions to fill gaps in the table of organization. Tebba Girana was now third platoon's sergeant. Dav Grott had been promoted to corporal and had second squad. Jez Aivish had become first squad's leader following the death of Heyes Wurd. Ben Frehr still led third squad and Kai Eathon still had fourth. In fourth platoon the changes were even more extensive. Weil Jorgen was still platoon sergeant, and Wil Nace still led first squad, but the rest of the platoon had seen 90 percent turnover in three years. In third and fourth platoons combined, only twenty-seven of the men under Lon's command had been there when he became platoon leader.

The changes went right up through the organization. Colonel Gaffney had been succeeded as regimental commander by Colonel Ian McGregor, who had previously commanded the regiment's 3rd Battalion. But McGregor had died—mysteriously, some said—in an accident that should not have happened . . . and should not have been fatal in any case. Now Colonel Medwin Flowers had the regiment (and its seat on the Council of Regiments), and 2nd Battalion was commanded by Hiram Black, who had been promoted to lieutenant colonel on gaining the new post.

Tuesday morning, 10 September, Lon held his platoons in formation after the battalion's duty parade had been dismissed.

"If you've made any plans for this weekend," he told his troops, "get them canceled before noon today. Don't get your hopes up though, it's not a contract." He paused briefly to scan the ranks. Only his two platoon sergeants had been told what was coming. Lon had received the orders late the previous afternoon.

"This afternoon we'll be shuttled over to the Nassau Proving Range near Bascombe East. Beginning tomorrow, and continuing through Friday of next week, we will participate in field testing of a new piece of equipment that could be extremely valuable to us . . . if it works the way the brain-boys say it will. I can't tell you anything else about it now. No fatigue drills or training this morning. Get your areas squared away, get ready for movement. Dismissed."

He did not linger. The platoon sergeants were already calling orders to squad leaders. Lon headed into the barracks, aiming for his office on the second floor. His own kit was already prepared, but there was always red tape to tie in pretty knots for the chain of command to play with. In garrison, the bureaucratic fodder seemed to multiply on its own.

Captain Orlis was waiting in Lon's office. He gestured Lon around to his seat behind the desk. "You'll have quite a bit of company on your little jaunt," Orlis told him.

"I figured that," Lon replied. "Brain-boys to evaluate the tests, techies to make any adjustments, that sort of thing."

"In spades and doubled," Matt said. "If your preliminary tests come off, don't be surprised if you get spectators from the Council for the last rounds next week. That's unofficial, confidential, and you didn't hear it from me. This is a biggie. If it works, it could make a world of difference to us.''

Lon nodded. ''I read the file. A safe way to get munitions and food to troops on the ground when a shuttle landing is impossible sounds great. But if it's as simple as the, uh, prospectus makes it sound, why wasn't it done a century ago?''

''Wouldn't surprise me if we've been working on it that long. The code number on this item should give you a clue, XRS-one-seventeen.''

''Meaning the first hundred and sixteen attempts flopped?''

''Some may never have gotten off the computer screen.'' Orlis grinned. ''Just make sure you and your men keep your heads down and listen to what the techs tell you. The buzz is that this one works.'' Lon did not ask about the captain's sources. Like most native Dirigenters in the Corps, Orlis had his own network of relatives scattered throughout the munitions industry.

''What ship is being used for that end of the tests, do you know?'' Lon asked.

Orlis shook his head as he got to his feet. ''Haven't heard. Not that there aren't plenty they *could* use. Look sharp on this job, Lon. It might not be a contract, but it is important.''

2

Since this was not a paying contract, there was no parade of buses through Dirigent City to the civilian spaceport. Lon's platoons were bused to the landing strip on base and loaded on two transport shuttles. Lon rode the first shuttle, with third platoon. Fourth platoon was on the second shuttle. Neither group was crowded, even with barracks bags and a number of crates of cargo that had already been aboard when the troops arrived.

"Not the item we're to evaluate," Lon told Sergeant Tebba Girana in response to a direct question. *Perhaps the control units,* he thought, but he did not share his guess, since he was uncertain. There were numbers stenciled on each case, but those offered no clue to the uninitiated.

"Why all the secrecy?" Girana asked. The men were all in combat kit, complete with battle helmets. Girana talked to his lieutenant over their private circuit.

"I don't know, Tebba," Lon said. "I guess a lot of people think they have a lot riding on what we're going to do."

"I hope it works. I've been too many places where counting bullets was more than an exercise for the quartermaster."

"You and me both, Tebba."

The flight to the Nassau Proving Range, three hundred miles east of Dirigent City, was almost casual. The training transports were not as powerful, or nimble, as attack shuttles, and there was no reason for the pilots to attempt

records along the way. The flight remained solidly subor-
bital.

Ten minutes before the shuttles' ETA, Lon stood and
moved to where all of the men in third platoon would be
able to see him. He clicked his radio over to a channel
that would also connect him to fourth platoon in the other
shuttle—flying formation a hundred yards to the right.

"There's no drill on landing, men," Lon started. "We
disembark in an orderly fashion, unload our gear, and
move toward our temporary quarters. We've got the rest
of the afternoon to get squared away. The job doesn't start
until tomorrow morning. I'll give you the schedule as
soon as I get it. We're going to be up to our necks in
outsiders, people from Corps R&D, techies and so forth,
and no doubt a few civilians as well. Mind your manners.
They've come up with a gadget they think will make it
possible for us to get essential resupply in the field when
a shuttle can't get in. For those of you who have been in
combat, you know what that can mean. Let's do the job
right."

Lon no longer felt self-conscious making speeches like
that, and he no longer looked for reactions from his
men—boredom or suppressed laughter.

The barracks, mess hall, and other troop facilities at Nassau Proving Range were almost primitive. They had been
built by troops of available material—logs and rough-
hewn beams and planking, the chinks filled with clay.
Over many years the buildings had been improved now
and again, to add the comforts of base, but they retained
their rustic look. *Like a fort out on the western frontier
in North America a thousand years ago,* Lon thought as
the caravan of trucks approached the stockaded compound
where his men would be living for the next ten days.

Laboratories and inside testing facilities were different.
Those buildings had been constructed of plascrete, composites, and metal, offering ideal conditions for the techs
and others who would use them . . . and any visiting VIPs
who might come to observe tests. Set well apart from the

cruder-looking troop facilities, the "permanent" buildings lined several hillside terraces, with plascrete bunkers on the top of the hill offering a safe vantage for observing tests that might be dangerous—an explosives range was in the next valley to the southeast.

The only civilian staff onsite when Lon's platoons arrived consisted of only six people, two maintenance men, and four who worked in the kitchen. A platoon of military police served to guard the facility. None of the military or civilian technical staff who would be in charge of the tests had arrived yet.

"They'll be coming in first thing tomorrow morning," Lieutenant Shaesel Ourf, the commander of the MP platoon, told Lon when they met in the troop compound.

"Just as well," Lon said, looking around. "Give us a chance to settle in first without them tripping over us."

Ourf grinned. "I can bounce that all day," he said. "I like it best here when it's just us and empty space."

"This a permanent post for your lads?"

"We rotate the duty, draw three months here every two years. A platoon that's lucky sees nothing but nature."

Lon grinned. "Sorry to spoil your luck."

The MP lieutenant shrugged. "Fall of the cards. We've had six weeks of the good life. Life's a bit casual here, most of the time. A lot of us look forward to it."

"Food all replicated, or do you get fresh in?"

"When it's just us, it all comes out of the machines, but I've been alerted that there's a supply transport coming in this evening with vegetables, fruit, and meat. They like to treat the brain-boys and techies right, and when the nobs eat fresh, so do the rest of us. Evening chow is at seventeen hundred hours. You'll join me?"

"Honored," Lon said. They were, for the time being, the only officers on base. "What about the town, Bascombe East?"

Ourf chuckled. "Calling it a town is a bit much. Two hundred or so permanent residents. They provide civilian workers here and for a small armory and replicating factory." The Corps had dozens of scattered sites, insurance against any attack against the world that might disrupt production in and around Dirigent City. "One pub, one restaurant, hotel, general store. Fifteen miles west of here. The only transport is what we have."

"Sounds cramped. They equipped to deal with soldiers on pass?"

"Maybe two squads at a time. You find out when your men will have free time, we'll do what we can to arrange transport. In any case, we've got beer in the dayroom."

Lon made an informal inspection of the troop bays to see that the men were settled in, and to answer the inevitable questions—mostly about the chance to get out and have a drink.

"You just got here, lad," Lon told one of the newer privates in fourth platoon. "We're here to work, in case you've forgotten." But he said it mildly, not as a rebuke.

"I don't know the schedule yet," he told each group of men. "Looks as if we won't know until the R&D folks get in tomorrow morning. Supper will be coming up shortly. After that, get comfortable. There's a dayroom across the way. Get plenty of sleep while you can."

On the inside, the barracks looked as modern as anything at the Corps' main base back in Dirigent City. Lon found his room rather larger than his usual accommodations. His gear had been set next to the bed. Junior officers did not rate aides to pack and unpack for them. They had to do for themselves.

Lon took his own advice and got a good night's sleep—a rare seven hours undisturbed. His room was between the troop bays where his platoons were billeted, and he was flanked by the platoon sergeants. In the morning, after a brief and informal reveille formation, they all went to breakfast, to find that the civilian cooks had already started using some of the fresh foods that had arrived the evening before—eggs and ham.

The shuttles bringing the research and development team started to arrive while breakfast was in progress.

"I guess that's my call," Lon said after hearing two shuttles come in for their landings. "My orders are to report to the team leader upon his arrival."

Lieutenant Ourf smiled. "Finish your breakfast, Lon. You've got plenty of time." He touched his left ear. There was a radio receiver plugged into it. "It'll be a while yet before they're ready for anything."

An hour later the two lieutenants walked to the lab offices on the lowest terrace on the hillside. Altogether, some three dozen people had arrived, along with two small ground-effect trucks and several pallets of crates. A lead sergeant with a Technical Corps emblem in the center of his chevrons directed them to the team leader.

"I'm Major Joseph Pitt," the man said after returning the salutes of the lieutenants. "Nolan, you brought the men who are going to do the testing?"

"Yes, sir."

"We'll have a lengthy briefing on the testing protocol after lunch, followed by instructions on the equipment and operating procedures. Field testing won't begin until tomorrow. My people will need the rest of today to get ready. The only delay might be if the weather turns sour. We want perfect conditions for at least the first round of testing."

"The XRS-one-seventeen will make it possible for a platoon on the ground to receive resupply of ammunition and food directly from an orbiting transport or a shuttle standing off out of the way of hostile fire," Pitt told the men of third and fourth platoons. Lon stood off to the side to be able to watch both the presentation and his men.

"Each platoon will be issued two ground-control units once the system becomes fully operational. It will add no more than twelve ounces to a soldier's load, and link through his helmet communications system. The supply capsule, a small rocket, will be launched by ship or shuttle on a trajectory to bring it within visual range of the target unit, which will guide the capsule into a soft—and extremely precise—landing, just where it's needed."

There was video, and a series of animated charts. Pitt turned over the podium to a gray-haired man in a white lab coat, who went through the procedure step by step as he narrated another animation.

Then the civilian went through the extensive safety protocols. "This is still experimental, you understand," he said, looking slowly around the room, as if waiting for nods of understanding from each of the soldiers. "We are dealing with explosive rocket fuels, and—in field operations—these capsules will also customarily be carrying ammunition. In our first tests, the target landing sites will be no closer than one hundred yards to any personnel on the ground. Later, if early results warrant the step, we will bring that distance down to more . . . practical limits."

"They want us to guide freakin' bombs right down on our own heads," Phip said to the men of his squad during the break following the orientation lecture. It would be fifteen minutes before the platoons were given separate close instruction on the operation of the units—hands-on instruction.

"Even your skull doesn't have a radius of a hundred yards," Lon said. Phip had not seen him coming. "Look at it the other way around. You've been places where ammo was just a memory. If this works, it boosts everyone's odds of coming home from even the worst contract."

Phip turned, not at all embarrassed. "I know that, Lieutenant," he said—they were on duty. "I just don't fancy being a guinea pig."

"They're not going to risk necks. The rockets will be coming in with inert cargo and just enough fuel for the range. Until they know it works and is safe." Lon looked around at the other men of third platoon's second squad. "They've got to have field troops to test gear, because we might see problems that the brain-boys would miss. But they're not going to risk anything they don't have to. Besides, we're going to have civilians hanging around.

Even if they might not worry too much about us, they're going to be mighty careful of their own necks."

Lon remained with the civilian briefing officer for an hour after he had dismissed his men. "I want to know exactly how it's supposed to go," Lon told the researcher. "I need to be at least as proficient with any equipment as any of my men."

The civilian blinked once, then nodded. "I suppose you do at that," he conceded. "Let's get comfortable. I'll take you through the whole procedure in the simulator, then explain exactly what's supposed to happen every step of the way."

By the time he had—literally—sweated his way through the guidance and retrieval of three simulated supply capsules, Lon's hands were trembling. He felt as if he had completed a strenuous physical workout. "Thanks," he told the civilian, Alec Deradier. "I hope it works that well in practice. This gizmo could make a big difference to us. I expect you know that."

Deradier smiled. "Not as well as you seem to, but I've heard the same from other line officers."

"I don't want to step on any toes, but I understand that R&D has been working at this for . . . well, a long time. Some special problem?" Lon spoke tentatively, not at all certain how Deradier might respond to what he might take as criticism.

For a protracted moment, the older man did not speak. He pursed his lips and appeared to be intently studying the tip of his nose. Then he cleared his throat. "Yes, a long time," he said then, very slowly. "We've had the theory well in hand for more than a decade. And, far longer than that, we could have produced a system that would allow a ship or shuttle to place a resupply capsule on the ground within, shall we say, a five-meter radius of its target. The problem arises because of the need for control of the incoming capsule from the ground. Combat situations can change quite quickly—I am told," he added with a self-conscious glance at Lon's face. "We would not want to land supply capsules where the enemy might get to them first, or where retrieving them might be too dangerous for our own people. That limits the speed of the capsule to what human perception and reactions can handle, which makes enemy intercept easier, and so forth. To balance all of this has proven difficult."

"Have the capsule reach the vicinity of its target at the fastest speed possible, still allowing for the man on the ground to direct it to a precise landing," Lon said.

Deradier nodded. "Exactly. An enemy surface-to-air missile does not have to limit its speed. There have been times when I have almost despaired of finding a workable solution."

"But now you think you have?"

"We hope."

Lon nodded. "I wonder if, perhaps, there is one consideration you might not have taken note of. I apologize if this seems presumptuous, but the reactions of a man in a real life-or-death combat situation can't be adequately approximated in safe field tests. The only way to know for sure, even if everything works perfectly here, is to try them with troops on contract, in a situation where they are faced with an immediate enemy and *need* ammunition to survive."

Deradier shrugged. "That is most difficult to test under any other circumstances," he agreed. "We have likely not given it the fullest of consideration for that very reason. But I might venture to suggest that the parallel is closer than you seem ready to concede. True, your troops will not have the fear and uncertainty of combat to heighten reflexes, but neither will they have any long regimen of too little sleep and constant worry and work to slow those reflexes. In any case, before we could proceed to that sort of testing, we must be satisfied with the controlled experiments."

Lon woke early the next morning, after a restless night. The simulations had played themselves back, with variations—mostly unpleasant—in his dreams. He had seen himself directing a life-saving capsule of ammunition and food in ... only to have it explode in a terrific fireball, consuming all of his men. There was a background of maniacal laughter to the explosion.

It can't happen like that, he assured himself when he woke trembling from the fears of sleep. *It's not possible, even in combat, and certainly not here and now. They won't let it happen.* But his hands needed a moment to stop trembling, and he could not wait to get into the shower to wash away the sweat that had come with his nightmares.

Breakfast was a hurried affair. Trucks were waiting to carry Lon's platoons to the testing area. The R&D people would go separately, carrying the control units and their monitoring equipment. Another team was aboard the shuttle that would be used to fire the capsules into the testing area.

"I want my squad leaders to be the first to try steering in the capsules," Lon told Deradier and Major Pitt. "That gives you experience and steady hands, and they've all been in situations where a barrel of bullets from heaven would have been welcome."

"Probably an excellent idea, Lieutenant," Major Pitt said, nodding. "It's something we didn't cover in our test protocols, and likely we should have. We've got a bit of leisure here. We're only going to fire one rocket at a time, and before a second is launched—if it is—we'll analyze the results of the first. So let's get your first man equipped, and Dr. Deradier will go through the procedure with him once more before the shuttle takes off."

Lon chose Dav Grott to make the first attempt, and hovered nearby while Deradier coached the corporal through the steps again, then attached the controller to Grott's helmet. "A simple joystick, nothing special at all," the civilian said. "Two buttons to control the maneuvering jets." He spent several minutes issuing maneuvering instructions then and watched Dav as he operated the controls. "Good. Good." Deradier nodded several times. "I think you'll do fine." He turned to Pitt. "Major, I think we're ready."

Lon's platoons were deployed in a permanent trench paved and lined with plascrete. Deradier and Pitt remained with them, close to the radio equipment that connected them to the shuttle that would launch the capsules. The rest of the R&D team was dispersed around the area, some in a bunker behind the trench, others in redoubts at the edges of the test area.

"The target is that red X in the center of the white circle out there," Deradier reminded Dav Grott. A large tarpaulin had been staked to the ground. "One hundred yards out. We're not looking for great precision, Corporal. You're not firing for a sharpshooter's qualification. Somewhere close to the target would be nice, but today we're more interested in the total maneuvering time once the capsule comes within control range."

Lon noted that he was sweating again. His hands were balled up into fists at his sides. *Almost like my first combat landing,* he thought, trying to force himself to relax. He was not too close to Dav. Grott was flanked by Pitt and Deradier. But he was close enough to hear Major Pitt talking to the shuttle pilot.

"Twelve minutes until the shuttle reaches the test area," Pitt reported after he finished that conversation. "Then we'll set up specific timing for the first capsule launch. Relax, Corporal. I'll let you know when it's time to tighten up."

Dav, wearing his battle helmet with the faceplate up, managed a weak grin. "I'll try to remember that, sir," he said.

The shuttle would make its run from south to north, releasing the capsule at fifteen thousand feet, six miles south of the target. The capsule's main rocket would accelerate the projectile until it was within a thousand yards—vertically and horizontally; then retrorockets would fire to start slowing the capsule. As soon as Dav spotted the capsule—with a lot of other eyes to assist him during the test—he would take over manual control to bring it into the target. *Fast enough to make it hard for an enemy to destroy it, slow enough so the primers on the ammunition aren't set off,* Lon thought. But the only payload this capsule would carry would be testing equipment to judge the impact and record the detailed course and second-by-second speed of the landing.

There was a twenty-second countdown before the launch. Eyes and cameras watched the sky, looking for the first sight of the capsule—the test units had been painted a bright red to make that as easy as possible.

"There it is!" A dozen men might have yelled that simultaneously. Once the rocket had been spotted, the rest went too quickly for anyone to do much more than watch. Except for Dav. He juggled his joystick and pushed buttons, biting his lower lip as he concentrated—so fiercely that blood was trickling onto his chin before the job was finished.

The performance was not polished. At the end, the watchers could see the capsule jiggling around, almost going into an end-for-end spin, but it did come to rest—with the force of an object falling from fifty feet—within thirty feet of the center of the cross on the tarp.

A cheer went up from most of Lon's men. Dav Grott nearly collapsed in exhaustion.

"It's too soon for cheering," Alec Deradier said, almost under his breath. Lon scarcely heard him. "Was it within the necessary parameters?" He turned to look at the blockhouse, where the main bank of instruments were housed. Several of his men were already hurrying toward the capsule, flanking the small wheeled cart that would bring it in for further examination.

3

It was Saturday afternoon before Lon got to look Bascombe East over. Lieutenant Shaesel Ourf drove him.

"My platoon sergeant can handle anything that comes up," Ourf assured Lon. "Doesn't really matter that we've got R&D people in. They pretty much stick to themselves, unless they want something." Ourf wore civilian clothes. Lon had to make do with a khaki staff uniform. He had not brought civilian clothes along.

"It's not as if they can't get hold of us if they really want to," Lon said. Both officers had pocket radios to connect them to their platoon sergeants and the research people.

"Well, it's not too likely that the R&D people will show up in town. If we see them, they're as likely to pretend they don't know us as anything. The civilians are booked at the hotel for the weekend, but the ones I've seen here in the past tend to stay with their abracadabra machines pretty much all the time."

"I couldn't wait to get away from it." Lon shook his head. In two days, only six tests had been run, with mixed results. One capsule had gone completely haywire when the retros were fired, and the shuttle had been forced to shoot it down before it could stray from the airspace over the proving ground. The other five had all been maneuvered in, but the time spent getting them in had been marginal—according to Deradier.

"I'd offer you the full tour of Bascombe East," Ourf said as they reached the town, "but you can see it all from here. My suggestion is that we head straight for the pub."

Lon laughed. "Sounds good to me. What are the locals like?"

"Peaceful sorts. Life runs a lot slower in Bascombe East than in the city. Like I said, a couple of hundred people live in town. Farmers come in from about twenty miles around, those who don't want to go as far as Donnelly or Jameson." Those were the nearest sizable towns—though neither could boast more than fifteen hundred residents. "Saturday and Sunday are the big days, even when there aren't soldiers in from Nassau. Folks come for dinner and maybe a drink or three. Later on, in the fall, they have a theater group, amateur stuff. Put on their shows in the hotel ballroom."

"Sounds like more fun than fancy balls at headquarters," Lon said. Ourf laughed but didn't argue the point.

The pub was The Winking Eye. Its sign was holographic. The eye did appear to wink as a person moved. Inside, there was an amber cast to everything. The lights were a dusty yellow. After the brightness of the clear afternoon outside, it seemed almost dark. Lon noticed the smell of beer as soon as the door opened, and felt warmth pouring out through the opening.

"That's one thing I've noticed," Ourf said softly. "They keep the place too damn hot for comfort. I guess they think folks'll drink more to cool off."

"Bet it works," Lon replied.

They headed directly for the bar. The barman grinned when he saw Ourf. "Afternoon, Lieutenant," he said in a loud, cheerful voice. "Didn't realize your lads were back at the Boomer. What can I get for you, beer?"

"Beer for both of us, Mr. Pine," Ourf said. "My friend here is Lieutenant Lon Nolan. He and his men are out at Nassau to help with some tests."

"Good afternoon, Lieutenant Nolan," Pine said. "First round's on me. Drew the short straw for guinea pigs, did you?"

Lon smiled. "I guess you could say that. Makes a

change though, and welcome at that. Pleasant place you have here.''

"I like to think so.'' He drew the beers while he talked and set them in front of the lieutenants. "If you'd like to eat later, we have a ripping good pot roast, with all the trimmings.''

"Sounds good.'' Ourf turned to Lon. "Mrs. Pine does the cooking, and you'd have to travel a far piece to find better.''

"My mouth's watering already, Mr. Pine,'' Lon said. "One of my best childhood memories is Sunday pot roast. I expect it'll taste every bit as good on a Saturday.''

"Just give a shout when you're ready to tuck in,'' Pine said.

Shaesel and Lon exchanged glances, then both turned back toward Pine. "Now seems as good a time as any,'' Ourf said.

"Find yourselves a table.'' There were two vacant. The other three had one or two people each, and there were four other customers at the bar. "I'll have Sara bring your supper out.''

"Sara his wife?'' Lon asked as they took seats at the table nearest the rear of the room.

Shaesel chuckled. "His wife's name is Mildred. Sara's his daughter. And something else!''

Lon had started to raise his stein but stopped before it reached his lips. "That good, huh?''

"Just wait till you see her.''

"You've definitely piqued my curiosity.'' Lon took his sip of beer, then adjusted his chair so it gave him a better view of the door that appeared to lead to the kitchen. He leaned back and drank casually over the next few minutes.

A young redheaded woman came out of the kitchen, carrying a tray. She wore a long white apron over a pale green dress. Even from across the room, she appeared strikingly beautiful. Lon's impression grew stronger as she came toward him. He set his beer down, almost missing the table.

"Two pot roast dinners,'' Sara announced when she

arrived. Her voice was cheerful, light, and she was smiling. "Good to see you back, Lieutenant Ourf." She gave Lon a sidelong glance.

"Sara, this is Lon Nolan. He's in at Nassau for the next week or so. Lon, this is Sara Pine." Lon didn't notice Ourf's grin. Neither did Sara. She was looking at Lon.

"Good afternoon, Lieutenant," Sara said. "A pleasure to have you here." She set the plates, napkins, and silverware on the table in front of the officers. "I hope you'll both enjoy your dinner."

"I'm sure we will," Lon said. He hoped he wasn't stammering but he wasn't sure. His eyes were too full of the view.

Sara smiled even more broadly, then turned and headed back to the kitchen. Lon stared after her, and was not even embarrassed when she glanced over her shoulder just before she reached the door and saw that he was still looking. She winked, then disappeared through the doorway.

"That," Shaesel said after a half minute, "is Sara." Lon was still looking at the door, as if hoping that she would come back for a curtain call. "Don't let your food get cold, Lon. And quit drooling. Officers aren't supposed to drool."

That took a few seconds to register. Lon turned back toward the table, shaking his head slowly. He looked at the food—ample portions of meat, browned potatoes, and carrots—then glanced at Shaesel. "Is she married or anything?"

Ourf had already started to eat. He paused with his fork in midair. "Not that I know of, but it's been a couple of weeks since the last time I was in here. Go ahead, eat. You don't want to insult her mother's cooking."

That seemed to penetrate. Lon started eating, but he had difficulty concentrating. He kept looking for Sara. When she came out with a tray for another table, Lon's head turned and he nearly missed his mouth with a forkful of food. He set the fork down and gave Shaesel a sheepish look.

"I don't usually get so distracted by a pretty girl," he said. "Never like this."

"At least it shows you're not dead. How's the food?"

Lon looked startled. Food was the last thing on his mind. "Good," he said after a hesitation. "Excellent, I guess."

"And you've been going at it like cold leftovers from the worst mess hall in the Corps," Ourf accused. "Take a deep breath, take a drink, and pay attention to what you're eating. You won't find better even in the senior officers' mess at headquarters."

It was difficult, but Lon did manage to focus on his food for a couple of minutes. It *was* good, the best he could remember, and it deserved to be savored. "I'm really not like this most times," Lon said after pausing to take a long drink of beer. Sara had gone back to the kitchen.

"I'd almost say that she seems quite taken with you, too," Ourf said, catching a hint of Sara looking out through the kitchen door, holding it just barely ajar. "Too bad you're only here for a week."

Lon blinked twice, then looked directly at the other lieutenant. "Have you always had this trace of sadism?"

"Always," Ourf said, laughing. "My greatest failing. I guess that's why I joined the MPs."

Sara came out to ask how the meal was. "Excellent, as always," Shaesel Ourf said.

"The b-best I can recall," Lon stammered, feeling his face flush, and feeling even more embarrassed at the way Sara grinned at him in reply.

"Can I get either of you another beer?" she asked then.

"I think we could both use one," Shaesel said, sparing Lon the chore of another reply.

"Right away," Sara promised, heading toward the bar.

"You ought to get out more," Shaesel said, leaning closer to Lon. "A pretty girl always get you so tongue-tied?"

"Not like this." Lon took a deep breath. "Never like

this. Is it just me, or does she affect everyone the same way?''

''More or less, at least the first time.''

''What about you? You have designs on her?''

Ourf laughed. ''My wife would kill me. That's something else about being a military cop. There's no pressure to stay single until you're over the hill. MP companies go out on combat contracts only a little more often than pigs fly. Long contracts with a lot of time in between, mostly. My company hasn't been off-planet in fourteen years. But if I were single. . . .'' He didn't bother to finish the thought. He didn't have to.

Lon hurried to finish his beer before Sara arrived with its replacement. ''I'll be back to clear your plates away when you've finished,'' she said, smiling but looking only at Lon.

''I swear, you must have affected her the same way she affects you,'' Shaesel said after she left again. ''I see her quite a bit, see her smile and then forget a new lad, except for normal courtesy, but she's going out of her way. Maybe you ought to chat her up, even if you're only going to be here a week.''

Lon nearly choked on the food he was attempting to swallow. He coughed a couple of times into his napkin, then washed the food down with beer. ''I don't know if I'd remember how to act,'' he said. ''Back in the city, there are the girls of Camo Town and the princesses at the formal balls, and I don't think Sara fits either category.''

''You're right there, but then, officers are supposed to be resourceful.''

Lon looked at the kitchen door, then toward the bar, where Sara's father was busily wiping the counter. ''I should have a word with Mr. Pine, tell him that my boys will be around for the next week, that sort of thing.''

''He's a good sort. Anyone from Nassau gets a little rowdy, he gives me a call and we come and slap a killjoy on the lad's arm and make sure he pays for any damages and apologizes. Then it's all been said and done. Never had the same lad get out of line twice here—mine or visitors in like your lot.''

"Still . . .''

"Finish your supper. Then you can compliment him on his wife's cooking, too,'' Shaesel said with a chuckle. "This is a real homey place, not like anything you've ever seen in Camo Town—unless it's changed a lot since the last time I was there.''

"Probably not,'' Lon said. Two minutes later he had finished eating, and he started glancing toward the bar again.

"You should talk to Sara instead of her father,'' Shaesel said, looking unconscionably amused. "I know I would be, were I unattached.''

"One thing at a time,'' Lon said, well under his breath. He pushed the chair back and got to his feet.

"Take your beer,'' Ourf advised. "Talking's thirsty work.''

Lon almost managed to knock the glass over trying to pick it up without looking. He went to the bar, and took up a place near the end where Mr. Pine was standing.

"Sara could have brought you a refill, Lieutenant.''

Lon glanced at his beer. "I wanted to have a word with you, sir,'' Lon said. Pine nodded. "As Lieutennant Ourf said, I'll be at Nassau for the next week. With my two platoons. I imagine that most of the men will be in, when they get a chance. The first probably sometime in the next hour or two.''

"Always happy to see 'em,'' Pine said. "I did five years in uniform myself, back when I was a lot younger, and single. Might have stayed in if I hadn't met the missus.''

"They're good lads, but . . . well, some of them aren't used to quiet, respectable places like yours. I don't *think* that any of them are likely to cause trouble, but if any of them *do* get a little too . . . boisterous, just let me know and I'll get them straightened out in a hurry.''

"Not to worry, Lieutenant. If I can't keep 'em quiet, I just have a word with Lieutenant Ourf and he handles it. Never a ruckus. I do know what it's like.''

Lon nodded, took a drink of his beer, then said, "And please tell Mrs. Pine that the food was the best I can recall. It was absolutely delicious."

Pine grinned as if the compliment had been directed at him instead of his wife. "She'll be pleased to hear that, Lieutenant. She sets great store on her talents in the kitchen—and they are considerable." He patted his stomach in emphasis. "But why not step back into the kitchen and tell her yourself. Come along, lad. I'll introduce you."

Lon felt an instant of panic, but he followed Mr. Pine to the far end of the bar and into the kitchen. Sara was just coming out, carrying food for one of the tables. They did not actually come close to a collision, but Lon felt all sorts of warnings going off in his head as they passed within inches of each other. Sara Pine was two inches shorter then he. She looked up and smiled, and from such close range, the effect was devastating. Lon felt his heart fluttering. And then she was gone, through the doorway and into the public room.

"Mildred, here's a young man I'd like you to meet," Mr. Pine said, not quite shouting to his wife, whose back was to him. She was working at the stove.

Lon could see the resemblance between Sara and Mildred Pine. In her time the mother might have been every bit as beautiful as the daughter. She was still comely, in a matronly way, with a little more weight; her hair was darker than Sara's, more brown than red; the face was fuller, and showed a few lines. She wiped her hands on her apron as she turned.

"Mildred, this is Lieutenant Nolan. He and his lads are out at the Boomer for the next week. Lieutenant, my wife."

"Mrs. Pine." Lon nodded. "I told your husband that the pot roast dinner was the best food I could recall. It was."

"Why, thank you, Lieutenant." She beamed at the compliment. "It's nice to be appreciated." She paused for a second, giving her husband a look that Lon could not decipher. "You say you'll be around for a week?"

"I'm afraid that's all," Lon said, surprised that he felt regret. "We're to go back to Dirigent City next Friday."

"A pity," Mrs. Pine said. "Still, I guess a lad in uniform can't pick and choose where he gets to serve."

"Not unless he's the General himself," Mr. Pine said with a chuckle. "I hope you've got plenty of food on hand, Mildred," he added. "The lieutenant says his lads will start coming in fairly soon, and if I know soldiers, they'll be hungry."

"We can feed more than a couple of platoons, as you know full well," Mildred said. "You'd best make sure you've got a couple of fresh kegs ready to hook to the taps. Soldiers will be more thirsty than hungry."

"There's plenty of beer, and everything else," her husband said, feigned indignation over her suggestion that he might not be prepared. "But I'd best have my own supper now, before they arrive. I'll have Sara watch the bar for a bit, while I eat." He turned toward the door, turning to Lon at the same time. "Perhaps you'll keep her company, Lieutenant," he said as he led Lon to the public room. "I know she'll enjoy that."

Lon could not even stammer a reply.

"Well, Lieutenant, how are you enjoying our quiet little town?" Sara asked when she arrived behind the bar and went to where he was standing—a little numb.

"What I've seen, I like fine," he managed. "But please, my name is Lon."

"And I'm Sara." She giggled, and Lon felt as if his head would explode from the surge of blood that rushed to his face.

"It is a nice town," Sara said, seemingly oblivious to Lon's predicament. "But, well, one of these days I'd like to live in Dirigent City. See a little more. Here, everyone knows your business, and everything else about you. It's like being on display twenty-five hours a day. Nice folks, but still . . ."

"There's a lot to be said for a place like Bascombe

East," Lon said. "Always a friend close by if you need a hand. People who know you and care. A big city can be a lonely place."

"Oh, sure. I know all that. But it would be nice—for a change at least, a few years maybe. Be on my own. Work at a job where I actually got paid, except for the occasional tip." She was smiling, even through the implied criticism.

There was a brief gap in the conversation, which Lon filled by taking several short drinks of beer.

"There's one thing I've wanted to ask," Sara said, appraising him openly. Lon set down his glass and met her gaze.

"Your accent," she said. "You're not originally from Dirigent, are you?"

He shook his head. "I was born and raised on Earth. I've been here more than three years, though. Closer to four."

"Earth? Really?"

"Really," Lon said with a smile, not surprised at her reaction. He had encountered that response quite often. "Eastern North America."

"My family was originally from New Zealand," she said. "Came here centuries ago."

"I've seen pictures of New Zealand, but I never got there," Lon said. "I didn't do a whole lot of traveling."

"I've looked at just about everything on the nets about Earth, especially New Zealand," Sara said. She shrugged. "There's a lot of time for stuff like that here."

Lon was unaware of the slight sigh he emitted before saying, "I don't expect I'll ever get back. Dirigent is my home now, and better—in a lot of ways—than Earth. Not nearly so crowded."

Mr. Pine came out of the kitchen and moved behind the bar again. "Thanks, Sara," he said, giving her hand a squeeze. "You both look as if you could use a breath of fresh air. Why don't you take the lieutenant out for a short walk, Sara. Show him around. Your mother and I can handle things around here for fifteen minutes or so.''

Is everyone trying to set me up? Lon wondered as he fought a sudden surge of something that felt a lot like panic.

4

Lon held the door for Sara, then followed her out of The Winking Eye. It was not quite sunset, though the sun was hidden behind the buildings of Bascombe East and the forest that surrounded it. After the warmth of the pub, the temperature outside felt almost chilly. But welcome. Lon felt gooseflesh rising on his arms. *Maybe not just from the temperature,* he thought. Sara had not seen, but Shaesel Ourf had raised his beer in salute, in front of a broad grin, as the two left.

"I think my father put you on the spot," Sara said, moving away from the door, then turning to face Lon. He moved closer.

"Maybe, but I'm glad he did," Lon said, and he was rewarded with a slight blush from Sara.

"He does everything but throw me at young officers who come around the way you did. I'm sorry. That's the way he is. He moans about there being no good 'catches' here, then goes into high dramatics every time I suggest that I could move to Dirigent City. Says he can't bear the thought of me alone in the big city, with whatever dangers he's dreamed up most recently."

Lon had no idea what to say. He felt as if anything that might come out would sound foolish. But to keep from standing mute he said, "Your father suggested we take a walk. Shall we?"

"If you'd rather go back and drink, I'll understand."

"I can drink anytime. A chance like this . . . who knows?"

She smiled and lowered her blue eyes. "At least until

we find a place where we can sit," she said in little more than a whisper. She took his arm and they started walking.

At first they were both silent. Lon was glad for the respite. There were too many things rushing around in his mind. He needed to get control of his thoughts—and fears. The latter revolved mainly around the possibility (quite great in his imaginings) that he would make a complete jackass of himself and suffer terminal embarrassment. He needed to use the biofeedback techniques he had learned to slow the way his heart was pounding. *I never felt like this even going into combat,* he thought, squeezing his eyes shut for an instant.

The few businesses in Bascombe East flanked the main street, occupying little more than a short block. There were houses beyond on either end, and more off of the one crossroad. There were a few other pedestrians out, but no one gave any obvious notice to the young couple.

"I do wish I was going to be here longer than a week," Lon said when they came to the end of the block. "And I've got no way of knowing if I'll ever get another chance for duty at Nassau." Then he realized how his words must sound and stopped, flustered. "I'm being presumptuous," he said apologetically.

Sara held his arm more tightly. "I wish you were going to be here longer, too," she said. "I was afraid that I was just having foolish girlish fantasies, though." She turned more toward him then, leaning almost against him.

This can't be happening, Lon told himself as he hesitantly leaned toward her. *This is like something out of some sickening romance vid.* Almost without the active will of either of them, they kissed, tentatively at first, then almost with desperation. Sara put her arms around Lon's neck, and he put his arms around her body, and they pulled each other into a deeper embrace.

"I never believed in love at first sight before," Lon whispered when the kiss finally ended. Their mouths were no more than an inch apart. *Lieutenants aren't supposed to fall in love,* he thought. *It's not on the program.*

"I did," Sara replied. "I always believed in it."

A week. I'm only going to be here a week. His mind started racing again, and the edge of panic now was different than before. It was no longer acting foolish he was afraid of, but that a week—the few hours of it he might manage to spend with Sara Pine—would not be enough to make plans . . . and make certain that this sudden mutual infatuation held any substance.

"I think my brain has gone AWOL," Lon whispered, leaning his forehead against the top of Sara's head, rubbing against her soft hair. The fragrance of her shampoo or perfume was too heady to resist. "There's so much to say, so much to think about, but all I want to do is hold you tight until I'm sure this isn't some bizarre dream come to torture me."

"I know," she said. "I feel the same way. My head's all awhirl. I keep thinking my heart's going to bounce its way straight out of my chest. I've never felt this way before, Lon." She pulled back a little and stared into his eyes. It was the first time she had called him by name. "Lon," she repeated.

"Sara."

That exchange brought them to another kiss, not so deep or prolonged as the first, more with tenderness than passion.

"We're making a spectacle of ourselves here," Sara whispered—breathed—when it ended. "We should at least move around the corner."

"Or right out in the middle of the blinkin' street so folks won't have to crane their necks," Lon said. Then he thought, *I can't believe that came out of me. My God, my men will be coming into town any minute.* "But maybe you're right," he said with an unaffected sigh. It would not do to have his men arrive and spy their officer in a passionate clinch in the middle of the street. "This might be considered 'conduct unbecoming an officer.' "

As naturally as if they had been doing it for years, they moved side by side, Lon's arm around Sara's shoulders, her arm around his waist. She leaned her head against him as they walked, turning the corner away from the town's business street.

What the hell are we going to do? Lon wondered. *There's no manual to cover this.*

"There's a gazebo in the park." Sara pointed across the side street and ahead. "There are benches inside, and it's about as private a spot as we could find."

Not private enough for what I really want, Lon thought, but he did not ask questions. He simply steered them across the vacant road toward the park and into the gazebo that appeared to be its centerpiece. He saw no one else in the park or along the way. It was nearly dark behind the trellises that bounded six of the gazebo's eight sides.

They sat on one of the benches that lined the trellised sides of the structure. Rather, Lon sat on the bench and Sara sat on his lap, sideways, her body twisted so she could get her arms around his neck.

"I think I'm a little out of my depth," Lon said. "There's so much to say, so much to do, but I can't think straight."

"I don't want to think. I just want to enjoy, and dream," Sara said. She closed her eyes and scooted around a little so she could lay her head on his shoulder.

For a few seconds Lon let his eyes close as well, holding her, enjoying the feel of her weight on him, and the incredible thrill of her. Then his eyes popped open, and his body gave a start. *I'm still presuming,* he thought, as shocked as if he had received a stiff electrical jolt.

"Sara?" He waited until she opened her eyes and looked at him. "I think maybe I'm still taking too much for granted."

"What do you mean?"

"Well, I . . ." He stopped, swallowed, then tried again. "I mean, well, we just started. . . ." And stopped again.

Sara giggled. "I feel that way, too."

He held onto her as if she were a life preserver and he were adrift on a hostile ocean. "We're both *assuming*, but we haven't *said* anything."

"There'll be plenty of time for words," Sara assured him.

He stroked her cheek. "We do need a few words now," he said. "Like, 'Will you marry me?' "

"Of course I will," Sara said, her tone suggesting that the question was unnecessary. "Now kiss me again. Let's leave the thinking for later."

Lon was not certain how long it had been since they had left The Winking Eye. "Your father's going to be wondering where you are," he said eventually. They were still snuggled up together on the bench in the gazebo. They had moved hardly at all in however long they had been sitting there.

"He knows I'm safe," Sara said, not opening her eyes or offering to move.

"The pub might be busy now." Lon did not try to get a view of his wristwatch. He was certain that too much time had passed. "There could be sixty or seventy of my men in there all wanting a drink at the same time."

Sara's sigh was extended and overdramatic. "I guess you're right," she conceded. "Papa will want a hand."

They walked, but not rapidly, their arms around each other again. "I'll get in every evening I can while we're here," Lon said, feeling some urgency to get at least *something* in the way of planning going. "We'll have time to figure out how we're going to handle things."

"I'm not worried," Sara said. "If nothing else, I'll do what I've been threatening to do for the past year, move to Dirigent City and get a proper job."

It would be nice to have her close, in a place of her own, Lon thought, but then he started thinking of Camo Town, and the jobs that were most easily available to young women there in bars and bordellos. "Let's worry more about doing it right," he whispered. "We both need to cool down and do some hard thinking."

She giggled but said nothing.

•　•　•

Three trucks had arrived from Nassau. They were parked on the street outside The Winking Eye. Lon and Sara almost tore themselves apart from each other before he opened the pub door, but she would not surrender his hand until she saw the crowd inside. Lon thought he heard the ghost of a moan from her. The bar was more crowded than she could remember seeing it. Soldiers were standing three-deep in front of it, and her father was having difficulty getting to everyone fast enough to suit them.

"I've got to help," Sara said plaintively, turned toward Lon. She didn't wait for any response, just gave him a quick kiss on the lips and hurried away.

In something of a daze, Lon wandered back to the table where Shaesel Ourf was still sitting. Lon ignored the welcoming calls from several of his own men, mostly because he was not aware of them, or even of the huge grin on Ourf's face as Lon nearly fell into his chair.

"Did I see what I think I saw?" Shaesel asked over a laugh that seemed to have neither beginning nor end.

Lon blinked several times and looked for a beer in front of him. There was nothing there. He shook his head slowly. "I don't know what you think you saw, but I seem to be engaged."

Ourf's laugh died. The look of shock that came over his face was almost a reflection of the look that Lon still wore. After a moment he whispered, "I'll be damned." When Lon did not respond, Shaesel repeated himself. Several times.

"Yeah, me, too," Lon eventually said. He shook his head again, still not completely certain he was awake and that everything that had happened was more than a dream.

"Beg pardon, Lieutenant."

Lon blinked and turned his head. Tebba was standing next to him. "What is it, Tebba?"

"Are you okay, Lieutenant?" Girana asked. "You look a bit . . . well, *funny*."

While Lon was gathering himself for some sort of coherent reply—not certain *what* to say—Lieutenant Ourf started laughing again. "Stand easy, Sergeant," Ourf said.

"Your lieutenant has just been through a very trying experience."

"Sir?" Tebba asked, puzzlement in his eyes and voice.

"It's okay, Tebba," Lon said, finally finding some voice of his own. "I'm just a little out of it at the moment."

"You'll have to excuse him, Sergeant. He means what he said." Shaesel leaned as far across the table as he could get without standing. "You might want to keep an extra-sharp eye on your lads to make sure none of them gets too boisterous in here. It seems your lieutenant has just gotten himself engaged to the proprietor's daughter."

Ourf's laughter started again when he saw the sergeant develop his own stunned look. Girana's mouth fell open. Then he closed it and turned to look at the girl behind the bar. "Her, sir?" he asked.

"Her, indeed," Ourf agreed. "Very much, indeed."

Monday morning seemed a universe and aeons removed from Saturday morning. Lon had slept not at all Saturday night, and Sunday he had only been able to get to sleep with a patch. He disliked using medical aid for sleep, but knew that he had to have a clear head—or a reasonable facsimile thereof—for the new workweek.

The weekend felt as if it had been a crazy dream. He had managed only a few more minutes of conversation with Sara after they returned to the pub. Her father had even left the bar unattended for two of those minutes while all three Pines talked with him in the kitchen. Sara's parents seemed overjoyed at the prospect of having a stranger carry off their daughter. Lon had found that a little unnerving.

"They know you're an officer in the Corps," Sara explained when they finally had a moment alone. "They both have the highest respect for that. Papa is sure that anyone who becomes an officer and serves for any length of time has to be honorable and everything else he wants for me."

"I hope I don't disappoint them, or you."

"You won't."

The utter certainty in her voice had been frightening for Lon. On the drive back to Nassau Proving Range, Shaesel Ourf had been quiet, mostly. Lon had been too distracted for conversation, and wasn't even certain he had actually heard the other lieutenant whisper, "I don't believe it. I just don't believe it." When they reached the troop compound at the range, Ourf had promised to provide whatever help he could. "Get you a car so you can get into town whenever you've got time," he promised. Lon had nodded, numbly, and barely managed to find voice to thank Ourf.

On Sunday Lon had driven to Bascombe East and spent all afternoon and part of the evening there. Sara had been working when he arrived, dealing with the end of the dinner rush—mostly locals. When her father saw Lon come in, he told Sara to take the afternoon off. "You two need to spend some time getting to know each other," he had told them, speaking softly so no customers would hear.

It was a delightful eight hours for Lon, even though he found himself half dazed through much of it. Remembering details was difficult. They were hidden behind a mist of love . . . or infatuation. They had talked about themselves, and each other, sharing personal histories. Sara had been curious about how Lon had come to leave Earth for Dirigent, and he told her the story of how the top graduates in his class were going to be co-opted for service in the federal police, and the subterfuge that the commandant of the academy had perpetrated to get some of his best students off-world to have a chance to soldier. "All I ever wanted to be was a soldier," Lon told Sara, and she had merely nodded, accepting without question. She had asked about the contracts he had been on, but did not press for details past the bare outline he gave her.

Tentatively, they made plans. Lon would go back to Dirigent City and make arrangements, get the necessary permission from his battalion commander—or whoever had the final say—to marry, and so forth. They would talk every evening—duties permitting. And as soon as

Lon had everything prepared for them in Dirigent City, he would return to Bascombe East and they would be married in the village's only church. *As soon as possible.*

"Lieutenant Nolan?"

"Yes, Dr. Deradier?" Lon blinked and focused on the civilian. "Sorry. I guess I was wool-gathering." Monday had started immediately after breakfast, with a briefing on the test results from the previous work—a lot of numbers, charts, and technical jargon that Lon sometimes had difficulty following.

Deradier smiled. *He knows, too!* Lon thought. He had the feeling that everyone at the Nassau Proving Range, and everyone who lived within twenty miles of Bascombe East, knew of the whirlwind romance and engagement.

"You're not expected to follow all of the technical folderol here," Deradier said softly. "We realize it isn't your area of expertise. But it's time to move into areas you should follow."

Lon nodded, feeling sheepish and certain that his face was again turning crimson. It had been doing that a lot in the past forty hours . . . approximately every time someone said something suggestive or gave him what he considered to be a suggestive look.

"We are moderately encouraged by the early results," Deradier said, raising his voice and gesturing to include the others at the conference. "The simulations we've run based on the successful tests—that is, all but the one capsule that went its own way from interior malfunction—suggest that with this system we can achieve a better than fifty percent success rate in the field—that is, have more than half of the capsules arrive at the target safely, without being shot down by enemy forces. The actual projection to this point is fifty-three point seven percent. While that is not entirely satisfactory, it is promising. We hope that more data points will enable us to revise that estimate upward, dramatically." He paused to take a sip of water.

"More to the point. We want to make certain we are able to get as many data points as we can this week. To that end, we will attempt to run four separate tests each morning and afternoon. And, if today and tomorrow provide the results we hope for, we do plan to run one series of tests at night, most likely Wednesday night into Thursday morning.''

''At night, Doctor?'' Lon asked. ''I'm not so certain that my men are ready for that. It's difficult enough to track those capsules in daylight. In the dark, even with our night-vision systems . . .'' *It will mean one night I won't get to see Sara,* Lon thought, but that had not occurred to him until he had mentioned his practical reservations.

''Actually, it might well prove simpler in the dark, Lieutenant,'' Deradier said. ''The control system hooks completely into your helmet electronics, not just into your communications systems. Your men will have more precise tracking data onscreen as well as a visible representation of the capsule.''

''We'll have an opportunity to try that in simulation first?''

''Of course.''

On Tuesday Lon operated the controls for one of the tests. He felt the tension from the moment the controls were attached to his electronics, felt his muscles tighten. At times he held his teeth clenched.

''Just relax, Lieutenant,'' Tebba whispered. ''It's a piece of cake, really. The real thing's easier than the sims. Better depth perception. Just don't get jerky with the joystick.''

''Thanks, Tebba, I'll try.'' Girana was the only one of the men in third and fourth platoons whom Lon had felt comfortable confiding in about his adventures. He never snickered or made jokes, the way Lon knew Phip Steesen and Dean Ericks were certain to once they had a private opportunity. Lon was thankful that that chance had not yet come.

All of the reassurances in the galaxy could not completely quell Lon's nervousness about the test, but it was

enough to force him to focus on what he had to do—
totally shut out any thoughts of Sara.

The shuttle was in the air. Three tests had already been
run that morning. Lon's would be the last before lunch.
He listened to the proceedings. He could hear the conversation between test control and the shuttle pilot, with
Deradier adding comments when appropriate. The countdown to launch started.

And ended. Lon had the track of the capsule on the
head-up display of his faceplate, along with the numbers
describing its speed and course. He tried to slow his
breathing, pace himself, trying to *feel* the progress of the
capsule. The target circle was closer than it had been the
first two days, only thirty-five yards from the trench where
he and his men were waiting. His focus was complete,
and—although he did not realize it at the time—he relaxed, for the first time since he had first seen Sara Pine
in The Winking Eye.

The capsule came into visual range. Lon worked the
joystick and control buttons with a light touch, keeping
his eyes on the capsule, with only occasional glances at
the ground target. A retrorocket burst, a quick attitude
adjustment. More braking. Then cut power completely.

His capsule hit twelve feet from the center of the target.

"Excellent, Lieutenant!" Deradier's voice was the first
Lon heard. "Most excellent. The raw numbers look very
good. Congratulations."

Lon let out his breath. *I guess I can still function as a
soldier,* he decided.

Deradier and his colleagues decided to run night tests both Wednesday and Thursday, adding the second night after seeing the preliminary results of the first. Lon managed only a couple of short complink conversations with Sara, and found it difficult to conceal his disappointment at not having another chance to see her before he took his men back to Dirigent City.

"I'll get everything there taken care of as quickly as I can," he promised. "Then I'll be back."

"I'll be waiting," Sara said. "Call whenever you can."

Lon sat quietly on the transport carrying him back to the Corps' main base. He felt more depressed than he had on the shuttle that had taken him away from Earth on his exile. No one was wearing helmets, so Lon did not have the mask of a faceplate to hide behind. But he was withdrawn, and there wasn't a man in the lander who did not know why. Lon had heard some of the talk, and could guess at how much more there must have been behind his back. Now he was too glum even to feel the touch of paranoia that had initially inspired in him. His platoon sergeants, Girana and Jorgen, had provided as much of a buffer as possible, and neither had complained at their lieutenant going into town every evening they were not running tests while they had to alternate. Lon promised himself that he would find a way to make that up—that and everything else he owed them.

Lon had spoken to Captain Orlis by complink several times. Lon had alluded to his new situation without coming right out and saying that he wanted to get married as soon as possible. The captain had clearly seen that something had changed. "I'd rather wait until we can talk face to face, Captain," Lon had said when Orlis probed for the cause. "I need to get a few things sorted out in my own head first."

As far as Lon was concerned, the flight from Nassau to Dirigent City might have been instantaneous. He was oblivious to virtually everything. The pilot's announcement that the transport was on its final approach came as a shock. Lon's mind was still in Bascombe East, under The Winking Eye with Sara.

Lon was surprised to find Captain Orlis waiting at the landing strip. Lon turned the platoons over to their sergeants, to get the men onto the buses that would carry them and their gear back to barracks, then went to the captain and saluted.

"I didn't expect to see you here, sir," Lon said after Orlis returned the salute.

"I just had to see for myself," Orlis said.

"See what, sir?" Lon asked. "That we made it back safely?"

"That one of my lieutenants hadn't suddenly turned into a babbling idiot."

"Sir?" There was no hint of censure to Orlis's face or voice, which made his words all the more difficult to comprehend.

"If you had been as incoherent in your work this week as you've been talking with me, I would have heard about it from Major Pitt, or the regimental commander. But I've had nothing but commendation for the whole lot of you, so it has to be something else."

Gradually Lon realized what the captain was talking about, and that started him blushing. "I did say I wanted to talk about it in person rather than by complink, sir," Lon said. "It's personal," he added.

Orlis shook his head but could not hide a smile. "I did gather that much. Get in the car. Tell me on the way in."

Even in person, Lon's tale verged on incoherency. Orlis

mainly kept his eyes on the road, following the buses. A couple of times he did glance to his side, to look at Lon.

After Lon finished, Orlis remained silent for a moment. Then he said, "I don't suppose there's any creature in the galaxy quite as pathetic as a lovesick lieutenant."

Lon was unable to reply to that.

"I should have suspected," Orlis said. "Just about anyone else, I suppose I would have. You met a girl and fell so madly in love that you can't wait ten seconds longer than absolutely necessary before you marry her. Have I got that part of it more or less right?"

"Yes, sir," Lon said—with difficulty.

"And you'd like me to rush through the red tape for permission and so forth, help you secure quarters, that sort of thing, maybe even choose drapes?"

The words stung, even though Lon *thought* the captain was teasing, having fun at his expense. He sucked in an involuntarily deep breath. "I don't know about the drapes, sir," he said, which occasioned another of Orlis's glances.

"Well, at least you've got a little starch left in your breeches," he said. "Tell me about her, without the breathless moans of passion."

So Lon tried again, from the start, how they met, how that meeting had affected him. It took time as he tried to compose each sentence fully in his mind before he spoke it. They arrived at their destination before Lon had finished. Orlis parked the car behind the barracks and sat without moving, fully watching Lon now, patiently listening through the entire recital.

"I guess I got hit pretty hard," Lon said after there had been an extended silence at the conclusion of his story.

"There was a time when an officer with less than ten years' service who came to his commander with a request like yours would have been closely examined to see if he were still fit to be an officer in the Corps," Orlis said. "Before my time, but recently enough that some of the captains and majors I served under when I was a new lieutenant remembered, had been affected by the . . . well, it was never officially taboo, but discouraged in the strongest ways possible short of prohibition. A lot of officers still have reservations about married men serving at any rank, for reasons I'm sure you're aware of."

Lon nodded. "A married man can't be so totally committed to the Corps. He has other responsibilities. And so forth."

"At great length. On the other side of the ledger there are studies that indicate that married officers and noncoms make more stable leaders, that what they might lose in reckless bravery is more than offset by increased maturity of judgment. I tend to side with that group myself, but, of course, I'm also married. I had been in the Corps just a few months short of ten years when that happened, by the way."

"Yes, sir, I know," Lon said.

Orlis looked at him for a moment before he spoke again. "It's clear you're not going to be a hell of a lot of use to me the way you are, so I guess the fastest way to get back a fully functional lieutenant is to marry you off as fast as possible."

"Thank you, Captain," Lon said.

"Okay, you've had the good news. Now I've got to take the air out of your balloon. It doesn't look as if it's going to be possible right away. This isn't official yet, but I've had warning that we're probably going out on contract . . . very soon."

"How soon? It wouldn't take Sara and me long once we get the official approval."

Orlis shook his head. "Sorry, Lon. Remember, this is unofficial, you didn't hear it from me, and I better not hear any rumors coming back. It doesn't go beyond the two of us, not even to your Sara." He waited for Lon to nod before he continued. "There is an offer on the table, I understand from very good sources, that would involve at least one and possibly two full regiments. And of the regiments that aren't short a battalion or more just now, we're number one on the duty list. If the Council of Regiments accepts the contract, we might have no more than twenty-four hours' warning before shipping out."

Lon could almost feel his heart plummeting out of his chest to roll on the floor of the car. "Yes, sir," he said, sounding as glum as he felt. "Will the men be under any restrictions while we wait, sir?" he asked after perhaps a minute.

"How could there be restrictions when there's nothing going on?" Orlis asked, feigning innocence.

Lon nodded. "I see what you mean."

"Now, if it will ease your mind, a little, anyway, I'll start the ball rolling for you. Make the request official, marked to my attention, and I'll get it forwarded to battalion right away..Now, go on, get inside, see to your men, then sit down at your complink and type out that request."

Sara answered the complink call at The Winking Eye. Seeing her made Lon both happy and sad at once—happy to see her, sad to be so far away and not know how long it might be before they could be together.

"I hoped it was you," Sara said, almost breathless with excitement. "I love you."

"I love you, too. We got back safely and I've already put in the request for permission to get married."

"Do you know how long it will take?"

Lon shook his head. "Processing marriage requests from junior officers isn't near the top of anyone's list of priorities, but my captain said he'd push it through as quickly as he can." He didn't like not being able to tell her it might be considerably delayed, that he might go on a contract before they could get married, but he took Matt Orlis's warning seriously. "The request went to battalion an hour ago, but I doubt that anyone there will even look at it before Monday. And after that, hard telling how long it will be. It could never be soon enough for me."

"Or for me," Sara said.

They talked for a few minutes, idle talk, content more to look at and listen to each other. Then Sara said, "I've really got to go and help." She paused for an instant, then giggled. "You know, when I go to Dirigent City, Papa may actually have to break down and hire someone to help in the pub. He's going to *hate* that part of it.''

After ending the connection to Bascombe East, Lon stared listlessly at the complink monitor. It was suppertime. He knew he should go to the mess hall. It was either that or go to the canteen, or into Camo Town, and buy supper. He did not want to spend money needlessly, not when he was facing the added expense of a wife, but he also felt no urge to go to the mess hall. He had just about convinced himself to go anyway when there was a knock on his door.

"Come in," Lon said, using the arrival as a spur to get him to his feet. Phip Steesen and Dean Ericks came in together. They had changed into civilian clothes and were obviously ready for Camo Town and a night of gentle debauchery.

"Like to come into town with us?" Phip asked after Dean shut the door behind them.

Lon smiled but shook his head. "You'll have to do the town up without me tonight, guys. I'm not up to it."

"You're not going to pull a Janno on us, are you?" Phip asked with a seriousness that surprised Lon. "Get married and run to civie street?"

"I am getting married, but I'm not planning on leaving the Corps. You saw Sara, everyone in both platoons did." The ones who might have passed up the chance to go into town for a few drinks had all gone in once rumors started to circulate that their lieutenant had gone madly, head over heels in love. Lon had not been so totally oblivious as to miss that.

"Janno didn't plan to leave either, when he got himself hitched," Dean said.

"I'm not Janno, and Sara isn't Mary," Lon said. "Look, I know we haven't had much chance to talk the past few weeks. Maybe over the weekend we can get off for a couple of hours and talk over a few beers someplace quiet. But not yet. I've still got some work to do getting my head straight. And right now I've got to put some food in my stomach. Get yourselves off to Camo Town, and don't water your beer crying over me.''

Supper seemed tasteless, suffering through Lon's memories of The Winking Eye and Sara. After the meal he went to the officers' club and had a drink, but he found no pleasure in that either, so he went back to his room. He set a program of music on his entertainment unit and lay on his bunk, staring at the ceiling . . . thinking of Sara.

Near ten o'clock, she called. The last customer had left The Winking Eye. The nightly clean-up ritual was almost finished. They talked for nearly two hours, until it was clear they were both so tired they were having difficulty keeping their eyes open.

"Tomorrow," Lon said. "I'll call tomorrow."

And tomorrow, and tomorrow.

Monday morning, Lon nearly slept through his alarm. He stumbled through his morning ritual and went to breakfast in something of a personal fog, his mind not completely alert.

I hardly know who I am anymore. It's as if I turned into somebody completely different the second I saw Sara. Thinking of her brought a smile to his face and helped perk him up. It made the food taste better as well. He had nearly finished eating when Lead Sergeant Jim Ziegler came to his table.

"Captain would like to see you, sir, as soon as you finish breakfast," Ziegler said.

"Two seconds, Sergeant." Lon took a last sip of coffee, then pushed his chair back. His first thought was that it must be something about his request for permission to marry. That was quickly overtaken by the far more likely possibility that it had to do with the contract Orlis had alluded to on Friday.

"Any idea what the captain wants?" Lon asked as he left the mess hall with Ziegler.

"He didn't say, Lieutenant, and it's too early of a Monday for me to try guessing."

Lon chuckled. "I heard all of that."

Ziegler smiled. "Yes, sir." Alpha's lead sergeant was one of only a handful of enlisted men in the unit who were married. He also had twenty-five years of service in the Corps, and was as important to the functioning of the company as its commander or either of its lieutenants. He was one of the men Lon had sought advice from in the confusing first days at Bascombe East.

Matt Orlis was eating a doughnut at his desk. He waved Lon into a chair. "Back to the usual schedule, Lon," the captain said after taking a sip of coffee. "Your platoons have fatigue details today and it's back to the contract office for you."

Lon nodded. "Any news, sir?" he asked, his voice cautious.

Orlis smiled. "Not about anything. You keep your ears open, you might hear something before I do, but you'll be totally surprised if you do, right?"

"Totally," Lon agreed with a grin.

"I had a short chat with Joe Pitt yesterday," Orlis said then, leaning back. Lon needed a second to connect the name: Major Joseph Pitt, Nassau Proving Range. "They only have the most preliminary workups yet on the tests, but Joe says it looks extremely promising. He was already talking about the possibility of doing more extensive field tests during the winter war games."

"It did look good," Lon said. "Men need more than three or four tries to get the hang of it, even after the simulators, but it's something I'd sure like to have when we really need it."

"You and everyone else who's ever been there," Orlis said quietly, seriously. "Maybe this time it'll be a go."

Maybe I'll get a chance to nose around and find out where this world is that we might get a contract for, Lon thought as he walked to Corps Headquarters. He chuckled at the fanciful image, knowing he would do nothing of the kind. *I'll find out soon enough if it turns up. No need to go looking for grief.*

The Contracts section occupied much of the north wing of Corps Headquarters, on the ground floor and the first basement level. The largest part of Contracts was OSI, the Office of Strategic Intelligence. Its job was to collect information on all of the settled worlds possible: political, social, and economic conditions; enemies and allies; possibilities for employment. OSI maintained one of the most extensive databases in the galaxy. Most of the information was available to any officer in the Corps. OSI conducted investigations, when possible, before contracts were accepted and troops committed. With minimum round-trip transit times between worlds approaching a month, it was not always possible.

During his weekly tours with Contracts, Lon had been shuffled from office to office with seeming abandon, working in two different OSI departments as well as in the contracts assessment department, which was Contracts' other primary division. He never knew until he reported in where he would be working any Monday. This time he was told to report to the audit office of OSI. That had nothing to do with finances. It was responsible for checking the accuracy of recent database entries. It was, in Lon's opinion, the most boring assignment in Contracts.

It was almost a relief when Captain Zim, the officer in charge of the audit office, came to the complink Lon was working a little after nine o'clock and told him to report to the commanding officer of Contracts.

"Yes, sir," Lon replied, logging off of the database while he spoke. "Any idea what it's about?"

"Something the colonel wants you to look at," Zim said.

Lieutenant Colonel Jorge Ruiz had his office on the first floor, with two windows facing the courtyard that held specimens of cannon spanning the previous thirteen centuries.

"Come on in, Nolan." Ruiz was extremely informal inside the section's office space, standing on little ceremony except when it might be necessary to impress off-world visitors. "Have a seat." He waited until Lon was seated on one of the leather and bonewood chairs that faced his desk before he continued.

"This might seem like some type of pop quiz to test how well you've learned your lessons here, but it's not," Ruiz said. Lon lifted an eyebrow. "I want you to examine a file and suggest a course of action. Unfortunately, I can't give you as much time as I'd like. Take until eleven-thirty hours. Reach your conclusions and have your reasons ready. We'll discuss it over lunch in the senior officers' mess."

"Yes, sir," Lon said.

Colonel Ruiz gave him the file name. "I'll tell Captain Zim that you're not to be disturbed, that you're working a special project for me."

The interview took less than five minutes. Lon returned to the audit office and keyed his password and the file name into his complink. After less than a minute of scanning the preamble to the file, he knew this was the contract Captain Orlis had hinted at.

6

Arguably, the food was no better in the senior officers' mess at Corps Headquarters than at any other mess
on base, but it was served on fine china, with fancier
flatware and crystal glasses. The tables had real linen ta-
blecloths. The salt and pepper shakers were crystal. Soft
music played in the background. Waiters provided table
service.

"Well, what's your opinion?" Colonel Ruiz asked Lon
after they had ordered lunch and the waiter had left.

Lon shrugged. "From the material I had to inspect, sir,
I see no substantial distinction in the merits of the claims
by the two colonies on Aldrin. They arrived separately
from Earth, both with valid charters. They have remained
separate throughout the intervening five centuries. There
is nothing to suggest that either is morally preferable to
the other. Now they have both begun to expand their numbers to the point where they are competing for the same
new territories. I see no reason why the Corps should not
feel free to accept a contract from either side, if one is
offered, but—you do want my personal opinion, Colonel?" When Ruiz nodded, Lon said, "I think we might
best serve Aldrin by offering mediation service between
the two colonies, if necessary backed up by peacekeeping
troops to provide a buffer until political agreement is
reached."

"You think that mediation and peacekeeping would be
the Corps' best proposal?" Ruiz asked.

"Based on the material available to me, yes, sir."

"And if one or both sides declined that proposal?"

"Well, sir, if *both* sides declined, then I don't see that the equation has changed. There is still no real difference between the two. However, if one accepted—honestly and not as some sort of transparent ploy—while the other declined, then I would suggest that we might favor the side that had accepted the offer, if they proffered a contract."

Their lunch arrived, and the conversation was tabled until the waiter was gone and they had tasted the food.

"One more question, Nolan," Ruiz said after dabbing at his lips with a linen napkin. "Hypothetical. Supposing that the Corps offered mediation and peacekeeping, one side accepted and the other declined, but it was the side that declined our offer that was willing and able to contract for military services?"

This time Lon hesitated before he ventured his reply. "I wouldn't presume to offer an opinion based solely on the information I read this morning, Colonel. I think it would depend on the reasons this side advanced for declining the offer of mediation and peacekeeping, and what our own investigations of those reasons turned up."

Colonel Ruiz was silent for a time, not paying attention to his food or really looking at Lon.

"I do know one thing, Colonel," Lon said. "Going in on a contract. The men like to think that they're on the side of the good guys. If they thought otherwise, I'm not certain that their performance would be quite up to the same standard."

"I know that, Nolan. I haven't been a desk soldier all the time. The question only arises in a case like this."

"This is an actual situation, sir? Something pending?"

"It's for real, Nolan." Ruiz sounded tired. "One we've been butting our heads against for months. Your analysis, by the way, was excellent. The questions you raised are among the very ones that the Council of Regiments has been debating. We've had a team of observers there for quite some time, trying to get agreement to mediation and peacekeeping."

"We just wait for something they see or hear to tip the balance one way or the other?" Lon asked.

Ruiz made a gesture of helplessness with his hands, then shook his head. "Let's say that a decision would be a lot simpler if there were a lot of other contracts being offered."

Lon had not been sworn to any special secrecy over the job Colonel Ruiz had asked him to do, nothing beyond the routine confidentiality he had been warned about his first day in Contracts. After work that Monday, Lon sought out Captain Orlis.

"That information I didn't hear from you?" Lon said in a hushed voice. "I wouldn't bank on it—not soon, anyway. It all looks rather iffy."

Matt Orlis nodded. "I know. But I suspect that the Council will eventually choose to put men to work."

"But maybe it will take long enough for Sara and me to get married first," Lon suggested.

"Patience. It's in the works. Just keep your pants on."

"Well, Captain, I'm here and she's there, so I don't have much choice about that."

There was an interview with Lieutenant Colonel Black over the request for permission to marry. Another interview with the Corps Personal Welfare office—that one included a questionnaire that was part psychological profile and part analysis of his ability and willingness to support a wife and family. "We need to know everything possible in order to help in the most efficient manner," Lon was told.

Two weeks after Lon's return from Nassau Proving Range, there still was no word on his request, or on the possible contract on Aldrin. Lon's Monday duties were switched. He remained with his platoons, while Carl Hoper went off on some other variety of detached duties.

Each evening during the week, and several times on Saturdays and Sundays, Lon spent time on the complink with Sara. After two weeks, both were showing impatience, especially when they talked. "Daddy says there's no way to rush the Corps,'' she said several times. "That we just have to wait as best we can.''

"My captain tells me pretty much the same thing,'' Lon admitted. "I think he's tired of me nagging him about it.''

"Lon, I've been thinking. I could move to Dirigent City. I've got a bit of money saved up from my tips. Get a small apartment close to you. That would be better than going crazy waiting so far apart.''

Lon's heart started thumping harder. "I'd love that, Sara, but—really—I think you'd better stay with your folks until we can get married. I'd worry too much about you alone here. Let's do it right, the way we planned. Maybe it won't be so much longer after all.''

Three days later, word finally came.

The contract, not the request for permission to marry. Twenty-four hours after that, Lon and his men were aboard the battalion transport *Long Snake*, heading out-system with the rest of 7th Regiment, en route to Aldrin.

"Two colonies have coexisted peacefully for centuries,'' Lon told his platoons during the first briefing aboard ship. "Aldrin East and Aldrin West are among the oldest settlements planted directly from Earth that are not in either the Confederation of Human Worlds or the Second Commonwealth. They have shared the only continent that has what they consider to be acceptable climate and conditions. Apart from their reluctance to deal with each other, they have been physically separated by a mountain chain that runs from northeast to southwest.'' Lon had charts of the world projected on a wall monitor so the men could see what he was talking about. "Both colonies have grown considerably and are feeling population pressures that have forced them to expand into areas they consider less than ideal. The area where the conflict between them came to a head is here, south of this peninsula.'' He pointed to an area that lay nearly on the planet's equator.

"Another tropical paradise?'' Phip Steesen asked.

"I don't know where we're going in," Lon said. "There has been, according to the last reports, some minor skirmishing there, but our client, Aldrin West, is far more concerned over what they see as an attempt to invade their core regions to the north, well into the temperate zone."

He paused. "We've had people on Aldrin for nearly a year, trying to get the two sides to agree to employ the DMC for mediation and peacekeeping. As long as there was no fighting, the Council of Regiments declined to accept a contract to help impose the will of one colony on the other. It was only when Aldrin East sent settlers and troops across the continental divide into this large tropical plain on what traditionally had been Aldrin West's side of the continent that we started to gear up for this contract. When word came that Aldrin East was also sending troops across the mountains here"—he pointed out the area on the map—"we got our orders. We know a lot about the top people in each colony, and have better than average data on the size of the armies each side can field. Not perfect, but better than we have most times.

"Both colonies have long maintained standing armies. Both have increased the size of those armies over the past several years to meet the threat each saw from the other. Each has its own munitions industry and a well-developed economy. East can field credible opposition, and that includes a sizable air fleet, which is why we're taking a full fighter squadron to support our effort. We're talking about national armies here, but the level of professionalism appears to be high on both sides.

"The mission we have contracted for is to repulse the invasion of West's heartland, and to evict the soldiers East has sent into the area under dispute in the south. We will not attempt to force relocation of civilians there but will prevent any new Easterners from moving in. We are to do what we can to minimize antagonizing the civilian Easterners. The Council of Regiments still hopes to turn this contract into one of mediation and peacekeeping once we're on the ground."

"I know one way we could make peace between them," Platoon Sergeant Jorgen said when Lon asked for comments and questions. "But I sure hope that's not what the Council has in mind."

"What's that?" Lon asked.

"Make both sides so mad at us that they'll kiss and make up and all turn against us." That brought uneasy laughs from some of the men, openly worried looks from others.

"They won't do that unless they get full payment for the contract in advance," Phip said, but his quip sounded nervous.

"Nothing has been said about anything like that," Lon said. "We go in and do our job. The contract team will continue to try to persuade both sides to agree to mediation, with 7th Regiment available to make certain there are no additional incidents. And 12th Regiment has been alerted to possibly reinforce us, in either role. If conditions deteriorate before we arrive, 12th might already be on the way when we land. The contract officers have authority to request that on their own."

"How long a contract is this?" Tebba Girana asked.

"The maximum duration under the initial contract is six months," Lon said. "If necessary, under conditions spelled out in detail in the contract. That means that if we get the war won faster, we get paid off and head for home sooner. If we do turn this into a peacekeeping effort, the time could be longer. But, as I understand the way the Corps works these things, we're not likely to stay longer than six months. If it goes beyond that, 7th would probably be rotated back to Dirigent and another regiment brought in to replace us." *I sure hope it doesn't run that long*, he thought. *This is one time I'd like to be in and out as fast as possible. I wouldn't even complain if we got there and turned right around to go home without even landing.*

The voyage to Aldrin seemed interminable to Lon, as if there were weeks between Q-space transits instead of three days. Lon studied the database on Aldrin until he had large sections of it virtually memorized. He scanned the maps, concentrating on the area where the invading army was supposed to be headed, and on the area in dispute to the south. He studied photographs and video, and read Aldrinian news accounts that the contract officers had relayed to Dirigent. He played the game of planning the campaign for himself, decided how he would use the regiment to fulfill the contract in the fastest, most economical manner. And, every day, he wrote long letters to Sara, knowing it might be weeks before he would get a chance to send any of them. When he could think of nothing else to write, he added long accounts of his memories of Earth—knowing they would interest Sara. He spent an hour or two working out in the gym every day, pushing himself, as always.

Most nights he slept only with the aid of a sleep patch. He took that step on his own, knowing that Captain Orlis would order it if he saw any sign that Lon was not getting a decent amount of sleep. *I've learned some of my lessons,* Lon told himself one night just after he put the patch on his neck. *No one has to tell me to keep myself in order now. I can do what I have to do.* He was asleep almost before he finished the thought.

"We won't be going in hot," Lieutenant Colonel Black told his officers. The staff meeting had been called six hours after the Dirigenter fleet came out of its final Q-space transit in Aldrin's system. The ships were on course, two and a half days out. "That's the word as of this minute, subject, of course, to change, but the intelligence looks good. The invading army is still in the mountains, moving rather slowly on the ground. They've been forced to leave behind most of their ground transport and move on foot. Apparently Aldrin East didn't feel confident enough of air superiority to try to move its troops across the mountains by air, even though they have the shuttles to do it, and fighter aircraft to cover them." He shrugged. "We are not privy to the reasoning behind the decision. Our representatives are no longer welcome in East, nor have they been able to continue talking with East's leaders even by complink." He coughed lightly, an affected gesture. "That might have something to do with the fact that we're on our way in. It seems that West broadcast the news, with a 'get out while you can' type of, ah, suggestion. There is no indication that news of our approach has scared East into abandoning their efforts." He paused. "I guess it was worth a try, but it does mean that we have no element of surprise going for us, which makes it that much better that we're going into a safe zone, to be moved into position later, if our mere presence on the ground doesn't scare East into turning around." He smiled. "That does appear unlikely. It would be nice, though. Remember, until we're told different, we would prefer to avoid a major fight. We hope to make both sides see that it would be far better to find a peaceful solution to their differences." That was being emphasized, on every level, at every possibility. "That means that, subject to the requirements of security, we treat the civilians of East with kid gloves and do not go, ah, overboard even against armed combatants. We protect ourselves. We do the job, but with such restraint as is militarily feasible."

Several rows back, Lon frowned, his head bent forward. He had studied military history during his time at The Springs, the North American Military Academy on Earth. The idea of limiting efforts against an armed enemy brought images of disaster to mind.

"Nolan?"

Lon was surprised to hear Colonel Black call his name. He looked up. "Sir?"

"You look as if you've just bitten into a rotten gavvie."

"Sorry, sir. What you said brought something back to me. Military history, sir. Iraq. Vietnam. Korea. *Restrained* warfare."

Black nodded. "I know the references, Nolan." He looked around the room. "For any of you who might not know what Lieutenant Nolan is talking about, I suggest you log on to the database and check them out. He is referring to three wars that took place on Earth in"—he looked at Lon as if for some confirmation—"the twentieth or early twenty-first century."

"Second half of the twentieth, sir," Lon said.

"Yes," Black said, nodding. "The point I want to make here is that the limitations on one side in each of those wars were imposed by civilian political leaders, not by military commanders on the scene. In this case, any limitations will be designed and overseen by Colonel Flowers on the advice of his CIC"—Combat Intelligence Center—"and the battalion commanders. We are not going to allow our men to be placed in unnecessary jeopardy to satisfy the whims of civilian politicians. We will use such restraint as possible without those complications. We place the safety of our people first." He focused on Lon then. "I trust that satisfies your concerns, Nolan?"

"Completely, sir," Lon said—not *too* much of an exaggeration. Nothing, short of leaving Aldrin to its own devices could do it completely.

Intelligence on conditions on Aldrin came in almost hourly as the DMC fleet approached. Some came from the government of Aldrin West. More (and more reliable) information came from the Dirigenters who had been on the world to secure the contract. Lon logged on several times each day to keep track of the latest changes, and passed on some of that information to his platoon sergeants and squad leaders.

"We get down there, I want to make sure we're as prepared as we can be," he told Girana and Jorgen. "This could be a touchy contract. We don't want mistakes that might complicate matters."

"I've got no argument with that, Lieutenant," Girana said. "I looked up those wars on Earth you told us about." Lon had mentioned them to his platoon sergeants after bringing them up at the officers' briefing. "Scary, the things that happened because the civilians were tying the army's hands."

"Well, Colonel Black promised that we won't have anything like that, Tebba. But we don't want to screw things up on our own, either."

"We'll do our best."

Lon nodded. "We all will." *And hope it's enough.*

Seventh Regiment was twelve hours from shuttle launch. There had been no changes in the announced plan. The regiment would land in safe areas, well away from any chance of fighting. The only threat—seen as minimal—was that Aldrin East might stage an air raid, trying to catch the shuttles on the way down. But Aldrin West promised to have its air force up, and Colonel Flowers planned to have the fleet's squadron of Shrike fighters out to provide protection for the shuttles as well.

The last day before grounding on a contract was always free of duty, except for those with command responsibility. Men slept and ate, fortifying themselves against the possibility that both food and slumber might be in short supply. Squad leaders tried to make sure that the rookies, men who had never been on a combat contract before, did not get *too* nervous. Officers and noncoms took time to study the operational orders. But they, too, tried to get in as much food and sleep as possible.

Lon was lying on his bunk, eyes closed, but he was not sleeping. He had given himself a schedule. Ten hours before the programmed launch of the shuttles, he would put on a sleep patch to make certain he got six hours. Now he was going over the files on Aldrin again, working to keep from forgetting anything that might prove vital later. *Like cramming for a test at the academy,* he thought during one break in his concentration.

The knock on his door was soft, as if whoever was on the other side did not want to wake him if he were asleep. "Come in," Lon said. He did not open his eyes until he heard the metallic noise of the door latch. Then he swung around to sit up on the edge of his bunk.

"Hello, Phip," Lon said, smiling as Steesen came in and shut the door. "Something on your mind?"

"Just checking, Lon. You going to be all right on this?" There was no mistaking the concern in Phip's voice—concern of a soldier for his commander, and the concern of a man for his friend. "I mean, you've got Sara on your mind now."

Lon stood face-to-face with Phip. "I'll be okay. Thanks for asking. But I've had time to get my head straight. I think." He grinned. "Anyway, I've got ninety-eight of the best men in the Corps looking after me."

Phip grinned back. "Sometimes I forget you're no rookie anymore. We've been through a lot, on contract and on pass."

"We have that, Phip."

"I see that cadet that Lieutenant Hoper is training, and I remember what it was like when you first came to us."

Lon laughed. "Yes, I know I was once that raw. But once we get home from Aldrin, Officer Cadet Esau O'Fallon will get his lieutenant's pips, like I did after Norbank." O'Fallon had been with the company eleven months, waiting his chance to earn his commission in combat.

Phip started to say something but bit it off. He had nearly mentioned that it was on Norbank that Lieutenant Arlan Taiters—Lon's mentor during his apprenticeship—had been killed. *Not at all the thing to say now,* Phip told himself. But mentioning Norbank had brought the same memory to Lon.

"I'll be okay, Phip," he repeated. "I have every intention of staying smart and alert, to make sure I get back to Sara. You can tell the others that I've got my head on straight."

"I think everybody knows that. I just figured I'd better come in, see was there anything distracting you. Anyway, compared to what we've been through before, this looks like it might be a far sight smoother."

"I hope so, but don't count on it. There are thirty million people on Aldrin, and the two colonies don't like each other. We could end up smack in the middle of that, like getting between a couple of lovers who are having an all-out brawl."

Phip shook his head. "We've seen a couple of those, too, haven't we? That one in the Purple Harridan, the one the MPs had to come in to break up?"

"I remember." That had been a year before, the worst incident of violence that Lon had seen on Dirigent . . . apart from the mock violence of combat exercises. A man and a woman had gotten into a knock-down, drag-out fight, the kind that breaks furniture and totally disrupts business. The other soldiers in the bar would have broken it up, except that the woman—a *civilian*—was clearly able to defend herself, giving as good as she got. That had not saved her boyfriend, a private in 3rd Regiment, from court-martial, conviction, and discharge with prejudice from the DMC after receiving a dozen lashes in front of his regiment. "Whatever happened to that gal?" Lon asked.

Phip shook his head. "I don't know. Haven't seen her in six months. Probably back with her boyfriend by now, or training recruits in hand-to-hand fighting." He laughed. That was unlikely. The Dirigent Mercenary Corps did not have any female soldiers, and all boot training was done by combat veterans.

A meal, sleep, another meal. Two hours before his men were scheduled to board their shuttles, Lon was dressed in camouflage battledress, ready. In a few minutes he would go to spend time with his men, stopping briefly with each squad, chatting, trying to spot potential problems, and trying to reassure his men—both about the coming work and his own calmness. If his men saw that he was easy about what was to come, they would be, too. *As long as I don't run around like a chicken with its head cut off,* he reminded himself, recalling how he had been the first time in—until Captain Orlis put him straight.

"We're not going to have anyone shooting at us first thing," he reminded his men. "We've got good intelligence on the ground, and we're going to land far from the enemy. We won't be going in with rounds in the chamber and safeties off."

"They gonna have dancing girls to meet us?" someone in fourth platoon asked.

"I don't know. It's not on the program," Lon replied.

"We're in good shape, Lieutenant," Tebba Girana said, "the best I can remember going in on a combat contract." Lon was with his two platoon sergeants in his cabin. They still had forty-five minutes before moving to the shuttles.

Weil Jorgen nodded his agreement. "The idea that we're not going to have to fight our way off the shuttles makes a big difference," he added. "I've had a couple of men suggest that they might not feel so good if that was coming. 'Been so long we might be rusty,' one of them told me. This way, everyone figures they'll have a chance to ease into anything."

"When it comes, it may still come in a hurry," Lon said. "I wouldn't encourage that 'ease into it' idea."

"I won't, but they're ready. It may be a long time since we've been in combat, but we don't let no rust accumulate."

"I know, Weil. You and Tebba supply all the oil that's necessary. I'm not worried about preparedness. And, with a fair bit of luck, this might turn out to be an easy contract. But we can't count on that. It could turn ugly fast, and there are a lot of Aldrinians carrying weapons, on both sides."

Both platoon sergeants nodded. They had seen the intelligence estimate that each side had more than a hundred thousand men under arms, more than half career soldiers. East and West each had maintained a standing army for generations. The colonies had never trusted each other.

"It's a big place, lotta people," Tebba said. "Not like most worlds we get to, not all concentrated in one or two places."

"No, it's not," Lon agreed. West had a half dozen cities whose population was above a quarter million, and Syracuse, the capital, had well over a million residents. There were scores of smaller cities, as well as the more common towns and villages. The population distribution was similar in Aldrin East. There were probably no more than two dozen colony worlds anywhere with more people. And the amount of tolerable land area was smaller than average. *That's the whole problem here,* Lon thought.

Lon inspected his troops again, superficially, in the troop bays before the platoons marched to the armory to draw weapons and ammunition and move on to the shuttle hangar. There was no audible joking. The mood was serious—business-like among the veterans, nervous among the rookies—but not extreme.

Second Battalion would be landing near the town of George's Gap, three hundred miles east of Syracuse, two hundred from the nearest enemy troops. The other battalions would land near other towns, in an arc roughly centered on the point of the enemy advance across the mountain chain that separated the colonies. Aldrin West had its own troops farther east, with units doing what they could to harass the enemy and slow their advance.

"It looks as if they've been playing it smart," Captain Orlis had told his lieutenants and Officer Cadet O'Fallon during their last private talk before landing. "Keeping their risk to a minimum while holding up the enemy columns. A damn good piece of generalship, from the reports I've seen."

"If they're so good, why do they need us?" O'Fallon asked.

"Maybe West would rather spend money than blood," Carl Hoper suggested. "They have no emotional stake in us."

Lon thought that O'Fallon flinched at that.

"As long as we do the job, we're as expendable as bullets," Hoper added, and Lon was certain that O'Fallon flinched this time. *I suppose I would have, back when I was going in the first time,* Lon thought, trying to be fair to the younger man. *He's never been in combat.*

"That's our job, O'Fallon," Orlis said. "That's why there's always going to be a market for professionals like us."

"Yes, sir," O'Fallon said, not quite stuttering.

The attack shuttles did not attempt a "hot" landing, accelerating into the atmosphere to get their passengers down and out of the boats as quickly as possible, but the ride was not as gentle as a civilian shuttle. The video monitors spaced around the bulkheads of the troop compartment in Lon's shuttle gave them a good view of the town below, and the small hydroelectric dam set up across the river in the gap that had given the town its name, George's Gap. The landing zone was on the north side of the river, away from the settled part of the community.

There were no dancing girls to meet the soldiers. Until after all the shuttles were on the ground, there was no one at all. Only after the last boat touched down did a car come across the top of the dam. The troops had been formed up by company by then, with their supplies stacked behind each platoon.

Colonel Black had passed the "stand easy" order.

"Can't tell there's a war goin' on here," Phip muttered.

Lon did not turn, but heard Tebba tell Phip to stop talking in ranks. *I hope it stays that way,* Lon thought.

The first few hours on Aldrin were an almost giddy experience for Lon. Gravity was 6 percent below Earth normal, 4 percent below what he had become used to on Dirigent. The atmospheric pressure also was low, but despite that, the air seemed "rich"—higher in oxygen.

"A man gets to breathing hard, he could get so lightheaded he'd float away," he commented to Captain Orlis while the men erected tents that had been brought down by supply shuttles. The battalion was setting up camp a half mile from George's Gap.

"We'll get used to it," Orlis said. "A couple of days and this will seem like normal."

"I'm not worried about here, but what's it like up in those mountains?" Lon asked. "If we have to meet East's army too high, it could get to be a problem. Back on Earth, operating a mile above sea level took careful acclimation."

Orlis nodded. "That's one of the reasons we set down here. The plan is to give us two full days here. Then we'll move east, higher, get into position in front of East's line of advance with two or three days in hand. I know it's been covered before, but warn your men against the ultraviolet danger to eyes again. We don't want problems."

Lon nodded. The men's molecular health maintenance systems would prevent long-term disability from UV exposure, but the medical nanobots needed time to operate. "I'll make sure the word gets to everyone, Cap."

The captain grinned suddenly. "You weren't with us on Blayne. That was about eight years ago. Blayne's just a little more massive than Mars, minimally breathable atmosphere. Gravity forty percent of normal. Winds over a hundred and twenty miles per hour. Blayne wouldn't have been worth much but for its minerals—gold, uranium, and several transuranic elements. There was a large mining colony, and people who wanted to raid the world to make a lot of quick money. We spent eight weeks there, and a couple of weeks getting readjusted to full gravity when we got home. This is a piece of cake compared to that."

The real surprise of the first day came an hour before sunset, when the western sky turned lilac, the color deepening as the sun moved closer to the horizon. The sight was novel enough to draw the attention of even the most jaded of Lon's men.

"Any idea what causes it, Lieutenant?" Phip Steesen asked.

"Not offhand. Must be something organic in the air, spores or something like that. It wasn't mentioned in the

files on Aldrin. I'll check on it." *Later,* he told himself.
For the moment he just wanted to watch it, like most of
the other men standing out in the open and staring into
the west.

Two days later, 2nd Battalion was a hundred miles east
of George's Gap and fifteen hundred feet higher. The
lilac-colored sunsets continued, but with diminished intensity. Lon learned that his guess had been correct. The
phenomenon was the result of airborne spores, rising in
the afternoon heat of the river valleys. It was an annual
event, lasting three to five weeks. The spores were for a
native tree that was almost like southern pine in appearance, but the wood was softer, unsuitable for use in construction. According to the report Lon got, its only
"saving graces" were the colorful displays the spores
provided and the tree's citrus scent.

The battalion made camp again. Twice daily, the officers gathered to hear the latest updates on the progress of
Aldrin East's invading army and the delaying actions the
DMC's hosts were taking. More detailed tactical maps
were provided of the area where the regiment was expected to be inserted to stop East's advance completely.

"Two full days here," Colonel Black told the officers
as soon as the second camp was established. "Then we
bring the shuttles in after dark to move us into position.
If East keeps coming, we wait there for them, pick our
ground, and prepare. If they change course, we move to
intercept them—most likely on the ground, as long as
that's practical. We hit them with everything we've got,
including Shrikes. Try to score heavily enough that they
give up or turn for home."

The enemy force numbered more than eight thousand,
nearly twice the size of 7th Regiment. Aldrin West had a
battalion, five hundred men, involved in the delaying action. They were moving three more battalions into position to support the mercenaries in what was hoped would
be the decisive engagement.

"If that doesn't settle the matter favorably, Colonel

Flowers is ready to send a message rocket back to Dirigent to order 12th Regiment here to back us up," Black said. "We will withdraw to wait for them, not try to stay engaged no matter what. The government of West has been notified of that decision, which seems to have had something to do with their decision to put four full battalions of their own troops into the fight."

There were no civilian communities close enough to the enemy's line of advance to be in early danger, or to complicate matters for the defenders. George's Gap was the nearest large town, and the nearest village was thirty miles west of the battalion's current camp.

A more businesslike way to run a contract, even if we do end up with one hell of a pitched battle, Lon thought after that briefing. *No do-or-die heroics, no taking impossible orders from the contracting government.*

Twenty hours before the scheduled move from the battalion's second camp, it started to rain. For the first few hours it came as a series of isolated showers. Then the rain became constant, and heavier, pushed by a thirty-mile-per-hour wind. Before the rain, the daytime highs had been in the upper seventies. The day of the rain, the temperature never got above fifty-five degrees Fahrenheit, and by sunset, when the battalion broke camp, the temperature had fallen to forty-eight.

"So much for your 'another tropical paradise,' Phip," Lon mentioned while the folded tents were being stacked.

"I don't mind the chill," Phip replied, wiping water from the faceplate of his helmet, "but I could sure do without the ice water. How long is this stuff supposed to keep coming?"

"At least through the night," Lon said. "Maybe through tomorrow morning, too."

"Great. Just great." Phip moved away, shaking his head.

Nothing wrong with a little rain, Lon thought, grinning behind the cover of his visor. *Until you have to sleep in three inches of water and mud.*

The battalion formed up by company and used darkness
and the high forest to cover their movement from any spy
satellites that might still be operational. Colonel Black set
a hard pace. His goal was for the battalion to cover fifteen
miles—most of it severely uphill—by dawn. Ten-minute
breaks each hour were all he permitted. The rain continued, with only a few short halts. In the morning, the battalion made camp in the rain, the men taking what care
they could to stretch tarps above them when they settled
in to try to sleep for a few hours.

"Give us tents when it's nice and sunny, then take them
away when the weather gets rotten," Girana said as he
got ready to settle in himself for three hours. Either he or
Weil Jorgen would be awake, on duty, at all times. The
men would stand watch one hour in three, even though
the enemy was—supposedly—still more than twenty
miles away.

"Just to let us know this isn't a lark," Lon replied.
"There are good trees overhead to keep off the worst of
it, and to hide us. Try to keep the men from frolicking
out in the open, in case there's anyone watching."

"I've already told them to keep their heads down. You
sound like you enjoy this," Tebba accused.

"It could be worse, Tebba. This could be snow and
sleet and the temperature sixty degrees colder. Or it could
be as steamy as New Bali." Lon could not give himself
the "pleasure" of trying to sleep yet. There was a battalion officers' call first. Colonel Black wanted to share
the latest information.

"We'll stay put today," he said after congratulating his
officers on the distance they had covered. "Move another
eight miles after dark, then set up and wait for East. The
good news is that the rain should end before noon. The
bad news is that it doesn't look as if the temperature's
going to get any warmer. 'Unseasonably cool' is how the
meteorologist put it. Maybe forty for the low tonight. We
can deal with that even though we can't have any open
fires." The thermal insulation of DMC battledress would
hold in body heat. Helmet faceplates would keep any

breeze from faces. Gloves. "After your men have had their first round of sleep, put them to cleaning weapons. We're getting close enough that the chance of the enemy pulling a surprise can't be ruled out, no matter how good we think our intelligence is."

The colonel paused before he added, "The way things look now, we could be seeing combat not much more than twenty-four hours from now. I want us as ready as possible."

Despite his earlier show of cheerfulness, Lon did not manage any sleep while the rain continued. It eased off by midmorning and was over before noon, but the ground remained wet, water continued to drip from the tree he had his bedroll under, and the sky remained threatening well into the afternoon. He did manage to doze, off and on, but never anything that was satisfying or restful. He was almost relieved when it was time to pack his bedroll and get ready for the evening's march.

The battalion did not make as good time the second night. The pace was slower and the breaks longer. Colonel Black did not push his men. It helped that they had little more than half as far to go. The sky started to clear after sunset, too late for there to be any hint of the air show to the west. *I don't think even that would have picked me up tonight,* Lon conceded. When they finally reached their destination, a self-heating meal was welcome more for the warmth of the food than for its taste. The battalion ate before it started preparing defensive positions and planting electronic snoops and land mines farther out, before scouting patrols were sent off to get a better view of the land than they could get simply from photographs taken from orbit.

"We'll be on half-and-half watches," Lon told his platoon sergeants. "With a little luck everyone might get two hours of sleep before trouble reaches us." And before anyone could try to get that minimal ration of sleep, foxholes had to be dug, other defensive preparations taken.

''Don't let anyone slack off just because we haven't heard a shot yet.''

Lon cleaned his own rifle and pistol for the second time in sixteen hours. Then, once his men had their emplacements ready, Lon finally allowed himself a chance to rest. To wait. Sleep came, but it was not particularly restful.

8

Colonel Flowers and the commander of the Aldrin West forces had chosen their positions carefully—a bucket into which East's invading army was expected to funnel. Flowers' 2nd Battalion lined the bottom of the bucket, with one battalion of Wester soldiers on their right. The rest of the Wester battalions committed to this battle were along the south side of the bucket, with two of the other DMC battalions on the north. The final mercenary battalion, 4th, was behind the lines as a reserve. The Dirigenter ships were placed to give the best possible intelligence of the anticipated battlefield from above, with two shuttles providing closer coverage—staying thirty thousand feet up and ten miles away laterally.

"I've just come from battalion," Captain Orlis told his lieutenants. "The enemy shows no sign that they suspect we're here. They *are* moving cautiously, but that's to be expected, since West has been harassing them since they reached the continental divide six weeks ago.

"They're moving down this ravine toward us, one platoon in front, most of a company two hundred yards back, and the bulk of their force another two hundred yards behind them. They have a series of patrols out on either side, from squad to platoon in strength. Five miles behind the main force they have a supply train—some small floaters, more pack animals—guarded by a battalion of infantry. The total force is between eight and ten thousand—according to the intelligence we have."

"Pack animals?" Carl Hoper asked, incredulous.

Orlis nodded. "Makes a certain kind of sense. I'm surprised they've been able to get any floaters at all across the mountains. There are no roads, no improved stretches of ground. Shows that they did their preparatory work well, mapping out a route that would let them use at least a few trucks.''

''If they've got good dispersal, scouts, and flankers, then we're not going to have tactical surprise against the main force, are we?'' Lon asked.

''Probably not,'' Orlis agreed. ''We're going to try to neutralize the flankers silently, but *that* would be iffy even if our people were doing it on both sides, but with West handling things on the south, I can't see it happening. There's almost certain to be an alarm. But there may be a certain amount of confusion on East's side of the action. They've had alarms enough. We hope they'll think it's just another harassing raid and keep coming. We let the point come all the way down the funnel, until we can spit in their faces if necessary, holding off any action until the battalions on either side take the enemy main force under fire.''

''There's no place between here and there where that force could detour to one side or the other, right?'' Hoper asked.

''Not and take their vehicles along,'' Orlis said.

Lon shrugged. *We'd abandon vehicles if we had to, without a second thought. But they've brought them this far. It might not be an easy decision to make.* ''The pack animals they're using—native or from Earth?''

''I don't know,'' Orlis said. ''The reports say they're equine in appearance, but whether that means horses, mules, burros, or something similar that developed here is anybody's guess.''

''It *could* make a difference.'' Lon thought he had heard something approaching exasperation in Orlis's voice. ''Horses, mules, and burros have different capabilities, and might react differently to the, ah, stress of a firefight. The training and treatment they've had would influence that too, of course.''

"You mean stampede the supply animals to starve out the soldiers?" Hoper asked.

Lon shrugged. "I hadn't thought it that far through. It might be possible, add a little confusion if nothing else."

Orlis stared at Lon, then said, "I'll pass your thoughts up the line, just in case. I guess there have been more far-fetched ideas that proved useful, but I can't think of any offhand."

I'm not used to sitting still and waiting for an enemy to walk up, Lon thought a couple of hours later. *We always try to be mobile, to spring up on the enemy where they don't expect us. Not this.* Waiting with an outward show of calmness was not easy. The act required concentration. But he knew the importance of showing his men that he was unflappable.

I'm not used to pitched battles involving fifteen thousand men either, he conceded with a half grin. It was rare for the DMC, rare anywhere. Even Earth had not seen a battle that large in centuries. He felt a mixture of apprehension and anticipation. He had studied many large battles in his almost four years at The Springs—battles fought with spears and swords, lances or muzzleloading rifles, or machine guns and artillery. *The weapons change more than the tactics,* Lon thought with almost cavalier abandon. It was not a proposition he would have to "prove" in class.

East's army stopped shortly after sunrise. There was some discussion on the officers' channels about the possibility that the enemy might make camp short of the waiting defenders. It did appear that this was more than just a ten-minute break. DMC scouts reported that many of the enemy soldiers were preparing meals or eating. Sentries were being posted. Patrols were sent out to either side.

"Wait to see if they're just relieving the flankers," Colonel Black told the scouts. "We'd rotate that and the point units as well. Watch for anything that looks like they're digging in for an extended stay." East had not been setting up camp until late morning during the time the DMC fleet had been watching from space. Then they had settled in for six to eight hours before starting out again.

Twenty minutes passed before the scouts nearest the enemy main force reported that it did look as if the flankers were simply being relieved. Patrols were coming back in. No trenches were being dug. The scouts saw no sign of snoopers or mines being planted.

Just a meal stop, Lon thought. *Maybe an hour altogether, give or take a few minutes.* He squeezed his eyes shut, concentrating. *They've been out on this march for two months. They might take more time, maybe even two hours.*

He tried to imagine what soldiers would feel like after two months of marching through rugged terrain, up one side of a mountain chain and starting back down the other—cold, wet, hungry, and sore. *Unless they've got one hell of a lot of motivation, they must be having morale problems by now.* Then he shook his head. There had been precious little in the database concerning public support in East for this war. *They want more room, more space to live, and they think they can only get it at the expense of West. Is that enough?* It was not until the word *Lebensraum* came to mind, along with its historical connotations of twentieth century Nazi expansionism and Earth's most violent war up to that time, that Lon decided that, just maybe, it would be.

Given the motivation of an approaching enemy, a trained soldier can erect quite a nest for himself in five hours, a trench buttressed and camouflaged, and as comfortable as conditions permit. He can map out zones of fire and commit salient points and distances to memory. The veteran does it automatically. The rookie needs to think through every step—and perhaps be reminded by his squad leader, and overseen to make sure he does it right. Lon's trench was typical. He had excavated it himself, digging down ten inches, piling the dirt up around the edges. Most of the hole was covered by a camouflage tarp bolstered by shrubbery. He had found a few loose rocks and added them to the front of the hole, then gone out in front to inspect his emplacement as well as those of his men, to make certain that none of the defenses would be readily apparent from a distance.

No one got much sleep, but each man rested as best he could—once the essentials were taken care of. Last among the essentials was food. Nearly everyone ate at least one complete meal pack. Some ate two.

Information was passed along the line of command. Matt Orlis received updates from battalion and passed them on to his lieutenants. Lon briefed his noncoms, and the squad leaders informed their men of anything they needed to know. *How close is the enemy? How soon will they be here? When does the shooting start?* The invading army remained in one spot for ninety minutes before resuming its march west, toward the positions held by the DMC and the regiment of Wester soldiers.

It was 1124 hours when Lon heard the first gunshots. The gunfire was not close or extensive. *One of the flanking patrols on the south must have run into West's people,* Lon decided quickly, since he expected the first contact to come there and since that was the direction the noise appeared to emanate from. For a few minutes there were exchanges of automatic weapons fire—long bursts, short bursts.

Lon listened to the intelligence channel, getting secondhand information. The DMC communication system was not directly linked to the system in the helmets the Westers used. There were only liaisons, DMC men with each Wester unit, and junior officers from West's army with each DMC battalion headquarters. It was five minutes before Lon received clear confirmation that his guess had been right. By that time the fighting had spread farther along the right flank.

Then there was a briefer firefight on the north flank, the one held by the DMC. That lasted no more than thirty seconds.

''The enemy main force has stopped, taken cover where

they are," Captain Orlis reported a few seconds later.
"Looks like their commanders are trying to figure out
what's up. I want everyone down. Don't give any of your
rookies a chance to foul things off by shooting early."

Lon passed that warning to his squad leaders. "Sit on
them if you have to," he added. "There's no enemy in
sight, and even if there were, we wait for the order to
fire."

East dispatched more men to help the flanking patrol
that was in action. Two minutes later, East's point started
west again—much more slowly than before, wary, looking for the earliest hint of another ambush.

Lon cranked the magnification to full on his helmet
faceplate, carefully scanning the draw in front of him,
knowing that the nearest enemy troops had to be within
five hundred yards. He breathed shallowly, when he remembered to breathe at all. He felt tension, the edge of
fear that no sane man could face combat without. He recognized the signs and understood them, used them to keep
him alert.

"Steady . . ." Captain Orlis droned the word, drawing
out the last syllable. Lon focused on the draw, out at the
limit of his visibility, knowing that the first enemy soldier
would have to step into view within seconds.

"Let them keep coming, right into our laps if necessary," Orlis said, and Lon briefly changed channels to
pass that reminder on to his men. "Wait for the order.
We want the main force engaged first, if possible," Orlis
added.

"Wait for the order," Lon echoed on his all-hands
channel.

Lon saw, or thought he saw, a hint of movement in the
distance, something more than a wind-blown branch. But
it was several more seconds before he saw it again and
was certain. A man in camouflaged battledress. A rifle.
The blank panel of a nonreflective faceplate. The enemy.

Lon moved his rifle until it was aimed at the distant
figure. He linked the weapon's sights to his faceplate as
he tracked the enemy soldier. Then he had an instant of

distraction. He thought of Sara, and that brought a knot to his solar plexus and a ludicrous twinge of guilt that it had been "so long" since he had last thought of her.

Not now! Lon told himself. *Keep your mind on right now, right here.* He blinked, swallowed, took a deep breath, and worked to concentrate on the approaching enemy.

There were more of the enemy visible now, moving cautiously, alert, not worrying about speed, just doing the job that point men were supposed to do—watching for any hint of the enemy.

Then everything started to happen at once—but not directly in front of Lon and 2nd Battalion. He heard over the radio what was going on. The enemy's main force had turned to its left and advanced against the Wester soldiers waiting along that flank.

At first the reports being relayed to the mercenary officers were fragmented, barely coherent at times, passed through the liaisons with the West units, then being rebroadcast on the DMC net. It took fifteen minutes before intelligence from CIC started to bring some coherence. The Eastmen moved in good order, disciplined, going straight into an all-out frontal attack so quickly that West had little time to prepare to meet it. East left behind just enough troops to delay any attack by the DMC units on their other flank. The point company, the unit nearest Lon, went to ground, ready to help repel any attack on what was now the right flank of their main force.

Do we go or not? Lon wondered. He did not ask. He had been an officer long enough not to bother his commander with useless questions. Either the order would come or it would not.

"Steady," he said on his platoon channels. "Wait."

East got to the high ground on the south side of the draw. Once there, they forced West's troops to pull back. "They're good, better than I expected," Lon mumbled after checking to make certain that he would not be broadcasting his comment. That came automatically now, the product of experience—and mistakes. *We'd be hard-*

pressed to do it better. That was perhaps the ultimate compliment.

"We're going to take on the enemy point," Captain Orlis told Lon after several minutes more. "Stay put, but give them something to think about. On my command."

The pause was just a few seconds. "Fire."

The concentrated rifle fire of an entire battalion against the nearest squads of the enemy was devastating. Leaves and small trees were shredded. Larger trunks were pocked. In a few small areas the ground itself looked as if it had been plowed. The Eastman soldiers tried to respond, but they took catastrophic casualties. The few who could, retreated quickly. After only two minutes, Captain Orlis passed the order to cease firing.

"Skirmish lines fifty yards apart," Orlis ordered. "Nolan, you've got the left; Hoper, the right. One platoon in front, the other behind."

Lon's third platoon would be in front. He would follow with fourth platoon—behind, where he belonged, so he would be able to see everything in front, able to respond to anything.

"Remember, there's a lot more of them out there," Lon told his men as the first skirmish line started to advance slowly. The entire battalion was moving forward, moving up the draw toward the earlier positions of the enemy point. "They may be the best we've faced, so no mistakes."

Second Battalion faced only light and sporadic fire as it advanced. The second skirmish line moved forward at the proper interval. Lon was in the middle of fourth platoon, two squads to either side of him. Occasionally he looked to make certain that his men were maintaining their position relative to the platoons that flanked them. The heaviest action remained farther ahead and well to the right, where the enemy main force had engaged the Wester troops.

The first skirmish line traveled a hundred yards before they encountered heavier enemy fire. The rest of East's point company opened up with rifle fire and grenades.

And, for the first time, Lon Nolan saw what mortars could do in combat. The DMC did not, as a rule, employ mortars, trading off weight for whatever advantage they might give. But Aldrin East had them, and the mortar bombs started falling, sending shrapnel flying, carving holes in the ranks of the mercenaries, and leaving small craters where they exploded.

"At the double!" Captain Orlis ordered. "Through it."

Lon did not have to echo the order. Orlis had used the company's all-hands channel. All Lon had to do was start trotting forward, looking to make sure that all of his men were doing the same. The mortars bombs were exploding along a narrow line. Apparently the enemy was not bothering to adjust their range, just throwing up a wall of shrapnel the mercenaries would have to penetrate to get to them.

The first skirmish line pushed through the curtain, taking more casualties, the men sprinting through the most dangerous area. The second line was still thirty yards from the heaviest concentration. Lon pushed himself. His breathing was labored, but he did not let that slow him. A glance to either side showed him that his men, most of them, were keeping pace. Everyone wanted to be through as quickly as possible.

This is insane! Lon thought as a patch of ground thirty yards in front of him erupted. He felt several sharp impacts off of his helmet, a heavier bump against his shoulder—but not the pain of shrapnel penetrating. A clump of dirt, or perhaps a small stone, had hit him.

Lon ran harder, straining himself to his limit. The bombs fell ten or fifteen seconds apart. If he could get through the target area before the next one hit . . .

The effort brought stabbing pains to his chest, flashes of white light across his vision. For a dizzying second Lon thought he would pass out. He heard a distant thumping—the sound of a mortar round being launched from its tube—somehow isolated from all the other noises of the battle. There was a long whistling after the shell reached the apex of its trajectory and started down again.

The explosion. Lon half-dove, half-fell forward, unable to go another step, almost oblivious to the impact as he hit the ground, unaware that many of his men had also gone to ground, if not always so precipitously. He gasped for breath, his chest heaving painfully. He hovered on the brink of unconsciousness for thirty seconds or more. As soon as the world stopped spinning and he could take in a breath without pain, Lon forced himself up to his hands and knees and looked to either side and then ahead. The first skirmish line was still moving forward, climbing the draw and keeping the enemy under fire.

"Up," Lon said. "Let's get the interval right again." Talking hurt. Getting to his feet brought another instant of vertigo. But that had to be ignored, conquered.

"You okay, Nolan?" Captain Orlis asked, also struggling for breath. He was to Lon's right, between his lieutenants, and he had also been moving quickly through the area the enemy had targeted with their mortars.

"Yes, sir. We're moving," Lon said, staggering forward as he spoke. "We'll be okay."

"Let's get to those mortars and put them out of action."

Lon did not bother to answer. He was moving forward with his men, concentrating on what lay ahead.

Second Battalion was stopped by an order from Colonel Flowers a hundred yards farther east. The enemy was moving again, pulling the rest of their troops over the rise on the south side of the draw, retreating.

"We're going to disengage," Orlis said after passing the order along. "See to our casualties and regroup."

"Get down and find what cover you can," Lon told his men. He moved his platoons closer together. "Weil, send your first two squads back to check on our casualties. I want all of the wounded treated as quickly as possible."

Lon stayed down for no more than a minute himself, still trying to get his breathing under control. The altitude and exertion had nearly been too much. But he had to see to his men, see who had been wounded. And killed.

9

Lon felt guilty for thinking, *We were lucky. It could have been a lot worse.* As if two dead men in third platoon and seven wounded were of little consequence. It did no good to remind himself that they were in the business of war and that casualties were part of the job. Compensating for the sense of guilt—irrational though it might be—he hovered around while medical orderlies tended the wounded and saw that those who needed time in a trauma tube got there quickly. The only good news was that no one in fourth platoon had been killed or seriously injured. One man had sprained a knee during the mad rush through the zone that had been blanketed by the enemy's mortars. Two hours of rest and a series of med patches over the knee would have him walking freely again.

The sounds of fighting moved farther east. The invaders were retreating in good order, and the troops of Aldrin West were following, harassing the enemy, making certain they kept retreating.

"Maybe this will end it, Lieutenant."

Lon turned and saw Sergeant Girana standing a little behind him. Tebba had his faceplate up and had not spoken over the radio. Lon lifted his own visor.

"I hope so, Tebba, but don't lay any wagers yet. This was just a skirmish."

"I know, but it helps to pretend that there's a chance," Tebba said, taking another step forward. "They've got good fighters here, on both sides. Disciplined."

Lon nodded. "That's what worries me. If this turns really ugly, we'll need all the help we can get."

"Long as East can't move a hell of a lot of troops across the mountains all at once. They don't seem to have the logistics, from what I've seen of the files on this place."

Lon chuckled. "Need a little light reading to help you sleep along the way?"

Tebba grinned and looked a little away. "I like to know what there is to know. Long as we've got the fleet overhead, I can't see the enemy moving overwhelming numbers this way."

"Figure that the enemy must have a contingency plan set up for this, Tebba. They sent a lot of troops across the border on foot, investing quite a few weeks at it. And there's the hint of trouble in the south, the area the dispute is over. I don't think it's going to be simple."

"If it was, West wouldn't have laid down good money to bring us in, and maybe a second regiment to boot. We don't often luck out and get paid for 'simple.' Any word what's next for us? Do we join the chase, or sit here and enjoy the mountain air?"

"I don't know." Lon shook his head slowly. "You've got to give the brass a little time to think it out. When you're not looking down the wrong end of a rifle barrel you get to thinking you've got all the time in the galaxy."

Second Battalion was the only one ordered to pull back. The other three battalions of 7th Regiment either held their positions or moved farther east, to guard against the possibility that the invaders would try to flank the pursuing Westers. A pair of Shrike fighters were on call, out of range of the enemy but close enough to join the fight in thirty seconds if needed.

"We'd still like to see this resolved without a full-blown war," Matt Orlis told his lieutenants when he briefed them. "The colonel is trying to get West's leaders to ease off on the pursuit as well. The fewer new grudges we add to the old, the more chance there is of getting the two sides to negotiate."

* * *

It was near nightfall before the withdrawing invaders managed to completely disengage. West's field commander gave up the pursuit. His men needed rest, and he did not want to risk getting too far away from reinforcement by the mercenaries. They had stopped moving east five hours earlier, over his protests.

Lon heard of the end of fighting when Captain Orlis told him to prepare for a battalion officers' call. "We'll be hiking over to Colonel Black's command post in ten minutes. If you haven't eaten in the last couple of hours, you'd better grab a quick bite while you can. I think we're going to be moving before long."

"Yes, sir," Lon said. He repressed the questions that came to mind. He would find out soon enough. In the meantime he took the captain's advice and opened a meal pouch. *Eat and sleep whenever you can. The next time might be a long way off.*

"We're in for a change of scenery," Black said without preamble once he saw that all of his officers had arrived. They sat or squatted in a semicircle around him. "The consensus is that the action here was intended more to keep the government of West too busy to take action in the south than as a serious attempt to invade the core regions of the western colony. To a degree, that strategy has succeeded. West has committed its top units to guarding against this invasion. And we're here." His pause was more for effect than to weigh his next sentences.

"It has kept West from interfering with the settlers East sent into the disputed region in the tropics. West may initially have missed the fact that East also sent troops into the area to protect those settlers. The government of West has decided that it is time to, ah, rectify the situation, to reaffirm its claim to that territory by dispatching troops and . . . political representatives." Hiram Black's slight smile was hidden from most of his officers in the dusk.

"I am not privy to the details of the negotiations that went on between Colonel Flowers and his staff and the government of Aldrin West. Suffice it to say that those talks have occupied a considerable portion of the colonel's time recently. The government wanted to send a large part of its own forces south, leaving us to worry about this invading army. Colonel Flowers feared that putting West's troops in might make the possibility of rapprochement between the two colonies more difficult. The upshot is that 2nd Battalion will be going south, while West's troops remain here to deal with the more immediate threat to their sovereignty. We will be accompanied by a detachment of civil servants who have instructions to assert West's dominion over the settlers in the disputed region. It will be our responsibility to keep those government representatives safe, and to deal with any military action taken by any troops from Aldrin East we find in the territory.

"We leave in ninety minutes," Black said after lowering his helmet visor to check the time. "We'll only travel half the distance tonight, grounding to give the men a decent night's sleep. The government people will join us in the morning, and we'll finish the trip then."

News that they were leaving the mountains was welcome to most of the men. It was enough for now that they were going to an area lower and warmer. They could worry about the next step later, after a night's sleep far from any chance of combat.

"Just as glad of it myself," Weil Jorgen told Lon after the men had been informed. "Change of pace, change of scenery, if nothing else. Maybe it won't be raining wherever we end up."

It had started raining on the western side of the mountains again, a slow, cold drizzle—just enough to make a foot soldier feel miserable.

"From what I understand, it's the wrong time of year for rain where we're likely to end up," Lon said. "And maybe hotter than New Bali. Remember, this area the people here are fighting over wasn't good enough for any of them until they started to think they had too many people to fit in the desirable areas."

Jorgen shook his head, smiling. "I was trying not to remember that, Lieutenant. 'Sufficient to the day are the evils thereof,' my daddy always told me."

Lon grunted. "What did he retire as—battalion lead sergeant?"

"Would've been regimental lead sergeant, but the man who had that job was too stubborn to retire when he should have," Jorgen said, with more good nature than his father would have. Lon had met the senior Jorgen once, at a Remembrance Day function. In his eighties, Weil's father still looked as if he could keep pace with any twenty-year-old recruit. And he had still talked with the assurance of a command lead sergeant.

The shuttles came in one at a time, loaded, and took off. There was no landing zone large enough for all of the battalion's transport craft to come in at once. The seriously injured and the dead had been taken out earlier. The wounded were aboard *Long Snake*, and many had already completed their hours in the trauma tubes that mended their injuries. Only two wounded men, who would require regeneration and rehab time, would be left aboard ship in the morning. The rest of the wounded would rejoin their companies before the second leg of the move.

Lon's platoons went out nearer the beginning of the series than the end. The ride was short and entirely atmospheric. They landed four hundred miles southwest of where they had started, at some distance from any large towns. But tents had been erected.

"No hot food or running water," Lon told his men once they had left the shuttle. "No soft mattresses either. But eat a ration pack or two and get what sleep you can."

"Sir, what time's reveille?" one of the newer men asked.

"Whenever it sounds," Lon replied. "Worry about it when you hear it. Just eat, clean up as best you can, and get all the sleep possible." They would post guards, but no one would have more than a single hour on that duty.

The platoon sergeants would pass along that bad news before they dismissed their men.

Lon took his own advice. Before the last of the battalion's shuttles landed to discharge their passengers, he was already in his bedroll, waiting for sleep. It was not a long wait.

There were no dreams to interrupt Lon's sleep. The first night out of trouble was usually peaceful for him. That more trouble might lie not too far in the future was not enough to disturb the pattern. Lon slept until he heard Tebba Girana call his name, then touch his shoulder.

"Sorry, sir. The captain said I should wake you."

Lon yawned and stretched, his eyes open just enough to see that there was daylight beyond the tent flap over Girana's shoulders and head, almost a halo around him. "What time is it?"

"Just past oh-seven-hundred," Girana said.

"The men?"

"Still sleeping. Captain said to give them till oh-seven-thirty."

Lon finished his routine of stretching and sat up. "The captain say any more than to wake me?"

"Officers' call at oh-eight-hundred. He said he thought you'd like some time first."

Lon nodded. *Nearly eight solid hours of sleep. I don't often manage that much in barracks.* That was something usually reserved for the trip home from a contract, when there was little else to do but eat and sleep, and no tensions of an upcoming campaign to spoil it.

"How long have you been up?" Lon asked.

"Jim Ziegler rousted me and Weil an hour ago," Tebba said. Ziegler was the company lead sergeant. "Told me to get my lazy carcass out of the rack and start earning my pay."

Lon managed a smile. He was too newly awake to make it a laugh. "Anybody got any coffee brewed?"

"Coffee and more, Lieutenant. Somebody come in and

stuck up a mess tent during the night. Hot breakfast waiting.''

That was enough to bring Lon to his feet.

A hot breakfast, even if the food was straight out of replicators, left Lon feeling almost cheerful. There had been plenty of hot coffee to go with the food. On top of a good night's sleep, Lon was almost able to put out of mind the fact that his men had already seen combat and might see more before they left Aldrin for home. He had gone to the mess tent before the enlisted men were wakened. Several other officers were there, taking their time with breakfast, savoring the unusual treat in the field of a meal that did not come out of ration packs. There were also a few noncoms, and a couple of privates who had been relieved from guard duty. Lon sat with Carl Hoper and the cadet he was training, Esau O'Fallon.

"How's he doing?'' Lon asked softly when O'Fallon got up to go for more coffee.

Hoper grinned. "Raw around the edges, about like you were the first time out. But he'll do fine. They don't send us the rejects. And the men accept him.''

Lon nodded. "That's good." There were always rumors in the Corps. At times they seemed to be the motive force for the professional army. Hoper had been a lieutenant for a long time. He was due to get a company of his own, and a captain's pips, sometime in the near future. O'Fallon was, more than likely, to be his replacement as leader of Alpha's first two platoons.

"You ready for hot weather?" Carl asked, watching O'Fallon return to the table.

"As ready as I'll ever be," Lon replied. "At least it won't be steamy jungle like New Bali.''

"From what I hear, we're going to this area at the best time of year," Carl said. "Hot but fairly dry, near the end of the growing season.''

"The settlers have been there long enough to get crops planted and ready to harvest?" O'Fallon asked.

Hoper merely nodded, but Lon said, "At least once."

"What's that supposed to mean?" Carl asked, and O'Fallon looked expectantly at Lon, who shrugged.

"Did you look at the recon video?" he asked.

"Of course," Carl said, and Esau nodded energetically.

"How about the earlier survey?" Lon did not wait for an answer. "I saw some of the material for Aldrin before the contract was signed, those Mondays I was working at HQ. I think some of these fields have been planted for at least two or three years, maybe more." Lon spoke softly, even though there was no longer any secrecy about any of the Aldrin material.

"West said that the 'new' intrusion of settlers was one of the reasons they wanted our help," Carl said.

"They did, but they were very careful not to say exactly when they arrived. And it wasn't until East started this invading army across the mountains that West finally convinced the Council to accept the contract."

"I don't understand," Esau O'Fallon said.

Carl shrugged. "West didn't tell us everything, kid. That's to be expected. A lot of clients tell us only what they want us to know about their situations. I'm sure the Council of Regiments took it all into account."

"I know they did," Lon said without saying why he was sure. "But I think it's also part of why we've been told to go easy, why the Council still wants us to try to set up a peaceful settlement between the two colonies."

"Couldn't we get in the middle and tell both sides to stop?" Esau asked. Neither of the lieutenants with him laughed.

"We couldn't be sure of getting paid that way," Carl said. "This *is* a business, in case you've forgotten."

The battalion officers' call was held in an open field under a clear sky. The temperature hovered at about seventy, and there was scarcely a breath of wind. Lon noticed birds flying, most at some distance. There was a smell of plowed earth—something he remembered mostly from Earth—in the air.

"We'll be boarding the shuttles in an hour or so," Colonel Black started after telling his officers to sit and make themselves as comfortable as they could on the long grass. The attack shuttles had remained on the ground after delivering the men to this temporary bivouac. The flight crews had been among the first people served in the mess tent that morning. They had slept in their shuttles. "An hour if the government people get here on time," he amended. "They'll have their own transportation. I'm not certain why they chose to rendezvous with us here rather than on the flight south." He shrugged. "Possibly just so they wouldn't have to be any prompter than they felt like. Civilian government officials." He spaced those last three words out carefully. "Not soldiers. At least that's what we've been told, but I have my doubts. I expect that there will be at least one senior representative of West's military establishment with the group." He hesitated, then shrugged. "I'm not faulting them for that. I'd probably do the same in that position." Black did not pace. He stood in front of his officers with his hands behind his back, almost at parade rest.

"We have one important restriction on our conduct in this area to the southwest," Black said. "We do not initiate hostilities. We defend ourselves as necessary. We respond, but we don't start anything, especially anything involving the civilian settlers. Any Eastman military units will be given the choice of withdrawing peacefully—that is, to return home—or disarming and accepting the sovereignty of Aldrin West. We are to protect the representatives of West from attack, by either the military or civilians. We are also—and this is to be kept quiet for now—to keep the representatives of West from doing anything overly drastic to the intruders, civilian and military. Once we are settled on the ground near the disputed settlements, our representatives will again attempt to make contact with the government of Aldrin East, and will also press West. The object is still to establish a truce and a peaceful means of settling the differences between the colonies. Our hope is that it will be easier to convince both sides to enter negotiations now that we are on the ground and the invading column of East's army has been turned back.

"I can't give you detailed instructions on what we will be doing once we ground. We will land and establish our normal defensive perimeter, then play it by ear. Questions?"

Matt Orlis got to his feet. "Yes, Captain?" Black said.

"I know a lot of this has to be off the cuff, Colonel," Orlis started, "but it sounds as if we're going to be standing around with our butts hanging out, waiting for something to happen. Are we going to get anything more precise in the way of rules of engagement?"

"Once that is possible, yes. Going in, the rules of engagement are these: One, we do not shoot first at anyone in the area, but we do respond—with the minimum necessary force—to any attack against us; two, we set up our defensive perimeter and keep the Eastmen out, but with minimal force, again without firing first. Beyond that, it will depend on what we find and how we are received. Just tell your men to keep their butts, and heads, down as much as possible until we know more."

Matt Orlis nodded and sat.

"We will retain three shuttles on the ground," Colonel Black said. "That will give us a little extra firepower if we need it. And we will be in constant contact with regiment and with CIC upstairs. If things get out of hand, we can have Shrike support in thirty minutes and ground reinforcement in hours. Or," he added slowly, "retrieval almost as quickly as we can get Shrikes in, if that proves necessary."

It was a sobering note to end the conference on, but there were no further questions.

10

Lon did not really listen to the banter among his men during the shuttle ride. He had the radio channel open, but with the volume low, the chatter became background. Lon kept his helmet faceplate down, and the tinted visor hid his expressions. Part of the time he brooded, thinking back over the officers' call and the chance that they might be exposed to danger that could be avoided . . . under different rules of engagement. *Let them shoot first, then respond. Target practice for anyone who wants to take the first shot.* Maybe it would work. Maybe it wouldn't. It was the uncertainty that bothered Lon.

And memories of Sara. At first, those were intrusions on his worries. Then, slowly, he concentrated on her, memories and plans, and the expression on his face softened. Eventually, and without his awareness, he smiled behind his faceplate. *I should have taken time last night to write her. Add a few lines to the message chip I've been working on. We might get a chance to send mail out soon. They'll be sending an MR back to Dirigent with progress reports.* He couldn't write in the shuttle with his men around, but he did start to compose a message in his head. It did not matter if he remembered the precise words later. The thought was there, and it helped pass the time.

There were few interruptions. Weil Jorgen had a question. The shuttle pilot passed along updates on their progress, especially as the landers approached their destination. The shuttles were not going in "hot." Lon gave the routine orders. Weapons would be loaded—just in case.

"Safeties stay on," Lon reminded his men. "We handle this like a drill, set up the perimeter and watch, but no firing without orders. Keep your heads down and your eyes open."

It was only in the last few minutes of the flight that Lon had to—reluctantly—put Sara out of his thoughts. There was too much to do. He opened his mapboard to look at the landing zone. It was open savanna, wild grasses and a few stands of trees, several miles from the nearest settlement but not as far from their cultivated fields. *Even if they react as soon as they see us, we should have time to get out into our perimeter before they can get to us,* Lon thought. It was some reassurance.

"I want the men out and in place faster than we've ever done it before," Lon told his noncoms. "No slacking off just because this isn't the usual thing." He thought that his voice sounded properly firm and disciplined, military, not indecisive or nervous. *It's okay to be nervous; just don't let the men know.*

In the last thirty seconds before touchdown, Lon checked his own weapons, rifle and pistol—loaded magazines, rounds in the chambers, safeties on. He closed his eyes for the length of two deep breaths, then opened them. He was as ready as he could be.

The DMC shuttles touched down together, in formation. Pilots reversed engine thrust and the landers skidded to a noisy halt, not one of them more than thirty yards out of position. The shuttle carrying the government team from Aldrin West came in twenty seconds later, separately, landing behind the last of the mercenary craft.

Lon followed his men out, moved with them out to their normal position on the battalion perimeter. The shuttles always landed in the same formation. The men always had the same relative section of the perimeter. By the time the Aldrinian shuttle came in—five hundred yards away— Lon's men were where they belonged, scraping out slit trenches to give them additional cover from any enemy. The delayed approach of the final lander created a delay

in getting the full perimeter closed. The men who were
assigned to that section of the oval LZ had to wait until
the people from Aldrin West were down.

The heat was apparent immediately as Lon left his shuttle, but it took a moment before it sank in. The heat from
the shuttle engines was always there after a landing, and
could be fairly oppressive no matter what the ambient
temperature of the LZ. Lon felt perspiration rise on his
skin, and dry almost immediately. The air was not desert-
dry, but it was closer to that than to jungle wet. The deep
grass of the savanna was turning brown, flowering heads
open to release their seeds. Only down near the ground,
the bottom five or six inches, was there any green left.
That portion of the grass was a little cooler as well. Lon
felt it in his hands.

There was no time for more nature observations. The
first minutes after a landing were far too busy for any
DMC officer. Lon had his men to see to. He had to coordinate with the platoon leaders on either side, and keep
track of what Captain Orlis and battalion headquarters had
to say . . . while digging his own slit trench and watching
for any approaching threat. He worked back and forth
among half a dozen radio channels, keeping track of as
many conversations. Controlled chaos.

At least, this time, the chaos was not multiplied by an
enemy attack. Around the perimeter word came back
quickly that there was no sign of any locals within a thousand yards. The approach of the shuttles, if not the landings themselves, had to have been observed by the
Eastman settlers. Sooner or later they would react—one
way or another.

Colonel Black waited ten minutes after the landing before he released those shuttles that were not being held
with the battalion. Part of the perimeter had to give way
to give those craft room for takeoff. Once they were gone,
burning for orbit, the perimeter closed again. By that time
the initial rush of work and worry had eased off. The
battalion was in place and ready for anything. Colonel
Black had his command post in the center of the triangle

formed by the three remaining DMC shuttles, at some distance from the smaller Aldrinian shuttle.

The next orders were for each company to send out a single squad to scout and plant electronic snoops in a wider perimeter around the battalion. In Alpha Company, first platoon drew the assignment, and Lon heard Captain Orlis tell Carl Hoper to send his cadet with the patrol. *I know what that's like,* Lon thought. O'Fallon would catch every sort of combat detail, and so would the squad he was assigned to, just because he was a cadet, working to earn a lieutenant's pips. The red and gold badge of rank was not *given* to anyone. No man who had not been through combat could command others in the Dirigent Mercenary Corps.

"Hoper, Nolan, come over to me," Captain Orlis said on the channel that connected him with his lieutenants.

Lon was content to leave his excavating. His trench was not complete, but he had made a good start. With a little luck, perhaps one or more of his men would finish the job while he was with the captain.

Captain Orlis had his company CP in the center of the section of perimeter he was responsible for, thirty yards behind the line. His headquarters squad had already excavated a sizable bunker and were extending telescoping poles across the top to hold a roof of sod. The captain was behind that area, sitting in the tall grass, his mapboard open on the ground. He gestured for the lieutenants to sit. Lon and Carl flanked their captain, close enough to see the mapboard easily.

"For now, sitting is about all we do," Orlis said, glancing up. "We've got eyes overhead watching that town closely. If there's any significant movement, we'll know fast. Colonel Black is meeting with the government people over there." He gestured with a thumb, vaguely in the direction of battalion headquarters. "The general idea, as I understand it, is that they're going to announce our arrival to the settlers, make their claim of sovereignty, and give instructions to the locals." Orlis tried to keep his voice free of any inflection that might seem editorial, but he was not completely successful. "If the locals accept the ultimatum, fine and good. If not . . ." He shrugged.

"We're going to keep patrols out, but they won't go near the town or farms." He made a gesture over the mapboard, indicating the prohibited areas. "At least not before dark. The duty will be rotated, but I doubt that we'll be sitting here long enough for every squad to get a turn." He paused. "I could be wrong, but I don't think so. And unless the colonel changes his mind, we'll only have two squads out at a time, instead of the four we have out now. Once your men are dug in, make sure everyone eats, then give your squads a turn at sacking out. Keep one on watch and let the others flake off. They're not going anywhere."

"How long do you think this might last, Captain?" Carl Hoper asked. "The sitting around, I mean."

"As far as I'm concerned, the longer the better," Orlis replied. "But I expect the Wester officials to give the settlers some sort of deadline to accept the ultimatum. If they don't accept it, we'll probably have to go to town. Honestly, Carl, I haven't been told more."

"Do we know where the Eastman troops are?" Lon asked.

Orlis shook his head. "There are no unidentified sources of military electronics. East has them, about on the same level as West, but if they *do* have soldiers here, they're maintaining electronic silence. They could be anywhere, maybe billeted with the settlers, maybe out camped under trees somewhere close."

"Are we taking the presence of Eastman troops solely on the say-so of West, or do we have independent intelligence?" Lon asked. "How certain is it that there *are* enemy troops around?"

A grunt was the captain's first reply. Then he said, "It's likely that there are at least *some* enemy soldiers in the region. That's the best I can tell you. Yes, it's mainly on the word of our, uh, paymasters that we anticipate that, but not entirely. There were radio transmissions the day we reached Aldrin, that were, shall we say, suspicious in nature.''

"Which means we don't have any real idea how many we might be facing,'' Carl said.

"I wouldn't go that far. I think we can be fairly comfortable with the estimate that it's not more than the equivalent of one or two companies. Unless, of course, the settlers are also soldiers, perhaps chosen on that basis.''

I don't like waiting, Lon told himself as he finished his trench. With too much time and too little else to do, he dug as if he were establishing a permanent residence, making the hole deeper than he would have under other circumstances, angling the sides of the hole enough to prevent cave-ins, piling the dirt and sod around the edge to give him even greater protection, and scooping out grenade traps at the bottom.

This waiting seemed worse than most. Over his years of military service on Dirigent, and his nearly four years as a student at the North American Military Academy on Earth, he had become almost inured to the inevitable waiting that sometimes seemed to occupy 90 percent of the waking hours of any soldier. Waiting in formation, waiting to eat, waiting for . . . everything. Then there was the more intense sort of waiting that came on contract, when a man knew that combat might be close. *A whole different beast,* Lon thought. But this waiting with no idea of when or how it might end was particularly trying.

Finally Lon stood in the center of his slit trench, knowing it was time to stop. *Before someone makes a crack about me trying to tunnel through to the other side of the world.* He shook his head. He might already be setting a bad example. After three years, the men who had been with him since the start could read his moods with uncanny accuracy. He climbed out of the hole and stood behind it, stretching to take the kinks out of his back and shoulders. He did a couple of knee bends then.

"Hard work'll do that to you when you're not used to it, Lieutenant."

"It feels good, Tebba," Lon said, recognizing the sergeant's voice. "Almost as good as running a mile race and winning." He turned. Girana was sitting in the grass a dozen feet away, even farther from his own foxhole.

"If you're just coming back to where you started, what's the hurry about it? That's what I never figured out," Tebba said.

"Is that smoke coming out of your ears? You're starting to turn philosopher again."

Tebba grinned. "It's how I cope with the waiting." His eyes shifted focus to the hole that Lon had so painstakingly dug.

"It's better waiting like this than getting shot at," Lon said quietly, the smile fading from his face.

"Any day," Tebba agreed, nodding.

"Tell me, the men start making bets how deep I would go?" Lon asked, walking over and sitting next to Girana.

"If they did, nobody let me in on it. I was just worried you would work so hard you'd fill that hole up with sweat."

"Thanks for reminding me. I had just about forgotten about the heat." Lon pulled a canteen off his belt and screwed open the top. "I trust you've reminded the men about not letting themselves get dehydrated?" he asked after he had taken three careful sips of water.

"A couple of times. I was about to remind you when you finally quit working."

Lon looked sheepish. "How long were you watching?"

"Oh, not all that long, I expect. Too much to do keeping after this gang of ours for spectator sports. Nobody much likes the waiting, even though they'd like the other even less."

"Life in the army, Tebba."

"All the way back to spears and clubs, I imagine," he said. "Some progress we've made."

"We've made some," Lon said, his voice going serious again. "When we fight, we don't have battles with a million soldiers involved. There aren't fifty thousand killed in a single day's battle. I guess we're getting somewhere.''

Lon's fourth platoon drew a patrol assignment. He handed it to Corporal Wil Nace and his men, the first squad. They were to cover the eastern sector, out to a thousand yards from the perimeter. Captain Orlis gave Nace the briefing personally. Lon sat in on it. *Go here. Don't go there. Report any contact, or any sign of enemy military forces, immediately. Be back in three hours.* Nace listened, nodded, and said, "Yes, sir," at the appropriate places.

"Nace is the best noncom I've got for this kind of assignment," Lon told the captain after Nace had gone to collect his men and move through the perimeter.

Orlis nodded soberly. "I know. He's like a ghost. Until some brain-boy comes up with a way to make soldiers really invisible, Nace is the closest thing we've got."

Lon actually managed to sleep for most of the time Nace's squad was out. He told his platoon sergeants he was going to take two hours. Partly that was show, to let his men know he wasn't nervous, or worried that the patrol might run into trouble. But partly it was a reaction to the waiting. He felt deeply tired, unable to suppress yawns or keep his eyes from watering. Sunset came while Lon was sleeping, lying on his side, his back against the angled dirt wall of the hole. Three feet below the surface of the savanna, the temperature was almost comfortable.

"Lieutenant, the patrol's comin' back in," Weil Jorgen said, speaking over their radio channel. He waited for Lon to speak, then repeated his message to make certain he heard it all.

"I take it they didn't run into any trouble?" Lon asked through a yawn.

"Beer run," Jorgen said. "Wil just gave me the rundown, after he reported to the captain."

"Make sure they eat before they turn in," Lon said. "They've been out three hours. They're due."

Weil's chuckle was very contained. ''They've done their share of walkin', that's for sure, Lieutenant. I'll see 'em down proper. You want to talk with Nace first?''

''Just long enough to tell him 'well done,' '' Lon said, and then he changed channels to do that. ''Get your men fed and settle in for a nap, Wil. We'll try to hold the noise down.''

The settlers had made no response to the ultimatum, not even an acknowledgment that they had heard the message—and it was as certain as possible that they had. CIC had taken over all communications channels relayed into the settlement by satellite. Anyone using a complink in the settlement would have heard and read the message. And it was being repeated on all channels every thirty minutes—continuously on the main news link. The deadline given was dawn the following morning. The ''or else'' was left undefined.

After midnight, Delta Company put a patrol out to the edge of the settlement without trouble and reported they had seen no sign of fortifications or soldiers. The next patrol sent in that direction, two hours later, was not so lucky. Lon was sleeping again by then. The sounds of a firefight woke him.

11

Gunfire, even at a distance, was enough to wake almost everyone. Squad leaders and their assistants took care of the few who seemed ready to sleep through it. Lon checked with his platoon sergeants and squad leaders, then concentrated on listening to the sounds of the firefight. It was clear it was just a skirmish. *Our patrol must have run into an enemy patrol,* Lon guessed. It was an easy hypothesis, confirmed by Captain Orlis within five minutes.

"Just stay alert, Nolan," Orlis said. "Delta is dealing with the contact. Unless it gets out of hand, we stay put."

That did not surprise Lon. Under the prevailing rules of engagement, any other course would have been remarkable. "Tebba, Weil," Lon said, switching channels. "Get the men fed. Tell them to stay alert but, at least for now, we're staying put. Eyes on their own section of the front."

Lon unfolded his mapboard, low in the trench so the slight glow from the screen would not give away his position. He adjusted the chart until he could see the blips of Delta's beleaguered patrol. There were no other blips, which meant that the enemy was not using helmet electronics—or had gear so advanced that the DMC's equipment could not detect it.

"Not likely," Lon muttered to himself.

The skirmish, more than three miles from the nearest point of the DMC perimeter, lasted less than a quarter hour. Disengagement was complete. Delta's patrol was on its way back, with its casualties, five minutes later. A full platoon from their company had gone out to meet them and get the injured to treatment as quickly as possible.

Lon waited for information. As quickly as the patrol's report could be processed, Lon expected that any pertinent information would be relayed. It would take longer for any change in plans to be decided on. Dawn was more than two hours away. That had been the deadline given to the settlers to respond. *There wouldn't be much point in doing anything serious before then,* Lon thought.

Exactly *what* the battalion would do if the deadline passed without response from the locals had not been announced, but there seemed little question about the only possible response—other than extending the deadline. The battalion would have to get out of its defensive perimeter and march on the town, try to move in and occupy it.

Wait for somebody to shoot at us. Lon let his face screw up in a momentary grimace. In his trench, with his visor down, there was no chance that anyone would see his expression. *Put troops all the way around the settled area, then march into town in skirmish line, ready, just waiting for someone to pull a trigger and start a fight.* It was not a happy thought.

He was distracted by an update from Captain Orlis. Delta's patrol had run into a six-man squad. Two enemy soldiers had been killed, three wounded, and left after first aid. One prisoner had been taken and was on his way to battalion headquarters for questioning. Delta had lost one dead, four wounded, one seriously enough to require speed getting him to a trauma tube.

"Put your men back on half-and-half," Orlis told Lon and Carl. "Unless battalion gets startling information from the prisoner, I expect we'll be moving shortly after dawn." The prisoner would be questioned, humanely, with drugs that would give him no opportunity to lie or remain silent and that worked too rapidly for a body's implanted medical defenses to offset them. Even if the molecular health maintenance system had been programmed with the exact formula of the truth drugs, it could not work quickly enough to neutralize them. Anything the prisoner knew would be divulged quickly. A similar drug was used to establish truth in criminal cases on Dirigent.

Lon took out a meal pack and ate after passing the word to his noncoms to put the men back on 50 percent watch. "Better make it forty-five minutes at a time," he added. "We can't count on more than about an hour and a half."

Night had brought quiet to the battalion's general radio channels. They were not officially observing electronic silence. The enemy knew where they were and could get a close estimate of their numbers. There had been no point in secrecy. The more nervous the settlers and their protectors got about the odds, the less likely it was that 2nd Battalion would have to fight. Night had brought its own peace, the men getting what sleep they could, and not doing anything to disturb those who were off watch. Even the firefight had only briefly increased the traffic.

The shank of the night, just before dawn, when people find it hardest to stay alert, Lon thought after finishing his meal—a breakfast of spaghetti with meat sauce, roll, and chocolate bar. There was almost a smile in his mind as he recalled long nights of cramming for tests at The Springs, when all of the stim patches in the world had not been enough to keep his mind functioning at full speed. *We'd sit there studying, yawning together. Pretty soon no one could stop.* He blinked rapidly, fighting back a yawn that came with the memory.

After the heat of the previous day, Lon was almost chilled sitting in his foxhole with no chance to move around. *Dry air heats rapidly and cools rapidly,* he thought, recalling a basic lesson in meteorology. He had wondered why an army officer might need to know so much about forecasting the weather at the time, when there were so many other topics whose importance had seemed so obvious. "Hell, even professional meteorologists still get the forecast wrong sometimes," he had joked to a few classmates. *I wonder where they've all got to,* he thought, and that took the humor from his thoughts. The top men in his class were to be denied the chance to be army officers—the goal they had sought for so long—drafted for service in the national police force. Some, like him, had left, aided by the academy's commandant. Most of those had intended to go to Dirigent, as Lon had, but none of them had made the journey with him, and he had not seen any of them since leaving Earth. He did not know if they had all changed their minds, been intercepted trying to leave, or had been turned down by the DMC.

Lon sat huddled up as protection against the greater chill that came over him, a chilling of the spirit as much as the body. He no longer felt homesick for Earth. Even before meeting Sara, he had overcome that. He missed family and friends, and he regretted the infrequent exchange of letters, but Dirigent had become home, in thought as well as in fact. Earth had become a place to escape, for those who could, long before the birth of Lon Nolan. The inescapable problem was that people could not emigrate fast enough to keep the population from continuing to grow. Doomsayers had been predicting a final "meltdown" of civilization on Earth for generations, always "imminent," always "inescapable." Someday they might even be right.

The call from Captain Orlis was a welcome distraction.

"Here's the poop," Orlis started. "There are about three hundred regular soldiers in the area, most right in the town, a few at another village twenty miles southeast. But count another two hundred militia among the settlers, some of them retired soldiers, the rest given three to six months of military training before being allowed to be part of this intrusion. No heavy equipment, no aircraft. The settlement isn't completely self-sufficient. They've still been getting items they can't grow or replicate on site from East. And the most they can muster is four mortars. The prisoner claims they have 'plenty' of ammunition but couldn't provide specifics. Morale is apparently good, despite complaints about the heat and conditions. It appears that these people were chosen as much for patriotic fervor as anything else."

"Doesn't bode well for a peaceful resolution, does it?"

"Nobody said it would be easy," Orlis said. "Just after dawn, Colonel Black is going to make one final direct appeal to the people of the town. He has the name of the military commander and the civilian mayor to work with, so that might help. But we are going to proceed on the assumption that it won't. As the colonel makes his broadcast, the battalion will start moving into position. Bravo and Delta Companies will move first. They'll be traveling farthest, to the far side of this town, spreading out to prevent any attempt by the garrison to escape. Alpha and Charlie will stay put until the other companies are set. Then we advance directly on the town, securing farmhouses along the way, going right into the settlement unless we come under fire first. If that happens, we respond, but still without going beyond the essentials of defending ourselves. What happens at that point depends on circumstances. We're still playing this by ear."

We could lose a few ears, and more, that way, Lon thought, but all he said was the necessary, "Yes, sir." *We walk forward like a row of targets until somebody starts knocking us down.*

"We'll have our three shuttles in the air ready for immediate response, and Shrikes not far away," Orlis said. DMC attack shuttles mounted rocket launchers and rapid-fire cannon. They were not as heavily armed or as maneuverable as Shrikes, but they might be able to fill in until the Shrikes could arrive.

"Anything from that prisoner on land mines or booby traps?"

"Nothing was said. Assume there are."

Lon shared the news with his platoon sergeants and squad leaders. "Make sure the men know that we're likely to be moving not long after sunup," he told them.

Lon lifted his helmet visor, then looked toward the horizon, watching for the earliest hint of dawn. For a time he concentrated on that, putting everything else out of mind, almost entering a state of meditation. But there was one nagging thought that would not let go completely. *We're going to have to fight before the morning is over.*

• • •

Along the eastern horizon, the black of night started to cycle through dark blues toward dawn. When the rim of Aldrin's sun showed above the mountains, the deadline would have arrived. Colonel Black would make his final appeal to the settlers from Aldrin East, and 2nd Battalion would start to move into place to furnish the "or else."

Lon had his squad leaders check their men. Then he got out of his trench and made the rounds of the section of perimeter his platoons were responsible for, talking to each squad—a few words here and there, encouragement, answering questions, showing himself to be confident and calm.

"Since we've got work, best to get it out of the way before the day gets too hot," he told one squad. "No need to have sweat complicate things." It got a weak laugh—more than it deserved, but enough. For Dav Grott's squad, Lon's jest was different. "I don't know of any pubs there, and the locals aren't likely to ask us in for a pint anyway, so enjoy the water in your canteens. Drink it like it was the best beer on Dirigent."

When the orders finally came for the company to form up for the move toward the disputed settlement, Lon was satisfied that his men were alert and as relaxed as possible. They would perform as the professionals they were supposed to be.

There was more waiting. The two companies that had the greatest distance to travel left the perimeter first. The others were on standby. Many of Lon's men took a few minutes to loosen up muscles that had been inactive through most of the night, preparing themselves. Lon continued to circulate, working the stiffness out of knees and back by walking. The sun rose, showing more of itself in a cloudless sky. The lower arc of the star appeared to be supported on top of the mountain range when word finally came for Alpha and Charlie to form up and move out.

Alpha was on the left, Charlie on the right. Lon's platoons were in the center, in two columns. Carl Hoper's men were to Lon's left. Three hundred yards away, Charlie moved south in similar formation, drawing farther away from Alpha as they moved toward their respective stations.

How close will they let us get? Lon wondered, thinking of the soldiers and civilian militia in the settlement. *When will the shooting start?*

12

The movements of 2nd Battalion were deliberate, slow. As Alpha and Charlie companies put more distance between them, they changed formation from platoon columns of two to a skirmish line. Each platoon had three squads in front and one trailing. The interval between soldiers in the front line grew to an average of eight yards. There were few stands of trees to complicate the movement of the companies. Each of those obstructions was investigated by a patrol first. Only when they proclaimed the trees free of ambush did the companies proceed.

Two thousand yards from the first cultivated fields, Alpha and Charlie Companies were given fifteen minutes to rest. The encirclement of the town was nearly complete. There would be considerable gaps in the ring, but that was intentional. The battalion was not attempting to establish a siege. Unless they met with serious resistance, they were going to occupy the town.

"I want everyone down flat," Lon told his noncoms when the order to halt came. "No heads sticking up above this grass we're in. Let's not tempt any Deadeye Dick with a rifle and scope."

Nearly everyone stared toward the town, peering through gaps in the wild savanna grasses, looking for any hint of the enemy. It was a nervous time. There was a grain field directly in front of Lon's platoons, across a strip some twenty yards wide that had been plowed to keep native grasses away from the settlement's crops. He guessed that the grain must be nearly ready for the harvest. The stalks were waist-high, with heavy heads turning a golden tan.

"A thousand men could hide in a field like that," Tebba Girana said over his radio link to Lon. "Long as they were still and didn't make the grain move against the wind, we'd be hard put to find them before they were ready to be found."

"I don't think so, Tebba," Lon replied. "We've got too many lenses looking down at this whole area. *We* might miss them, but the sky-eyes would see them, anything bigger than a possum."

There was a moment of silence before Girana asked, "What the hell's a possum?"

Lon laughed. "Small marsupial from Earth. Short legs, hairless tail. Maybe a bit bigger than an overfed house-cat."

"That where the saying 'playing possum' comes from?"

"Yeah. Story was that they'd play dead to escape threats. More likely, they get scared and just freeze up, even in the road with a car coming. Most I saw were roadkill." *Tebba must be unusually nervous,* Lon thought. *He doesn't normally talk more than he has to, going into action.* Lon glanced to his left. Tebba was more than fifty yards away, behind third platoon. Lon could pick him out only by where he was. With helmet and battledress, he could have been nearly anyone in the battalion.

"Just like a drill, Tebba," Lon said softly. "Don't go working yourself up to an itch you can't scratch."

Girana grunted. "I wouldn't have an itch if the fly-guys were spreading around a little metal first," he said. "Or maybe if those big shots from West's government were walking with us instead of sitting back there with their shuttle, all ready to get the hell out of here if things go bad in a hurry."

"They're not soldiers, Tebba. They'd just be in the way if they were with us," Lon said.

"Maybe so, but I'm starting to feel a little like one of those little yellow ducks in a carnival shooting gallery.

Knock down three and get a stuffed bear for your girl.''

"Maybe so, but remember, the sights on those shooting gallery guns are usually rigged so you're more likely to shoot yourself in the ass than hit three targets."

Tebba didn't respond. Lon had to switch channels for a call from Captain Orlis. "Another few minutes," the captain said. "We're waiting for Bravo and Delta on the other side. When we start up we keep going until we're in town or hit enemy fire."

"Yes, sir. We're ready." Lon switched to his all-hands channel. "We're got a couple of extra minutes waiting for the rest of the battalion. Let's keep this nice and loose. No need to tighten up. If trouble comes, you all know how to react. That means wait for an order to return fire. We still want to make nice if they'll let us. And they might. If they wanted to be nasty, we'd have had company last night, noisy company." *Sounds good to me,* he thought. He felt surprised that he was as calm as he was, not forced to put on an act for the men, the way he sometimes had to in the past. Even earlier this morning he had felt a little apprehensive about this mission, but no longer. His sweat was a product of heat, not nerves. Even Girana's unexpected jitters had not disturbed Lon. *Maybe it should have,* he conceded. *He's been in the business a hell of a lot longer than I have.*

The order to start moving again came. The platoons rose from the grass and started forward, rifles at port arms. Lon spent a few seconds nagging squad leaders to make certain their men watched their intervals. "No bunching up," he said. It was routine "officer noise," the kind that had often annoyed him when he was on the receiving end as cadet or trainee.

Looking ahead, even with his faceplate switched to magnify the view, Lon could see no people in the town. The place might as well have been deserted. *No, they're there, someplace,* Lon assured himself, *waiting.* He wondered if the settlers would indeed turn this into a fight, or just stall as long as possible then capitulate to save lives and avoid the destruction of their homes. *A lot of the men might have weapons, but they've also got wives and children.* Asking, *What would I do?* was unproductive. He had no wife or children. Yet. Even thoughts of Sara and marriage were not enough to let him trust his instincts on this. *Fight for something I believe in, or accept the inevitable and make sure the people I love remain safe?*

He followed his men through the grainfield. The stalks that were tramped down did not spring back afterward, but lay nearly flat, a clear sign of the passage of his soldiers, arrows showing their course and numbers. *We would know if any of the enemy was lying in wait,* Lon realized. *We'd know exactly where they were.* The native grasses had shown more resilience, slowly springing back after being walked over, but not the cultivated grain. *The grainheads are too heavy for the support,* Lon thought. *If it's not harvested on time, it would collapse under its own weight.* Lon had never farmed, or kept a garden, but his mother had always grown a few tomatoes and onions. *I guess I picked up some knowledge somewhere along the line,* he decided.

"Keep the pace down, Weil," Lon told the fourth platoon sergeant, noticing that his part of the skirmish line was starting to get ahead of its neighbors. "This isn't a race. We want to give the locals plenty of time to think about us coming, time to decide they don't want to fight us."

Jorgen was already dressing the line, passing the order to his squad leaders, undoubtedly more emphatically than Lon had given it to him. The line straightened quickly.

Lon noticed a lone bird circling high overhead. It made him think of the buzzards he had often seen on Earth, circling like that in the mountains, looking for dead meat. The buzzards got to much of the roadkill. As a child, Lon had asked his father, "How come we never see dead buzzards? Don't they die?" He could not recall, at the moment, how his father had answered that.

The skirmish line reached a point a thousand yards from the nearest buildings. Lon scanned the town again, still without seeing any human beings. "They're sure not going to welcome us with a parade," he muttered.

"The locals still aren't answering the radio," Matt Orlis said a moment later. "I just had that from battalion."

"I wish they'd say *something*, even if it was just, 'Go to hell,' " Lon said. "No change in the plan, is there?"

"No change," Orlis confirmed. "One way or the other, we make them commit themselves. At seven hundred yards, the colonel wants to slow the pace even more. One step at a time, as if we knew we were moving through a minefield."

"It's getting hot, so I guess that's better than running our tails off," Lon said, as much to himself as to the captain.

"That's one way of looking at it."

Lon told his platoon sergeants about the upcoming change. The line was still eight hundred yards from the first buildings.

A good sniper would have a field day now, Lon thought. *Like those ducks Tebba was worried about.* He could feel his muscles start to tighten, anticipating the possible need for quick action. It still was not fear. *Maybe I* should *be afraid.* He shook his head. This wasn't the time for self-analysis.

Seven hundred yards. Second Battalion slowed its pace. Lon scanned the near side of the town almost constantly, letting his sergeants and corporals worry about keeping the platoons in line. He caught a glint of sunlight off glass—someone peering out from the shadows behind an open window in one of the buildings. Lon mentioned the sighting to Captain Orlis. "It's the first hint I've seen of anyone in there," he added.

Lon flexed his shoulders. Walking hunched over for so long had started a cramp in his back. His shoulders ached as well. The web straps of his pack harness felt as if they were digging into flesh, though they were too well padded for that. His platoons marched out of one field of grain and through another plowed buffer strip (after it was checked for mines), then into more grain. The fields did not have wide separation between neat rows left for large harvesters to maneuver along—the way it was still done on Earth. The farmers would have smaller harvesters, robots that would separate grain from chaff and harvest both. No organics would be wasted. The inedible portions would be fed into replicators—raw materials for foods not being grown in the area. Wild vegetation would serve that purpose just as well, but humans still liked to grow some of their own food, even food animals, no matter the arguments that it was impractical, wasteful, that replicators could do the job far more efficiently, and produce meals indistinguishable from the "real" thing.

Five hundred yards. Lon saw more indications of human presence in the town, occasional movement, low to the ground or at the edges of windows and doorways. The settlers were there. Lon tried to figure the probabilities. How long would they wait to open fire? How disciplined were the soldiers, professionals and militiamen? When would one of the amateurs get nervous and let off the first shot? At five hundred yards, with little wind and a good firing stance, Lon could hit a ten-inch target nineteen times out of twenty. A nervous civilian would be lucky to come anywhere near a moving human at that range, even from a benchrest.

Four hundred yards. "Quack, quack," Lon whispered after silencing his radio, beginning to feel what Tebba had felt earlier. Nerves. His palms were sweaty. One at a time, he wiped them on his clothes. *I guess you're still human.* They might not be sitting, but they were nearly close enough to the settlers and soldiers from Aldrin East to be *standing* ducks. *Damn it! Do something!* he thought almost angrily, a sudden surge of emotion breaking through his studied reserve. *Either put up a fight or surrender.*

Two hundred yards. As the leading skirmish line hit that distance, a dozen rifles opened fire from inside the town.

"Take cover!" Lon's order was an echo of the one that Captain Orlis gave the entire company. Lon went down with his men, but kept his head up enough to look forward. The first shots had been farther to the right, near the junction between his fourth platoon and Charlie Company.

Thirty seconds passed before Captain Orlis came back on the line, this time on the channel that connected him with his lieutenants and platoon sergeants. "Hold your fire. Charlie's going to reply to the group that fired on it. No one else is to get involved."

Lon passed that order to his men as Charlie opened up. For nearly a minute, the men of Charlie poured rifle fire into a short section of the town's perimeter. Lon could not tell if the defenders were still firing, or if anyone else in the town had started. When Charlie Company stopped firing, there seemed to be silence around the settlement, but after a few seconds Lon noted that there was some scattered fire coming out, not coordinated, and not close.

"We're going in," Captain Orlis told his lieutenants. "Fire and maneuver. Two squads move while the other two provide the covering fire. I don't want wild shooting. We don't want a lot of civilian casualties. Tell your men to be careful and look for targets when possible, and to keep their aim narrowed to the areas where the enemy shooters are."

Lon passed on the orders and his platoons waited for the command to advance. The entire battalion would resume the constricting movement, tightening the ring around the settlers and the soldiers who were supposed to protect them.

That defense remained sporadic. Occasionally defenders along one section would provide a concerted effort, but never for long, and the fighting never became general. The Eastmen who had settled on territory claimed by their rivals hunkered down under the fire of the approaching mercenaries.

The leading squads of 2nd Battalion were still 150 yards out when the order was passed to fix bayonets. *That's it, for certain,* Lon thought as he attached his bayonet to the muzzle of his rifle. *We're going all the way in.*

"Halt the advance!" Captain Orlis ordered. Lon's men stopped in their tracks. They had scarcely had time to get their bayonets fixed. "Cease firing. Dress the line and keep the men down, alert. There's something going on. The settlers finally want to talk."

It's about time, Lon thought. *I hope they're ready to call it quits and this isn't just a stalling tactic.*

He did not worry as the wait extended past the first minutes. He was willing to let the Eastmen take all the time they wanted as long as the result was peaceful. "Get a drink and keep your eyes open," he told his men. "Hard telling how long we're going to be here." He took water himself, first a sip, then a longer drink. It wasn't noon yet and the temperature was already near a hundred degrees. Water was vital. Dehydration could drop a man in his tracks.

Ten minutes passed. Twenty. From habit, Lon had noted the time of the order. And when his radio came to life again, he glanced at his helmet timeline again.

"This is Colonel Black," the familiar voice said. "Stay alert, just in case, but it looks as if the fighting is over. We're waiting for the representatives of Aldrin West to join us, and then we're going to get up and walk right in."

I hope, Lon thought, closing his eyes for just an instant. *I hope it's not just a trick.*

13

Alpha Company was chosen to escort Colonel Black and the Wester government team. The rest of the battalion remained outside the town that the residents called Hope. Lon got his first close look at the supposedly civilian representatives of Aldrin West on the march into the settlement. There were twelve men. Six were described as police officers. They appeared military to Lon, even though they wore civilian clothing. Of the other six, the men chosen to begin West's administration of the captured settlement, Lon was certain that at least two were also military, officers of long service. They had the look, the bearing, of professional soldiers.

"Keep your eyes open," Lon told his men as they started moving into Hope. "If this is some kind of trick, we need to be ready. No doping off."

The town of Hope consisted of two dozen public buildings—commercial, industrial, and so forth—surrounded by more than two hundred residences, most with extensive yards and gardens. Lon looked closely at the buildings. The "new" had certainly worn off. Most had been constructed with plascrete and resin-based composites that could be nanofactured onsite to specification, but a large minority were built of wood, and all of those showed signs of weathering. Orchards planted in some yards had trees that were old enough to bear fruit. The center of the community was a large plaza. It was unpaved, and the grass was brown and sparse.

"This town has definitely been here more than a year or two," Lon commented on the radio channel that connected him with his platoon sergeants. "Look at it. I wouldn't be surprised if it's been here ten years."

"Half that, at least, Lieutenant," Weil Jorgen said. "Those apple trees on the left have to be that old or older. Nobody transplants or replicates them more than a year old."

It was no surprise to see trees and plants that naturally flourished in temperate climates doing well in tropical heat. Most terran flora that had been taken to new worlds had been modified for conditions wherever they were introduced. That had been going on since the start of the human diaspora. Genetic engineering, and the nanotechnology that allowed people to replicate goods from patterns—atom by atom—had been as vital to mankind's expansion as the mastery of Q-space.

The company of regular soldiers was drawn up in formation in the plaza, wearing soft caps instead of battle helmets. Their weapons had been carefully stacked twenty yards from the front rank of soldiers, flanking a flagpole that carried what Lon took to be the standard of Aldrin East—a white field with blue and red diagonals, surmounted by a golden sun. The officers stood in front of their men. Off to the left there was another series of pyramidal stacks of rifles. Those, Lon assumed, belonged to the militia, the "civilian" volunteers. But there was no formation of that unit. *We won't find any records saying who belonged either,* Lon guessed. *I'd bet anything those were destroyed to make sure there were no reprisals.* That would leave a cadre of trained men in the community, even if the regular army unit was taken out. *I bet they've got more weapons and ammunition cached somewhere the Westers will never find.* It was the obvious ploy. And Hope appeared to have been too carefully planned to miss that preparation.

A few civilians stood near the commander of the army unit, apparently the leaders of the municipal government. A few other civilians were visible on the fringes of the plaza, and in windows and doorways overlooking it. Most of the civilians were too far away for Lon to read facial expressions, but the nearest looked sullen and angry.

"They may have surrendered, but they don't look beaten," Lon commented. Tebba grunted. Weil did not reply at all.

Colonel Black had the company form up facing the defenders, just like regimental parade back on Dirigent.

"Nolan, come with me," Captain Orlis said. "Leave your rifle with one of your men. Hoper, you've got the company until I return." As Orlis and Lon moved forward, to stand behind Colonel Black and his headquarters staff, Orlis told Lon what was going on via private link. "We're here to make show. The colonel wants all of the company commanders and their junior lieutenants up close for the ceremony. The others are hurrying in from their posts around the town, so we've got a minute or two. We don't have to break our necks."

"What about West's people?" Lon asked.

Orlis gestured to the left with his head. "According to the deal that Colonel Black struck with the locals, their soldiers are going to surrender to us rather than to West. I don't know the details. The civilians will remain to the side for now. The idea is, Hope and its defenders surrender to us and we turn control over to West."

"A way for the locals to save face?"

"Maybe they just hate West too much to do it any other way."

The soldiers of East remained at attention while the mercenary officers assembled. Alpha Company was also at attention, and Colonel Black brought his gathered officers to that position as well once all of them had gathered.

"We'll move forward, halfway," Black informed the officers. "Their commander and senior officers will meet us there. Let's give them a proper show."

The groups of officers started to march toward each other, at about half a normal marching pace. When the two commanders were six feet apart, both groups of officers were halted.

"I am Lieutenant Colonel Hiram Black, commanding

2nd Battalion, 7th Regiment, Dirigent Mercenary Corps,'' Black announced. He had the visor of his helmet lifted.

"Major Anthony Esterling, commanding 2nd Volunteer Expeditionary Detachment, Aldrin East Defense Force,'' the other commander said.

Second detachment, Lon noted. *I wonder where the first is. Were they the people we fought in the mountains? Or are they somewhere else, waiting for their shot at us?*

"Colonel Black, when I spoke with you before, I indicated that I would only surrender my men, and the town that I was charged to defend, to you and your men. At this point, I wish to commit my men, and my civilian charges—men, women, and children—to your protection. We believe that we can trust you to act honorably and to protect us against drastic reprisals by the enemies of our people. The honorable reputation of the Dirigent Mercenary Corps is well known. Will you accept our surrender under that condition, sir?''

Lon blinked quickly several times. *Was all this worked out in advance?* He wanted, desperately, to see how the people from Aldrin West were reacting to Major Esterling's speech, but he was at attention, and the Westers weren't in his field of vision.

Colonel Black did not hesitate long enough for those civilians to object. "I will, Major Esterling. I promise you and the town of Hope that you will remain under the protection of the Dirigent Mercenary Corps until suitable guarantees for your safety can be arranged between the governments here.''

That's done it, Lon thought. *He's put the Corps right in the middle, between the colonies, right where the Council wanted us. He had to confer with Colonel Flowers first. Black wouldn't have dared to do this on his own.* Lon's desire to look toward the Westers grew.

"Colonel Black.'' The voice was unfamiliar and came from the side. Lon knew that it had to be one of the civilians. "Could I speak with you for a moment?'' There was command rather than request in the tone of voice.

Colonel Black did not turn. Instead, he spoke to Major Esterling again.

"You have my assurances, Major," he said. "If you will excuse me for a moment?"

Esterling nodded, a minimal gesture.

Black executed a sharp "left face" and strode to the Westers. Now Lon did permit himself to glance that way, almost surreptitiously. The leader of the Wester delegation took Black by the arm and walked him farther from eavesdropping ears. Lon brought his gaze back to the front, so he could not see what was going on, but Colonel Black had left open his radio circuit, so Lon—and the other DMC officers—could hear everything.

"You had no right to make those promises to these people," the civilian said, his voice low and controlled but obviously angry. "You were ordered to accept their surrender only, without terms, to place them under our control, to allow the government of Aldrin West to assume its proper and legal sovereignty over this territory. Your have exceeded your authority."

"I beg to differ, sir," Colonel Black replied, his voice showing no emotion at all. "I do not take orders from you or from anyone else in your government. My orders come from Colonel Flowers, and I was acting within the scope of those orders."

"Your promises are invalid. The government of Aldrin West will not honor them."

"The Dirigent Mercenary Corps does not count on your government honoring the promises made by it, sir. We honor our own promises. I will repeat, sir, so there can be no misunderstanding. The Dirigent Mercenary Corps will honor the promises I made to Major Esterling and the people of Hope."

"We shall see about that, Colonel," the civilian—Lon did not know the name of any of the government people—said. His voice was so tight with anger that he seemed to have difficulty getting the words out without sputtering.

"We shall," Black agreed. "Now, if I may return to Major Esterling? We still have to make arrangements for the disposition of things here, and to arrange accommodations for you and your people.'' The civilian did not respond, but Colonel Black had not waited for permission. He returned to the commander of East's soldiers in Hope.

"You have my word, Major,'' Black said. "And the word of my commander, Colonel Medwin Flowers, the senior DMC officer on Aldrin. If necessary, the entire Corps will support our promises to you and to the people of Hope.'' Black spoke loud enough to make certain the Westers could also hear him.

Both commanders put their men at parade rest, then resumed talking, more softly. Lon was surprised that the commanders were touching on each of the main points instead of leaving those arrangements to their staffs. After a few minutes the soldiers on both sides were given the "at ease" order, and Lon relaxed a little more. Now he could look over to where the Westers stood, still apart, in a tight group, turned inward, discussing the situation among themselves. While Lon watched, the leader of the Westers took out a small radio and started talking into it.

Getting new instructions, Lon thought. *They're not a happy lot, and their bosses won't be happy either. A few minutes more and Colonel Flowers will be getting his ear bent. There won't be any "on completion" bonuses voted for us here.*

He listened, but without full attention, to the discussions taking place a few steps in front of him. Details. Surrendered weapons would be under DMC control. East's soldiers would return to their barracks, once they had been inspected to make certain there were no munitions, and allowed their freedom within the settlement. The battalion of mercenaries would remain, for the present, in and around Hope, and would act as a buffer between the residents and the representatives of West. The local civilian government would continue to function until mutually acceptable arrangements could be made between the leaders of the two colonies. And so forth. Lon paid close attention only when the talk turned to living arrangements for his battalion. They would be quartered in separate locations, close in, a company at each site. Tents would be flown in. Local facilities for water would be extended to provide the basic amenities.

Apart from that, Lon concentrated on the civilians from West. He could not hear what they were saying, even when he adjusted the gain on the microphone on the left side of his helmet, but he could see their agitation. He realized that the consternation of the Wester delegation could translate to difficulty for the regiment, but it was too soon to worry. Cooler heads would almost certainly prevail. West could not afford to dare the wrath of the DMC. And any attack on 7th Regiment would guarantee massive reprisals.

The talk between the two commanding officers had gone on for more than a half hour before Major Esterling said, "Have I your permission to dismiss my troops, Colonel?"

"Of course, Major." Colonel Black nodded. A platoon from Bravo Company, summoned near the start of the discussion, had already inspected the barracks and nearby buildings. Lon assumed that their report had reached the colonel, but Lon had not heard what it was.

Major Esterling saluted and, after Colonel Black returned it, turned to face his soldiers and dismissed the formation.

Colonel Black turned to face the officers he had assembled. "Very well, gentlemen," he said softly. "Company officers, return to your men. You'll have detailed orders within the half hour. Captain Orlis, I'll want your company to remain here for the present. Your job is to guard the weapons that have been surrendered until we get floaters in to take them to the shuttles for transfer to *Long Snake*."

Captain Orlis said "Yes, sir" and saluted. Then Orlis gestured to Lon and they started back to their men.

We could be here a while, Lon thought. *I hope this is as hot as it gets.* It wasn't only the temperature he was thinking of.

14

One platoon stood guard directly over the captured weapons in the center of the plaza, out in the sun, with Captain Orlis's promise that no one would have more than fifteen minutes at a time. The rest of the company moved into the minimal shade of the buildings on the western side of the plaza. It was not long enough after noon for the shadows to extend far, but even a little protection from the sun helped.

The first platoon to draw the duty, one of Carl Hoper's, started an inventory, and made sure that all of the surrendered weapons were unloaded. The inventory and examination were finished by Lon's third platoon, which drew the second shift.

"Looks like not more'n a third of these rifles have been fired recently," Tebba told Lon afterward. All that remained was to wait for transportation to move the weapons to the shuttles. "I doubt many men cleaned their weapons for the surrender."

"Don't complain, Tebba," Lon said. "Would you rather have had them all firing this morning?"

"That's not the point, Lieutenant," Girana said in his "explaining" voice. "The point is, they could have put up a lot better defense than they did. And some of the magazines I looked at were only two or three rounds short of full. They could have made it one bloody fight if they'd had the heart for it."

Lon nodded slowly. "The regulars we faced in the mountains put more into their work. These people . . ." He turned through a circle. More people were visible, but most still kept as much distance as they could between themselves and the mercenaries.

"Maybe they'd have fought to the last man if it was Wester soldiers comin' in 'stead of us," Girana suggested.

"Good thinking, Tebba. I hadn't gotten around to looking gift horses in the mouth. I'll pass your observation along. It might help the colonel deal with both sides."

Lon walked to where Captain Orlis was sitting, in the shade, and reported what Girana had said, careful to attribute the observation properly. Orlis nodded, then passed the report along, with its source, to Colonel Black. The Corps made a fetish of encouraging everyone to offer suggestions, and recognizing those contributions.

"The colonel says to give Girana a 'well done,' " the captain said after completing his call. "I guess no one else *had* thought of it yet. He's going to pass it along to Colonel Flowers and the contract officers."

"I'll tell Tebba," Lon said.

"Better yet, we'll both go, and I'll tell him."

A switchover was being made. Third platoon was being relieved by second. The captain and Lon did not wait for the platoon to move into the shade, but met them in the center of the plaza. When Orlis gave Girana Colonel Black's commendation, Tebba looked almost embarrassed.

"Thank you, sir," he said. "It was just a thought that came to me when I saw the condition of those rifles."

Orlis shook his head. "An astute observation, and something that might never have occurred to the higher-ups if someone on the scene hadn't looked and done some thinking."

Third platoon moved into the shade. A few minutes later, two small trucks arrived, driven by men from one of the other companies in the battalion. Second platoon loaded the weapons and boxes of ammunition in the trucks and—except for one squad sent along to do the unloading at the other end—watched as the vehicles left, then moved out of the sun.

"When the trucks come back," Captain Orlis told Lon,

"they should have our tents. Our bivouac area will be in the direction of the shuttles, just past the edge of town, near that stand of trees." He pointed. The tops of the trees could just be seen over the intervening buildings. "The locals are extruding pipes to carry water out to the site. We should have that in place and running by sunset if everything goes right."

"Does it ever?" Lon asked.

"Once in a while, Nolan," Orlis said. "Like this morning."

The work of establishing camp was almost finished by sunset. Lon was with Captain Orlis, Lieutenant Hoper, and the cadet, O'Fallon, in front of the company command post. Colonel Black was holding an officers' call by radio, briefing them on the events of the day.

"Aldrin West is raising holy hell over my promises to the locals," Black said at the start. "Colonel Flowers and I anticipated that. It does mean that we have to be especially vigilant here, as much against the remote possibility that our employers might try something, ah, inappropriate, as against the theoretically greater chance that the locals, particularly the militia, might not regard the surrender as binding on them.

"The representatives of West chose to return to their shuttle and stay there rather than in Hope, at least for tonight. Bravo Company has one platoon with our shuttles to provide security. Against any eventuality," Black added.

"I want everyone else to maintain tight security around the camps. We'll run squad-strength patrols in and around Hope through the night. We'll set up a schedule, drawing squads from each company but Bravo, since they've got one platoon detached. I want the patrols commanded by platoon sergeants. They are to avoid any confrontations with the locals if possible. The guiding word is still 're-straint.' I want open eyes and ears. Tell your men to look at everything, but not to interfere with the locals unless they present an immediate hazard."

There were a few questions about details of the orders for the patrols, but nothing critical.

"I can't say how long this situation will continue," Black said. "I expect that it will be more than a day or two, possibly quite a bit longer. CIC launched an MR with a full report on the situation to Dirigent four hours ago. There have been regular reports since we arrived, so the latest news might not come as much of a surprise to the Council. But it will be at least twenty-eight days before we get a response to today's events."

A message rocket required as much time as a ship to get from one star system to another. An MR held limited room for cargo—less than one cubic foot. Everything else was propulsion, Nilssen generator, fuel, and the necessary control and navigational mechanisms. The Nilssen fitted to an MR was considerably smaller than those that moved ships through Q-space and provided artificial gravity, but they still accounted for more than 70 percent of the mass of an MR.

"Gentlemen, this next is very tentative, but once the newness of our presence here wears off, we hope there will be opportunities for some of you to meet members of the community on an informal basis. Colonel Flowers and CIC want more information on how these people really feel about the fighting between the colonies. We're looking for anything that might help us resolve the conflict without further bloodshed. And we need more data. Points of leverage."

That last phrase stuck in Lon's mind after the briefing was over and Captain Orlis, the acting battalion adjutant, had set up the duty roster for patrols that night. *Points of leverage.* Lon thought back to Tebba's observation about the captured weapons. *That was one,* he thought, happy that one of his people had found it. When he got back to his platoons, he brought his sergeants together and told them about the night's orders.

"Weil, you take care of the sentry duty for us. One fire team at a time, led by the squad leader. Coordinate with Jim Ziegler and whoever leads the detail from Lieutenant

Hoper's platoons. Tebba, you'll handle the one patrol we've drawn tonight. That means you and your first squad. We'll alternate the responsibilities night by night as long as this situation continues. I'll be going out with you tonight, Tebba, just because this is the first time for us. Weil, anything comes up while we're gone that you can't handle, check with the captain. I'll let him know that I'm going out." *I don't think he'll veto it,* Lon thought, wishing he had cleared his decision with Orlis first. But he had just made it.

"Lieutenant, I've got a question," Jorgen said. He waited for Lon to prompt him before he continued. "I know this is a touchy situation, but which side are we most worried about, the people who surrendered to us or the people who brought us here?"

"Our biggest worry is keeping our men safe," Lon replied. "We don't take either side for granted. I don't know which we need to worry most about, so we worry about both of them. Right now, the locals are closest, and despite the cache of weapons they surrendered, there's nothing to say they don't have more stashed where they can get at them once they think they've lulled us into complacency."

The early patrols into Hope that evening reported no difficulties. There was no real contact between them and the locals. Early on, the patrols did note that they were being observed, sometimes by people standing around in plain sight, but by four hours after sunset, when Lon got ready to lead his patrol, none of the locals was outside. There were few lights on either, especially in the outlying houses.

Dav Grott's squad, augmented by Tebba and Lon, moved in a well-dispersed formation, the sort they would have adopted going through territory where the likelihood of ambush was extremely high. Weapons were loaded, but Lon instructed the men to keep safeties on. "I don't want any accidental discharges. Remember, we do nothing provocative. We don't want to fight these people."

Hope was quiet. And the mercenaries made very little noise. Any talking was done in whispers, over the radio. Lon watched his men as well as the territory they walked through. It was never necessary to remind them to be alert. The possibility of duplicity by the locals was present in every mind.

Around the town and through it, the patrol came within fifty yards of every building, close enough that the dark could hold no secrets. Lon gave special attention to the barracks where the soldiers were, cranking up the pickups on his helmet to the maximum each time they came near them, listening for any sounds from within. But there were none, not even snoring. The buildings were too well built to leak routine sounds.

"Nice and quiet," Tebba commented as the patrol headed back toward camp. A patrol from Charlie Company was already on its way in, keeping the surveillance nearly continuous. "I hope it stays that way."

"You, me, and everyone else in the regiment," Lon replied. "We get in, get the men bedded down for the night. Tell them to sleep while they can."

Lon had no trouble staying alert while the patrol was in Hope, but after they had left the town and were halfway back to camp, exhaustion sprung its own ambush on him. He found himself yawning repeatedly, and the more he attempted to stifle the yawns, the more insistent they became.

Carl Hoper was already asleep in the tent he shared with Lon. There were no beds, nothing more than the bedrolls they would have slept on anywhere in the field. But the tent made a considerable difference, as much psychological as physical. Lon opened up his bedroll and twisted the capsule that inflated the air mattress. By the time it was ready he had taken off his pack harness and web belt. He sat on the inflated mattress to take off his boots, grateful for the relief.

With a little luck I might get five hours' sleep, Lon thought as he sat cross-legged on his bedding. A protracted yawn. He sighed, then maneuvered himself into the sleeping bag. He moved his helmet next to his head so he would hear a call on the radio, and felt for the position of his rifle and pistol—just in case. His hand remained on the butt of his pistol. Lon had already fallen asleep.

Lon jerked awake with a start. His forehead was covered with perspiration. His heart was beating too fast. He felt as if he were gasping for air. His hand closed around the butt of his pistol, and he started to sit up before he realized it had only been a dream that had wakened him. He let go of the pistol and took a deep breath, flopping back onto the mattress.

The substance of the dream had already escaped his memory. All he could recall was thunder, a constant drone of distant thunder that had somehow been transformed into the similar sound of artillery fire—big guns, howitzers or tank cannons, not the mortars he had faced in the mountains.

Lon knew how those weapons sounded, though he had never been in combat where either was present. The Corps had both armor and artillery, but they were ancillary branches, used only when necessary and practical. Lon had led his men in training exercises that included tanks or self-propelled guns. He had observed both on the firing ranges, part of his indoctrination into the capabilities of the Corps while he was a cadet.

He lay motionless, eyes closed, trying to get his body's rhythms back to normal so he could sleep again. But the sounds of the thunder, or artillery, echoed in his head. There was neither storm nor barrage anywhere near Hope. No attack was under way. The only sound close was the soft snoring of Carl Hoper five feet away.

This is ridiculous, Lon told himself when it became clear that he was not going to get right back to sleep. *You haven't even seen any artillery here, and you've never been afraid of thunder.* There was no overt danger close, no great likelihood of combat in the near future. *Ridiculous,* Lon thought again, with more force, as if the word alone might conquer the subconscious fears that had forced the dream on his mind. *It's not even likely to rain for at least another two or three weeks.*

Lon picked up his helmet and tilted it so he could look at the timeline on the visor. It was just after oh-three-thirty, the middle of the five hours he had hoped to sleep.

If I'm not going to sleep, I might as well do something useful. He got out of the sleeping bag and pulled on his boots, then strapped on his web belt and pistol and put on his helmet. *I can have a look around and make sure that the guards are where they should be.* And visit the latrine.

A slight breeze made the night more comfortable outside than in the tent. Lon felt sweat evaporating, rapidly enough to give him a chill even though the temperature was above seventy. He stood near the tent flap for several minutes, turning slowly and looking around, the night-vision system of his helmet giving him an excellent view. He spotted two sentries walking posts on the perimeter of the company's bivouac area. At least one of them spotted Lon. There was no challenge, though. Lon's helmet was switched on; a blip on the head-up display of the sentry's visor would tell him he was friendly.

Lon turned to gaze toward Hope. There was no haze of light above the town, the way there always was over Dirigent City or any sizable community on Earth. No neon signs or mercury-vapor streetlights. It was a farming town, with little nightlife. The sky was clear, pocked with stars strewn carelessly across the heavens. There was not a cloud to be seen, off to the limits of vision. No thunder would scar this night.

While he walked toward the latrine at the edge of camp, Lon spotted the two other sentries. He did not bother them and they did not bother him. By the time Lon returned to his tent, he had calmed down considerably. His pulse and breathing were approaching normal, and he was starting to feel sleepy again.

But sleep was still slow in returning. Eventually, though, it came.

15

Seventh Regiment settled in as if it might be staying indefinitely. In 2nd Battalion's camps around Hope, each morning started with calisthenics and running—before the temperatures neared their maximums, more than one hundred degrees every day.

Far to the northeast, the rest of the regiment established a similar regime in the foothills of the mountain chain that separated the two Aldrinian colonies. The invading Eastmen continued to withdraw, pulling back across the continental divide. The Westers who had been part of the fight in the mountains were east of the mercenaries, higher. They had not attempted to pursue the Eastmen to the far side of the chain.

"This is the position Colonel Flowers is taking with West," Colonel Black told his officers the day after the surrender of Hope. "We turned back the invasion in the north and accepted the surrender of the intruders in the south, according to the terms of our contract. What remains is for the governments to reach a political resolution of their differences. In the meantime we are on the scene and prepared to defend West against further attack, again, according to the terms of our contract." He gave no details of the various demands and protests that West's government was making. The turnover of Hope was high on the list, but they had taken no action to enforce that demand. No troops were being ferried south.

"If anything comes up, we'll know in plenty of time to react," Black assured his officers. "The fleet has West under as close scrutiny as East. We'll know of troop movements or the dispatch of aircraft as soon as they begin, if not before.''

Black vetoed the construction of defensive positions around the camps. ''No matter the intent, it might seem provocative to the people of Hope. They would assume that we were preparing to defend ourselves against them, and we can't very well tell them differently, that we're more worried about our employers than we are about them. If we let East know of the rift, that might be all it takes to bring about trouble.''

''I know it's better than fighting, but it's too damned complicated,'' Lon complained that afternoon after Colonel Black's briefing. Lon was sitting with Orlis, Hoper, and O'Fallon. They had been eating supper—battle rations—in the captain's tent. ''I'm beginning to wish that we could pack up and leave the Aldrinians to themselves.''

''Wish for a cold beer while you're at it,'' Carl Hoper advised. ''And a weekend in Camo Town. One'll do as much good as the other. No matter what, you've got to figure that we'll be here for another month at least. I can't see Colonel Flowers pulling us out without specific orders from the Council of Regiments. Right, Captain?''

Orlis nodded, chewing food. After he swallowed, he said, ''I expect it will be considerably more than a month. This is one time when I'll be surprised if we pull less than a full six-month tour. I doubt our job will be finished until the colonies reach some diplomatic compromise, and that could take a lot longer than six months. We'll just have to make the best of things, hope that we won't have any fighting to do before we go home. I don't mind earning my money this way, even if it is hotter than hell.''

''I don't miss the fighting, that's for sure,'' Lon said. ''I can put up with anything that lets me take home all the men I came in with, alive and healthy. But I wish they'd get off their asses and come to an agreement. Can't they see that they have to, one way or another? I mean, even on Earth the governments finally figured out that they had to operate as one entity.''

Hoper laughed. "Within very serious limits, as I recall," he said. "How many standing armies are there on Earth now?"

"About as many armies as continents, isn't it?" Orlis asked.

Lon nodded, reluctantly. "North American Union, Hispanic Confederacy, European Union, Pan-Africa, and Greater Asia. But there hasn't been a real war in centuries, and not many border squabbles. You have standing armies, because if you don't, there's never time to raise and train one when the need arises."

"Besides, putting men under military discipline is a social necessity on Earth, isn't it?" Orlis asked softly. "Especially when you select potential troublemakers and make them part of the solution rather than the problem."

Lon shrugged. "There's some of that, in some of the armies, I guess," reluctant to admit that even the North American Union found that expedient.

"But will all those armies be able to prevent the final collapse on Earth?" That was O'Fallon, speaking for the first time. All of the others stared at the cadet.

"Doomsayers have been predicting imminent catastrophe for a thousand years or more, since Malthus," Lon said. "There have been crises, but people always manage to keep society functioning, one way or another. Nanotech, the colonies, whatever."

"There were still some pretty scary die-offs," O'Fallon said, oblivious to the stares of the others. Only Lon was not looking directly at him now. "Plagues, wars, whatever. I studied Earth history a lot my last two years in school."

For a protracted moment, Lon merely stared at the meal pack in front of him. Thinking, *feeling*. Earth. Finally he took a deep breath and looked up, meeting O'Fallon's gaze. "You're pulling on the wrong strings, Esau," he said quietly. "I'm not a Terran any longer. I'm as much a Dirigenter as you are. Maybe more. I chose Dirigent. I didn't just inherit it as an accident of birth." *Maybe I didn't have a lot of choice,* he admitted to himself, *not as long as I wanted to be a soldier, but I could have stayed on Earth and been a cop.*

"Strings," Orlis said, letting the word hang until the others all looked at him. "I don't think anyone can escape the Earth strings. No matter how many generations our families have lived on Dirigent or Union or Buckingham, or any other world, the strings always go back to Earth. Think back, Lon, to when you first came to Dirigent. Do you recall the curiosity? The questions? All because you came from Earth directly instead of through genetic ancestry. I imagine you still run into that."

"Sometimes," Lon admitted. "Even Sara was excited at meeting a real Earthman. She had questions and preconceived notions, too." Lon looked at Esau when he said that. "You can't learn everything from a history text. Sometimes you can't really know a place without seeing it. I guess Earth, is both more and less than what people on Dirigent, and I suppose on other colony worlds, think. If you lumped together the populations of the ten most populous colony worlds, it wouldn't match the population of Earth even now, let alone in the early twenty-first century, when it reached its maximum. There are single cities, metropolitan areas, on Earth, maybe a dozen, that each have more people than the largest colony world mankind has settled. Of course there are problems. But with so many brains to tackle them, they do get solved, even if not always in the most efficient or elegant manner." He grinned. "Even if it's *rarely* efficient or elegant." It felt strange to be defending Earth. Strings. It was like the way he had been selected to look at the data on Aldrin, simply because it was assumed he would have a different perspective because he had been born and raised on the motherworld.

"I don't mean to press," O'Fallon said, "but aren't brains at the core of the problem, why it has to get worse until a time comes when Earth can't handle things any longer?"

"What do you mean?" Lon asked.

"As far back as I can remember, all the texts said that

the intelligence of people who leave Earth averages above that of those who don't leave, gradually weakening the brain pool or whatever you want to call it. That each succeeding generation is that much dumber than the one before.''

Lon laughed. "And, of course, the inevitable corollary is that people on colony worlds are inevitably smarter and growing smarter all of the time.''

O'Fallon's face reddened at Lon's laugh, but he did not back down. "Something like that,'' he insisted. "An easy assertion to back up statistically. Besides, it's logical.''

"A thousand years ago, that might have been true,'' Lon said. "When all mankind had was what nature provided. But we've been tampering with natural selection almost that long. And now there is no drain on the average intelligence from people with extremely subnormal intelligence. Genetics and medical science have virtually eliminated the causes of retardation, and we have the means to correct physical irregularities that arise after birth. Every generation the average intelligence increases, not just on the colony worlds but on Earth as well, and mechanical and electronic supplements to organic intelligence also improve.''

Orlis and Hoper had leaned back, observing the dialogue between Lon and O'Fallon with considerable humor. Now the captain leaned forward, ready to end the discussion, or at least move it to other topics.

"He's right, you know, O'Fallon,'' Orlis said. "The average ten-year-old student today, on virtually any settled world, can solve math problems that Hinrik Nilssen couldn't even imagine when he was solving the equations that led to the Nilssen Drive we rely on to travel between stars and to give us artificial gravity. And all this talk is giving me a headache. Let's table it.''

"Besides,'' Carl Hoper added, "this is one topic you can't argue with Nolan and win. He put a lot of study into it after he came to Dirigent, back when there were a lot of people ragging him about the poor, befuddled masses of Earth.''

• • •

After a week camped near Hope, Lon noticed the heat less. The routine had not changed. Second Battalion mounted patrols in and around the town at night, and took physical training first thing in the morning. There were no patrols in the town or near the satellite farms during the day. Late each afternoon Colonel Black held a briefing for his officers, generally with the news that there was no substantive news. The best he could offer was that there was no fighting going on anywhere on Aldrin. It was only at Hope that the mercenaries had physical contact with people from either colony. The bad news was there were no talks going on between the governments of the colonies, and contacts between headquarters of 7th Regiment and either side were rare, brief, and unproductive.

The people of Hope were slow to open up to the mercenaries. "I had hoped it would be faster," Black confessed to his officers a week after the surrender. "Maybe I was unrealistically optimistic. We did arrive as conquerors, not liberators, even though we stand ready to defend Hope if necessary."

"We don't have the right kind of contacts with them, sir," Captain Wallis Ames of Bravo Company said. "They see us sitting around out here during the day, surrounding their town. At night, if they see us at all, it's as an occupying force patrolling their streets to make sure they don't sneak up on us. How else *can* they see us?"

Colonel Black hesitated before he replied. "There's a lot to that. The problem is balancing our security with the desire to develop better relations with the locals. Colonel Flowers left the decision to me, how soon and how much we relax our security measures. We could substitute concealed electronic snoops for the patrols, but I'm not at all certain the locals would see that as any improvement. It would still indicate a lack of trust on our part, be an intrusion. We're going to be making a temporary adjustment starting tonight, cut the patrols down to a single fire team rather than a full squad. We'll leave a few minutes' gap between patrols as well, rather than have one going in while the previous one is coming out. The next step might be just to arrange better locations for offsite observation, stay outside of town at night altogether, or just run one or two quick patrols. Look, we're feeling our way, and changes could come quickly, depending on what happens. This town is still our best key to the puzzle of Aldrin. We can't afford to screw up.''

Two days later, just after morning exercises and breakfast, Lon was called to battalion headquarters—located in one of the rare stands of trees on the savanna. The rudiments of civilization had been brought in for Colonel Black and his staff, field desks and folding chairs, a small generator, electric lights. Colonel Black was sitting on one of the chairs in front of the two-room tent that served as his command post and quarters. There was a vacant chair near the colonel.

"Have a seat, Nolan," Black said after Lon saluted and reported formally. "Take a load off."

Lon sat, watching the colonel's eyes, trying to figure out why he had been summoned. Black noticed, and chuckled.

"Relax, lad," he said. "You're not in any trouble."

"That's always good to know, Colonel," Lon said.

"You know that I've been looking for an entrée with the locals. Looking very hard," Black said. Lon nodded. "Yesterday Matt Orlis suggested that you might provide it."

"Me, sir?"

Black nodded. "You're the only officer in this battalion who was born and raised on Earth."

"How does that make any difference?" Lon asked.

The colonel shrugged. "I'm not certain that it does, but I mentioned the fact that I had an officer who came from Earth, and Major Esterling raised an eyebrow and said, 'Is that so?' I told him that you had studied at Earth's premier military academy but left shortly before graduation to join the DMC."

"And now he would like to have a chat with me?"

Lon supplied, seeing where the discussion was going.

"He did indicate that he would like to meet you, and said something about one of his distant ancestors who attended the North American Military Academy and later returned to serve a tour as its adjutant."

"Did you tell him anything about the, ah, circumstances under which I left the academy?" Lon asked.

"Not in detail. But he has invited you along to lunch today. You and I both, actually. It's a step in the direction we want to take. You have no objections?"

"Of course not, sir." Lon hesitated, then added, "Even if for no other reason than to get a change of menu."

"We'll leave here at eleven hundred hours. Not to put pressure on you or anything, but this could be the opening we've been looking for, Nolan."

"Just because of chance?"

"A lot of military cusps come as a result of chance. Fortune. Apparently it's been quite a while since anyone immigrated to Aldrin directly from Earth. So we appeal to their curiosity. At least, *you* appeal to their curiosity. Sorry to put you on the spot like this, but I've got to take whatever steps I can here."

"I understand that, Colonel. So I'll be charming and do what I can to satisfy Major Esterling's curiosity."

"Something like that," Black said through a grin. "But gently, Nolan, gently."

There were no dress uniforms available, but Lon spent the rest of the morning making his battledress as presentable as possible for the meeting. Colonel Black had indicated they would carry no weapons, not even sidearms. No pack harnesses. They would have their helmets, to keep in contact with the battalion, but once they reached Hope, they would take the helmets off and carry them.

"Now I'm a diplomat," Lon told Matt Orlis when he described the meeting with Colonel Black. "Or a freak held up for public display." He shrugged. "That doesn't bother me, Captain. I'm used to being singled out because

I'm from Earth, and anything that helps us here is okay by me.''

"Just don't work too hard at it, Nolan," the captain had advised. "Let it happen naturally."

"Yes, sir. I've been telling myself the same thing."

"If I wasn't confident that you'd do us proud, I wouldn't have suggested using you."

Lon had time to sit in his tent and think before it was time to meet Black for the walk into Hope. *No pressure,* he told himself. *Like hell. They're all hoping that the fact that I'm from Earth will provide some sort of miraculous change. Put the kid from Earth on display and hope he'll charm the locals into thinking we're all something special. Like I'm some superhero from a vid, ready to save the galaxy all by my lonesome.*

His palms were sweating. There was a nervous knot in his stomach. He felt more aware of the heat than he had in days. The tent fabric did provide considerable thermal insulation, but it had never been enough for real comfort. *I can't let myself get so knotted up that I can't eat,* Lon thought. *They might think I was too uppity to share their food. It would be worse if I ate and then barfed it back up. A real diplomatic incident.*

He closed his eyes and tried to calm himself. It had all sounded so simple when Colonel Black first told him. It was the waiting that gave doubts and worries a chance to intrude. *Better if they'd sprung this on me at the last minute, or just invited me along to lunch without telling me why.*

Lon got up and paced, the three steps in each direction that the tent permitted. He would not go outside to do his pacing where his men would see, and wonder what had him so nervous. He had told his sergeants he would be going to Hope with the colonel, but he had not explained the mission further.

It was a relief when the time came to leave. At least

the waiting would be over soon. *Once we get there and get talking, it shouldn't be so bad.* He knew that would almost certainly be the case, but it did not still the butterflies in his stomach.

16

Battalion Lead Sergeant Zal Osier accompanied Lon and Colonel Black. Osier was the only one who was armed, and he wore only his pistol. His function as escort would be easy to explain. "Maybe he'll even get invited to lunch with Major Esterling's noncoms," Colonel Black suggested, though he added that he was not counting on it. "I'm just taking every chance for a little more of a wedge."

"The more I think about this, Colonel," Lon said, "the more it feels as if we're grasping at some awfully thin straws."

"You're not far wrong," Black conceded. "But just now those are all we have within reach."

Major Esterling's second-in-command, Captain Oliver Howard, met them at the edge of town. There were introductions, and Howard's explanation that he was to escort them to the officers' mess. "Major Esterling is overseeing preparations personally. He wants to make certain that everything is perfect."

I'll bet his mess sergeant appreciates that, Lon thought, taking care to hide the grin that wanted to come to his face. He looked around. There seemed to be more people about, out in the open, wearing their curiosity freely now. *It's like they know that something's up, and not just that there's someone from Earth coming in.* He kept coming back to that, but the walk had given him a chance to dampen his nervousness. The people had been out before the Dirigenters arrived, so it could not be that they were coming out just because three men came into town alone, two of them unarmed.

The garrison's barracks were a separate compound within the town, apparently as old as any of the civilian structures. The fence around the compound had been removed the day of the surrender—unilaterally, by the garrison. It had not been mentioned in the discussions. The mess hall, with separate facilities for officers and enlisted men, was at the southeastern corner of the compound. Stairs and a lift tube went from a separate entrance to the officers' mess on the second floor.

This was definitely not put up as a temporary structure, Lon observed as they climbed the stairs. It was too well built, too solid, and some care had been taken in the furnishing and decoration. An efficient air-conditioning system made the officers' dining room almost chilly. Lead Sergeant Osier was still with them. Captain Howard had suggested that the major would want to meet him, and that he was certain they would be able to make arrangements to keep the sergeant entertained and fed after that.

"I'm easy to please," Osier had said, a bit gruffly in Lon's opinion. "I've been a soldier for a lot of years."

It was clear that someone had been detailed to watch for their arrival. The four men had not been in the dining room fifteen seconds before Major Esterling came hurrying in from the other side, apparently from the kitchen or a service area.

"It was good of you to come, Colonel Black," Esterling said before he had quite reached the group. Black nodded. The East major came to a stop and glanced at Lon. "This would be your lieutenant from Earth?" he asked.

Colonel Black introduced Lon and Osier. "I know the sergeant wasn't included in your invitation," Black said, "but I find it difficult to function without my lead sergeant close."

"Of course. There are times when I think that most armies would never miss the loss of their officers as long as they had good noncoms to keep things going." He gave

Osier a salesman's smile. "Perhaps you would care to sample the fare in our sergeants' mess, Lead Sergeant," he suggested. "It will provide a change from field rations. That is," Esterling added, glancing at Black, "if your colonel can bear to have you a few yards farther away from him."

"Thank you," Black said. "Zal, you bring your appetite along?"

"Yes, sir," Osier said, looking at the colonel, then at the major. "Thank you for your invitation, sir. I appreciate it."

"Fine, fine. I'll have my command lead sergeant escort you." The man could not have been far away. He arrived within thirty seconds after Esterling summoned him. The Eastman major introduced the sergeants, then sent them off to eat

"Now, Colonel, Lieutenant," Esterling said after the enlisted men had left, "I hope you'll enjoy the little repast our chief cook has prepared."

The colonel's table was in a nook along one side of the room. The round table was large enough to seat six, but only four places were set, spaced equally around the perimeter. Lon guessed, correctly, that Major Esterling would sit at the rear of the nook, with his back and sides to walls, facing the portion of the room he could see. There was a white tablecloth. The centerpiece was a brass candelabrum with five electric candles. The china and silverware were plain but looked as if they were of premium quality. The napkins were linen, or a substitute indistinguishable from the real thing.

Esterling placed Colonel Black across from him. Lon was at the major's right, and Captain Howard sat in the final chair.

"We're usually not so formal except for dinner on Sundays and holidays," Major Esterling explained. "But I thought we should put on our 'company faces' for this occasion."

I'll bet, Lon thought, but he worked hard to keep a straight face. *Don't spook the deal, kid,* he warned himself. He felt relieved that Major Esterling had not started to ply him immediately with questions about Earth. The only reference to the planet had been the introductory question.

A mess steward arrived. "A little wine, gentlemen?" Esterling asked his guests, focusing on Colonel Black. "We have a fairly decent wine cellar, even if it's on the second floor."

"Thank you," Black said, nodding and smiling. "That would be a distinct pleasure."

Esterling gestured, and the steward hurried off to fetch the wine. "The one I have in mind is my personal favorite. The grapes are a hybrid developed on Aldrin from two terran varieties, Riesling and Gewürztraminer." He turned toward Lon. "I believe that both of the original varieties were European."

"The Riesling at least, Major," Lon said. "I'm not familiar with the second. I'm not even certain I could pronounce it."

Esterling laughed politely and repeated the pronunciation. "We also grow both ancestral varieties near the East Coast," he explained. "The Gewürztraminer produces a slightly spicy wine alone. And the Riesling makes a moderately sweet white wine."

The wine arrived. Major Esterling tasted and nodded his approval before the steward poured for all of them, leaving the open bottle behind.

"To peace," Major Esterling said, raising his glass in a toast. The others echoed the sentiment.

Lon was cautious with his first sip. Wine had never been his beverage of choice, but something to be drunk only when the occasion required it. He was pleasantly surprised by the taste, and allowed himself a second, more generous, sip before setting the glass back on the table.

"Very nice," Colonel Black said. "It teases the tongue."

Lon nodded. "Yes, nice indeed," he allowed.

Major Esterling beamed as if he had stomped the grapes and made the wine personally. He had no time to do more before a pair of stewards arrived bearing the first course of the meal.

Lon waited for the questions about Earth to begin, but Major Esterling talked about the food, wine, and the tribulations of service in a tropical climate. He did not refer to Earth, or to the current impasse between the two colonies on Aldrin.

He's trying to be the perfect host, as if this were some formal affair at his home base, Lon decided. *He wants to impress us with his etiquette and with the cuisine.* Virtually everything had been grown or raised domestically, most of it in or around Hope. Lon tried to keep track of the items the major talked about. After the dessert arrived and had been described, Lon thought, *He never mentioned the butter. Maybe that came from a replicator.* He viewed that deduction as a minor triumph.

There was another bottle of wine after dessert, a different variety, and cigars. Lon accepted the wine gratefully, the cigar with reluctance. He did not care for smoking, but did it when it was socially required. He lit his cigar, then brought it near his mouth just often enough to keep it from going out.

"Now, *this* wine is a straight Gewürztraminer," Esterling said after he had tasted and approved it. "From a special picking, berry by berry, to get only the finest fruit." He waited for his guests to sample the wine and voice their approval, then leaned back and turned his attention to Lon.

"Now, Lieutenant," he started, "I must confess I was extremely intrigued when your colonel mentioned that one of his officers had been born and raised on Earth, and attended North American Military Academy. One of my ancestors won his commission at The Springs, and later returned to serve as its adjutant for several years."

Lon nodded. "Colonel Black mentioned that, but I must confess that I don't recall any Esterlings among the lists of academy officials we were forced to memorize as plebes."

"Not an Esterling. My ancestor was Colonel Emil Marghazi."

"There's a Marghazi Hall at the academy," Lon said.

"Yes, yes," Esterling said, grinning and nodding happily. "Dedicated some years after my ancestor's death, just before several of his descendants emigrated, coming to Aldrin."

"Marghazi Hall. Part of the engineering department," Lon said, thinking back. "I had several classes in that building."

The connection firmly established, Esterling went on to question Lon about Earth for an hour, through two bottles of wine and a second round of cigars. The rest of his officers came to eat their lunches and left. The mess hall workers moved about as unobtrusively as possible, cleaning everything but the nook. The major asked about the academy and Lon's experiences there, and he asked about places on Earth that figured in his family's past. The Marghazis had lived near Niagara Falls, no more than a mile from the west bank of the Niagara River. Esterling did not probe into the circumstances of Lon's departure from the academy. He asked few personal questions. His interest was in Earth, not in the life of one man who had come from there.

Eventually it was Colonel Black who brought the conversation about Earth to an end, with apologies. "I would like to offer to return your hospitality, Major," Black said. "But you would find it far less elegant. We have only replicated field rations, and no wine. If it becomes possible, when circumstances are . . . less troubled than they are currently, I will be more than happy to entertain you in the officers' mess aboard our transport. The cuisine still will not match this, but I would be happy to share it with you."

"I hope the day comes soon when I will be able to accept your invitation, Colonel," Esterling said. "The current contretemps is most distressing. We had such high hopes when your government offered to mediate the dispute between us and Aldrin West. We were devastated by their refusal to entertain discussions that could have averted the conflict."

Colonel Black nodded solemnly. "It was not merely a soldier's normal distaste for war that made us work toward peaceful mediation, Major. Any world that is divided against itself is at a tremendous disadvantage in dealings with other worlds. It can be easy pickings for any united world or alliance that seeks to exploit their resources or populace."

"Unfortunately, Colonel, I am not the one you need to convince of that. Nor is my government. We were all in favor of Dirigentan mediation. It was West that blocked that, as you must know. But, even there, it is only the government that needs convincing. If their people were allowed the free expression of their will, I am certain that they, too, would have voted for peaceful resolution."

Lon was glad he was no longer the focus of attention. He was certain his face would have shown a startled look at what the major had said about the people of Aldrin West not being given any choice in what their government did. Colonel Black and Major Esterling had both leaned forward, their eyes in constant contact. Even Captain Howard was following the conversation between them, watching their faces. Lon might as easily have been invisible.

Is what he said just propaganda, or is it the truth? Lon wondered. *Everything I saw about Aldrin said that both governments were popularly elected democracies.* He tried to think back through the megabytes of information he had read about the world. *What was the source of the reports? How much of it was directly seen by our people? How much did we take on the word of West's government?* Colonel Black's face gave nothing away, but Lon could not conceive of the colonel missing the hints in what Esterling had said.

"Whatever the circumstances, eventually both governments will have to put aside old conflicts and unite if this world is to maintain its liberty," Black said. "You share the same world and the same heritage. Being at loggerheads over a small section of real estate is not practical.''

Lon found nothing else startling in the few minutes of conversation that remained before they left the officers' dining hall and went downstairs to where Zal Osier was waiting. Thanks were repeated, and farewells; then the mercenaries started the walk back toward battalion headquarters.

"How much faith can we place in what he said, sir?" Lon asked once the three of them were well outside Hope. "That about the people of West having no say in what their government does? That isn't what the contract file said.''

"I'm not sure, Nolan," Black said, his voice showing he was not paying full attention. He was thinking hard about what Esterling had said, and trying to remember the same details from the file on Aldrin. "We'll have to go over those files again, and check with Colonel Flowers and the men we've had on this world for so long.'' He stopped walking and looked at Lon. "You were working in the contracts office for a while, weren't you?"

"Yes, sir. Mondays over a couple of months. They gave me the Aldrin file to study and make recommendations on before the contract was accepted, before we heard that East had mounted an invasion. I studied that file very closely. I don't recall anything that suggested that West was not fully democratic.''

Black grunted as he started walking again. "Very few worlds are, as you put it, 'fully democratic.' Dirigent certainly isn't. There are always limits, once the population gets too large for everyone to take an intelligent, personal interest in all the affairs of the world. We don't require a government to be democratic before we accept a contract, and we generally do not attempt to dictate local politics to our clients. That would be impractical. But we do have certain values.''

"I know it was the fact of the invasion that let the Council conclude that we should intervene on the side of West, sir, with all of the limitations impressed on us about working to switch the contract to mediation,'' Lon said.

"When they asked me to assess the file before that news, I concluded that the merits of the two sides were equal, and was told that was the consensus, in the contracts office and in the Council of Regiments." Black nodded, punctuation to Lon's comments. "Is it possible that we came in on the wrong side, sir?" he asked.

"Of course it's *possible*," Black said. "Anyone can make a mistake, even the Council of Regiments. But since our primary goal was to get the sides to agree to peace-keeping and mediation, it's almost a moot point here."

They went on a little before Colonel Black spoke again. "Zal, did you pick up anything useful in their sergeants' mess?"

"I don't know how useful it might be, Colonel," Osier said, "but I did gather that the noncoms weren't too thrilled about fighting us. They were in Hope to defend the civilians against West, and they sure had nothing good to say about the people who paid our way here. A patriotic lot, and I think it was serious, not something they were putting on for my benefit."

"We get back to the CP, I want you to spend a few minutes and tell me everything you recall of the discussion. Nolan, I want you to stick with me as well. As soon as I'm sure I'm on top of everything the two of you can contribute, I'll want you both present when I call Colonel Flowers. Maybe we can give him enough pieces of the puzzle to solve it."

17

Three days later, Colonel Medwin Flowers flew to Hope before dawn. Only Lieutenant Colonel Black knew in advance that Flowers was coming. In the regimental camps to the north, between the two colonies, the fact of his absence remained a closely guarded secret. The other battalion commanders, and many of their company commanders, were in on the secret, but every effort was made to pretend that Flowers was still in his headquarters. The few communications from the government of Aldrin West were either taken by the executive officer or seamlessly patched through to Colonel Flowers.

Lon was wakened by Alpha Company's lead sergeant, Jim Ziegler. "Sorry to bother you, sir," Ziegler said as soon as Lon showed signs of life, "but they want you at battalion HQ, fast as you can get dressed and grab a bite of breakfast."

Lon sat up and stretched, his mind barely registering what the lead sergeant said. "Any idea what's up?" Lon asked as soon as he was able to stop yawning.

"No, sir. I just know what Colonel Black said."

That penetrated fully. "The colonel himself called?"

"Yes, sir. He said to get you up and tell you to take time for a quick breakfast first, but then you were to get over to his CP just as quick as you can make it."

"Okay. Thanks for waking me."

I wonder who he wants to impress with his tame Earthman today? Lon thought after Ziegler left. He felt sluggish, but did not linger. A summons from the battalion commander did not offer that luxury. Lon dressed quickly.

Some improvements had been made to the camp in the nearly two weeks since it had been established. There was now a mess tent with replicators and a stove, and the food was several steps above that in the meal packs they had been relying on.

Lon left his pack harness but carried his rifle and battle helmet. His web belt held pistol, canteen, and a pouch with four extra magazines for the handgun. The uniform of the day remained camouflaged battledress.

Ziegler had already informed the mess cook that Lon was coming, and the cook brought a tray to one of the front tables as soon as Lon came through the doorway of the tent. "I'll have your coffee in two seconds, Lieutenant," the cook said.

Lon smiled his thanks and nodded. He scarcely had time to sit and lift his fork before the cook returned. "Anything more you want, sir, just holler," the cook said.

"This should do fine. Thanks," Lon said. A few minutes of being awake had given his curiosity time to start nagging. This early in the day it seemed unlikely that he was being summoned to show him off to more locals. Beyond that, Lon had no idea what Colonel Black might want, and the fastest way to satisfy his curiosity was to get to HQ quickly.

He shoveled the food in methodically, chewing, and swallowing with the aid of large gulps of coffee.

Battalion headquarters was half a mile from Alpha's camp. It was not a particularly taxing walk. The sun had finally peeked over the distant mountains. Lon walked with his helmet visor up, to give himself the advantage of the almost cool breeze from the northeast. Sentries at the edge of Alpha's camp and near battalion headquarters passed him through without comment.

At first Lon did not even note that there was an additional shuttle in the field past the trees that held Colonel Black's command post and the headquarters detachment. There was no reason for the lander to be questioned. Scarcely a day went by without at least one flight in from the fleet or the rest of the regiment, carrying supplies or people.

There were lights on yet in the colonel's tent, and a sentry at the door. Again, Lon was passed through without question. Lon was startled to see Colonel Flowers with the battalion commander. They were sitting at a field desk, facing each other. A portable complink was open on the desk between them.

"Come in, Nolan," Black said. "We've been waiting on you."

"Yes, sir. I got here as quickly as I could."

"Nolan," Colonel Flowers said with a nod, "I hear you've been using that head of yours again."

Lon was uncertain what to make of the colonel's comment, but he nodded. "I try to, sir."

"Sit down, Nolan," Flowers said, gesturing to the remaining chair at the desk. "It's partly because of you that I decided to make this trip. I want to see for myself what's going on, meet these people in Hope, and Colonel Black suggested it might be easier to achieve what I want if I tote you along."

"I'll do whatever I can, of course, Colonel," Lon said, still puzzled over just what Flowers was talking about.

"Don't look so befuddled, Nolan," Flowers said, chuckling. "I'll explain, as far as I can. I want to talk with this Major Esterling. I'd like to enlist him as an ally, to give us a pipeline to his government, a more direct line of communications than we've managed so far."

Lon nodded. "I think he might be agreeable to that, Colonel. And he seems to think that his government might be looking for a way out of the current situation here."

"That is what we're going to test. Just for your information, for the present, what I would like most of all would be a chance to fly to East's capital, Landfall, to talk directly with their military and civilian leaders. Without, I hasten to add, having the government of West learn about the conference."

"Just off the top of my head, sir," Lon said after thinking about it for a few seconds, "it sounds as if this whole thing could be touchy on both sides—trusting that East's leaders would be as amenable as Major Esterling, and how West might react if they learned about it. But if it does work, it could be big.''

''No doubt about it,'' Flowers said. ''It could turn into a real fiasco. But only a handful of our people know I'm even here, and West isn't going to learn anything about my reasons from us. They might see that a shuttle makes the trip to Landfall, but that's no worse than a fifty-fifty proposition, and we'll do what we can to obfuscate the situation. In any case, the only way they'll know who is aboard the shuttle will be if they have a spy placed high enough in East's command structure.''

''Spy, sir?''

Flowers laughed at the startled tone of Lon's question. ''That's what I said. I suspect—presume, actually—that both sides have managed to plant agents in the other's ranks. That would explain some of the data we received from West.''

Lon couldn't find anything to say. The idea of spies seemed too extreme to deal with immediately. He shook his head slowly.

''The cloak-and-dagger stuff does still exist, Nolan,'' Flowers said. ''It may not be much like anything you may have seen in adventure vids, but there are spies. And conditions on Aldrin are as prime as they could be for espionage.''

''Yes, sir, if you say so.''

Flowers laughed again, but more gently. ''Maybe I shouldn't have mentioned it. The odds against any harm coming from the possibility are remote. Let's just deal with this one step at a time and see how far we get.''

''I had just talked with Major Esterling before you arrived,'' Colonel Black told Lon. ''I said I had someone else I thought he should meet, and that I would bring you along as well. He was agreeable, but curious when I declined to name the new person. He might suspect but did not say anything, ah, untoward. He will be expecting us.''

"Yes, sir," Lon said, since Black seemed to expect some comment from him.

"This time, at least, we won't have to walk," Black continued. "The colonel had a command car shipped down from the fleet. Lead Sergeant Osier will drive."

Colonel Flowers was in no mood to waste time. The three officers drank a quick cup of coffee, then went out to the command car, a ground-effect vehicle whose outer surfaces were painted in a camouflage pattern. The floater had been parked under a tree, and an additional camouflage net had been spread over it. Two privates from battalion headquarters pulled the net off. Sergeant Osier started the engine while his passengers were arranging themselves in the vehicle. The two colonels sat in back. Lon sat up front with Osier.

The trip into Hope was considerably faster by floater than on foot. Although the cabin of the command car was well insulated against the noise of the fans and engine, the ride was made in silence. It was only when they neared Major Esterling's headquarters that Colonel Black spoke.

"You'll stay with the vehicle, Sergeant," Black said. "Any of the noncoms you met the other day come by, feel free to get out and chat with them, but don't go wandering off. We'll want to know just where you are."

"Yes, sir, I understand."

"We'll be leaving our weapons with you, so that should be excuse enough for staying put if anyone questions it, and they shouldn't," Black continued.

"I'll handle whatever comes up, sir," Osier said.

Captain Howard came out to greet them. If he was surprised by the insignia on Colonel Flowers' shoulder, he did not show it. There was no suspense. Black introduced the regimental commander to the captain at once.

"Good to have you with us, sir," Howard said. "I'm certain that Major Esterling will be delighted as well. He's in his office, sir. This way."

Lon tagged along at the rear of the group. Esterling's

office was on the ground floor of the building next to the mess hall. The office was spartan but adequate, but showed no indication of being temporary or new. There were several chairs upholstered in what looked like leather.

Major Esterling stood to greet his guests and did show modest surprise—real or feigned—at the identity of the mystery man. "I am extremely happy to meet you, Colonel," Esterling said as the two men shook hands.

"And I am equally happy to meet you, Major," Flowers said, with just a hint of an upturn at the corners of his mouth. As soon as everyone was seated and Esterling indicated that he had sent for coffee, Flowers got right to the point.

"I've come here looking for your help, Major. I'd like to find a peaceful solution to the differences between the two colonies on this world, and from what Colonel Black and Lieutenant Nolan have told me, that is your desire as well."

"Completely, Colonel," Esterling said. "There never should have been any fighting. I'm not certain how I can help you, but whatever I can honorably do, I will, you may be assured of that."

"Is a peaceful solution also the desire of your government?" Flowers asked.

"Yes, sir. At least, to the best of my knowledge, and I have no reason to suspect that it is not so."

Lon, sitting to the side, was able to observe the others as they talked. No one was paying him any attention. Neither commander gave away anything by expression or tone. The talk had turned businesslike right at the start. The tones were crisp but diplomatic, appropriate between military men.

"If it can be arranged, Major," Flowers said, "I would like to travel to Landfall to talk with the leaders of your government directly, face to face, without knowledge of those talks reaching Aldrin West, ah, prematurely."

For the first time, Lon saw a definite reaction. Major Esterling blinked twice, working hard, but in vain, to keep surprise from showing on his face. There was also a significant pause before the major replied.

"That is a bold proposal, Colonel," he said. To Lon it seemed that the major was speaking slowly to give himself more time to think.

"A bold stroke is often the only way out of an impasse, Major, don't you agree?" Flowers asked.

Esterling nodded slowly, several times. "It might be possible, but I would have to relay your request through my headquarters to be taken to the civilian government at the highest level."

"Of course," Flowers said, nodding. "I am hoping it could all be arranged very quickly, and with maximum secrecy."

"I can call the chief of staff directly and explain the situation to him," Esterling said. "A little more information would help. For example, just how large a delegation do you envision sending to Landfall?"

"The three of us here; one other officer, Colonel Black's acting adjutant; the crew of my shuttle, that's three men; and perhaps six additional enlisted personnel to provide clerical and logistic support during the negotiations. If that would be acceptable to your government." Flowers made a gesture with the open palms of both hands. "We can make adjustments if necessary."

"It sounds reasonable, Colonel. Certainly, *I* see no reason why it might be unacceptable in Landfall." He paused, glanced at a blinking light on his desk, and touched a key. "Our coffee has arrived, gentlemen," he announced as an enlisted man wheeled in a cart with cups, a coffeepot, and condiments. The coffee was poured and distributed. As soon as the orderly left, Major Esterling said, "If you will excuse me, Colonel, I'll make that call now. Please, make yourselves at home. My communications center is just upstairs. I'll return as quickly as I can."

The three Dirigenters were left alone in Major Esterling's office. Lon did not need the minute shake of Colonel Flowers' head to know not to say anything that might relate in any way to what had happened. There was too great a chance that the office was wired for sound—and perhaps for video as well.

"They do themselves well here, sir," Lon said after tasting the coffee. "This coffee is good." He thought his voice did not give away anything of his nervousness, let alone his feelings about the prospect of accompanying his commanders to the capital of Aldrin East for clandestine negotiations. It was too soon for the latter to have really sunk in.

"It is good," Flowers agreed, though he had done little more than touch the cup to his lips. He closed his eyes briefly, wondering how far his gamble would take him. As a member of the Council of Regiments, he was well within his authority to take such a risk, but if his plan backfired, he also would have to take responsibility for whatever ills it brought. But this was what he had come south for, to do something, *anything*, he could to find an acceptable resolution to the problem of Aldrin. *Perhaps we were too quick to take a contract from West,* he thought. *Giving in to the pressures of finding work. If we had waited another month, given East's troops time to get closer to the population centers west of the mountains, perhaps West would have accepted mediation.* He did not sigh, even mentally, at the missed opportunity. The choices had been made. It was up to him to find an acceptable conclusion. One thing he did not worry about, even in passing, was the possibility that he—and the men he took with him to Landfall—might be held as hostages. Aldrin East could not be that foolish.

Lon worked hard at presenting a mask of untroubled serenity, as his superiors were doing. He kept his body as still as possible, save for drinking his coffee and refilling cups. As junior officer, he fell naturally into the role of server. Lon did not look around the office much. *Don't show any curiosity at all,* he told himself. *If anyone is watching, they have to see that we're all totally unconcerned about what happens.*

He avoided looking at the time. That would have required picking up his helmet to look at the display at the top of its faceplate. There was no clock visible in Major Esterling's office. Lon could not avoid thinking about the elapsed time, though. After he had poured coffee twice, he estimated that Esterling had been gone for a half hour or more. But it was not long after that when the major returned.

"My apologies, gentlemen," Esterling said. "It took rather longer than I expected." He sat, and leaned forward, his forearms on the edge of his desk. "I don't have a reply yet, but your message is being taken to the prime minister's office even now." He leaned back, spreading his arms. "I can't say how long a decision will take. Politicians. My guess—and I must stress that it is only a guess—is that I will have some reply from Landfall sometime today. You are welcome to remain here and enjoy our hospitality, such as it is, or, if you prefer to return to your camp, I will make certain that the news gets to you as soon as I hear anything."

"I'm tempted to take you up on your offer of hospitality, Major," Colonel Flowers said. "Colonel Black was very eloquent about the quality of that. But I suppose we should return to our camp to lessen any chance that my presence here will be detected prematurely."

"Of course, Colonel," Esterling said. "I understand fully."

"And when you do have word for us, Major, I would rather that it not be sent by means that might be intercepted. We don't have totally secure radio channels between us."

Esterling nodded. "If it is acceptable to you, I will deliver the response to your camp in person."

"Thank you, Major. That would be the safest possible way," Flowers said.

"So now we just bite our fingernails and wait?" Lon asked once the staff car was well on its way back.

"It would be more seemly without the nail-biting," Flowers said, smiling, "but that's about all we can do now. The ball, as they say, is now in East's court."

"It probably won't be a very long wait," Black said. "We only made an offer to go east to talk to them. If there is truly any desire for peace in Landfall, they shouldn't need much jawing to make the preliminary decision to talk or not."

"The more concerned they are about word of the meeting leaking west, the faster they're likely to act," Flowers said. "I wouldn't be at all surprised to have Major Black come out very early this afternoon."

"I'll make certain that the sentries know to pass him through and warn us of his arrival," Black said.

"Yes, we don't want any embarrassing difficulties over that," Flowers agreed. "You might as well pass the word now."

Black put on his helmet to use its radio. When he had finished, he took the helmet off. "We'll know the second a vehicle puts out from Hope. As soon as a sentry confirms that Major Esterling is coming, we'll have that relayed to the CP."

"We should have someone go to the perimeter to escort the major in," Colonel Flowers said. "Nolan? How about you?"

"Yes, sir, of course," Lon said quickly.

"Take this car," Flowers said. "And a driver. Offer to ride in with Major Esterling in his vehicle—assuming he comes by car. Give him the choice, his car or this one."

"Yes, sir."

Flowers turned toward Black. "Hiram, I'm going to proceed on the assumption that we're going to be going to Landfall, perhaps as soon as this evening. So let's get our team assembled. Captain Orlis is still your acting adjutant?"

Black nodded. "I expect to make the assignment permanent when we get back to Dirigent. He's due for promotion, and once the cadet earns his pips, he can take over Alpha's first two platoons and free Lieutenant Hoper for command of the company."

Lon kept his eyes forward. The rumor mills had already

postulated those changes, but this was the first official confirmation he had heard. From the day that Esau O'Fallon had reported, it had seemed likely. Seniority was far from being the only—or even the most important—qualification for promotion, but Carl Hoper was the senior lieutenant in the battalion. He was due for promotion to captain, and Matt Orlis was due for promotion to major, and a staff assignment. Those actions did not *have* to wait until there was a lieutenant to take over first and second platoons, but it would be . . . tidier if O'Fallon was ready to get his commission. *Carl's due,* Lon thought. *Past due. He's had his commission for ten years and he's earned his way on a lot of combat contracts.*

He felt only a trace of envy. Almost unnoticed, one thought did slide through his mind. *I hope it doesn't take me ten years to make captain.*

18

Lon hardly had a minute to himself. Black called to have Captain Orlis meet them at battalion headquarters. The four officers ate lunch while Colonel Flowers explained what had happened that morning and what he hoped would follow. Orlis showed no surprise at seeing the regimental commander. After the meal, Orlis and the colonels retreated into Black's CP, but Lon was told to stay close. A call might come at any minute that Major Esterling was on his way, and Lon would have to hurry then to meet the major at the perimeter.

"It's the most unusual situation I've run into in nearly twenty-five years in the Corps, Lieutenant," Lead Sergeant Osier said after sending his clerk to get coffee. "But maybe it's cockeyed enough to work."

"I hope so. But things could get sticky."

"Yes, sir, they could," Zal Osier agreed. "We could end up in the middle fighting either colony, or both. And from what we've seen so far, it wouldn't be a walkover for us."

A few minutes later, Lon left the tent to pace outside. *I'm just waiting, not showing nerves,* he reasoned. He had been told to stay close. Even if a few enlisted men saw him pacing, there would be no reason for them to think that his nerves were bad because of impending combat. It was hot, even in the shade, and there was scarcely a breath of air to temper the hundred-plus-degree heat. In a perverse way, the heat was welcome. It gave Lon something to think about besides the situation on Aldrin and waiting for a response from the "enemy" capital.

He tried to reason through the possibilities. If both sides were logical, there was no problem. Accepting mediation and finding a peaceful political resolution was the only answer. But Lon was not naive enough to expect logic to rule—at least not quickly. Had logic ruled, there would have been no fighting, no need for West to hire mercenaries. Lon's first guess was that East would accept Colonel Flowers' offer and that a trip to Landfall was in the offing. After that, East *might* accept the offer of mediation and the Corps' guarantee of safety until a binding peace could be negotiated. They had agreed to that before. But would West accept? They had been the ones to refuse mediation in the first place, preferring to fight.

West didn't want to face East alone in a war, Lon reminded himself. *They would have to stop to think if the alternative to accepting mediation was to face East and the DMC.*

But, again, that was only logic talking.

It was after two o'clock when Osier came out of the tent. "It's time, Lieutenant," he called. "There's a car coming from Hope. The colonel says we should leave right now."

Lon nodded. "You're driving?"

"Yes, sir. And the colonel said no weapons in the car."

"We won't need them," Lon said. His rifle and pistol were in Osier's half of the headquarters tent. Osier was not armed either. "Let's not keep Major Esterling waiting."

Lon rode in the rear seat. Standard military protocol. If Major Esterling rode back in this vehicle, he would be given the right side of the rear seat. In his own vehicle, the arrangements would no doubt be the same. The senior officer always had the right seat in the rear. That was a tradition that went back to Earth.

They reached the checkpoint on the perimeter less than a minute before the car from Hope. Lon got out and waited for the other vehicle to pull to a stop. Major Esterling was in the rear. His lead sergeant was driving.

"Good afternoon, Major," Lon said, saluting when Esterling opened the rear door of his car. "Colonel Flowers asked me to meet you and accompany you in. We can both go in your car, if you prefer, or my driver can take us."

"Thank you, Lieutenant. I'll be glad to have you ride with me," Esterling said. Lon nodded and went around to the other side of the major's floater and got in. He gave the driver directions to the battalion command post. Osier waited until they had gone a hundred yards before he followed.

"I don't think I'll ever truly get used to the heat here," Esterling said. "The area where I was raised almost never had temperatures reach a hundred, and plenty of snow in the winter."

"Yes, sir. Snow is fine, as long as you don't have to sleep in it. Where I was raised on Earth we got some snow each winter. Not as much as some places, but enough to let us know there were different seasons in the year."

"In Hope, there are two seasons," Esterling said. "Wet and dry. The dry season is a little hotter, but the humidity in the wet more than makes up for it. But the land is unbelievably fertile. We get two crops a year from most of the cultivated ground, different crops, adjusted to suit the season."

"You sound as though you know about farming, Major."

"In an amateur sort of way," Esterling said. "My family never farmed, but we lived in a farming area, and I used to visit and ask a lot of questions when I was a boy. There was a time when I wanted to be a farmer more than anything else, long before I decided on the army." He paused. "Most times I don't question that I made the right decision."

Sounds like this isn't one of them, Lon thought. *And that sounds like maybe you've got news Colonel Flowers isn't going to like.* It made the rest of the short ride more nervous for Lon. His stomach started to knot up.

●   ●   ●

Colonel Flowers asked Lon to sit in on the meeting. Captain Orlis was introduced as acting adjutant of 2nd Battalion. Lon waited for Esterling to spring his—presumably bad—news, nearly biting his tongue at the delay for amenities.

"I have heard from the office of our commander in chief," Esterling started when all of them were seated. "He has had instructions from the prime minister. Our government is not sanguine about the chances that West will accept any peaceful resolution to our difficulties, but the prime minister is anxious to explore any possibility."

Better than I thought! ran through Lon's head.

"In that spirit, he is delighted—that is the word I was instructed to use—to accept your offer to lead a mission to Landfall for talks. I am to invite you to make the journey, with the personnel you indicated, as soon as possible. The prime minister suggests that, since you desire secrecy, you depart after dark. Accommodations will be provided, and you will be given whatever time you need to rest after you arrive."

"We accept," Flowers said quickly. "I am most heartened by the decision of your government, Major, and I promise to do everything I can to bring about a peaceful and equitable solution to the difficulties between your two governments."

"Subject to your agreement, my government requests that I accompany you, as liaison and guide," Esterling said.

"I'll be happy to have you with us, Major. I would have asked you to come along in any case."

Esterling remained at Black's headquarters. Esterling's car returned to Hope with a corporal from the headquarters staff to accompany the driver. Two people had to be in the car, in case the Wester delegation observed. The other members of the team that would go east were brought in and briefed. Esterling was provided with a tent so he could rest. Dinner was served in battalion headquarters for him and the officers who were going to Landfall.

Three crates were taken to the shuttle. The men carrying them were told to give a show of effort, as if the boxes were heavy. In fact, they were empty, and were disassembled as soon as they were in the shuttle. It was all meant to help avoid any suspicions among the people from Aldrin West. The flight had to look routine, no different from the dozen other arrivals and departures that had taken place since the surrender of Hope.

Just before sunset, the shuttle's crew started their preflight checks. As soon as it was fully dark, their passengers were taken to the shuttle and boarded.

"We're going to make a burn for orbit on a trajectory to rendezvous with our fleet," Colonel Black informed Esterling. "But we won't rendezvous with any of the ships. As soon as we're lost in the clutter of radar returns, we'll go to full masking and make another burn, coming down near the south pole and flying north on East's side of the main continent. That should all combine to ensure that West doesn't know what's going on."

Major Esterling grinned. "Most devious, Colonel. I applaud you. I am out of my element here, but I accept your assurance that West will not spot the flight."

"Oh, they'll spot it—until we reach the fleet, that is. They'll see us approach our ships and have to assume that we dock. After that, we should be effectively invisible."

Lon settled back for the flight, having a good idea of the steps that would be taken to minimize the risk of detection. It would require a precise reentry burn, allowing the shuttle to coast until they were on the far side of the world and in the atmosphere. In space, the only thing about a shuttle that might be detected by ground or satellite instruments would be a rocket burn. There was no sure way to cloak that.

The DMC attack shuttle seemed deserted with so few people aboard. Major Esterling was flanked by the colonels. Captain Orlis was not too far from them. Lon and the enlisted personnel were farther away. On balance, Lon decided that he preferred it that way, even though he kept wondering if he was missing anything of importance. *At least I don't have to be overly careful of what I do or say,* he thought. And he could pay attention to the nearest video monitor, which gave him a succession of views of Aldrin.

Playing sightseer occupied Lon's mind nicely during the flight. He did not have the responsibilities of two platoons of men or the tension of approaching combat to keep him from enjoying the scenery, such as it was. He had made enough shuttle flights that there was no novelty left in the mechanics. Coming back in toward the world from the pseudorendezvous with the fleet, Lon found himself impressed by the vast expanse of Aldrin's ocean. He had seen Earth's Pacific Ocean from space, but compared to this world-spanning sea, the Pacific was a pond. Over thousands of miles there was not so much as one island large enough to be seen from the shuttle without magnification. And even though temperatures in the southern polar region were comparable to those of Earth's Antarctica, there was no extensive ice cap. Strong ocean and air currents prevented any large-scale accumulation of ice and snow. There were sheets of floating ice, sometimes many miles in extent, but they seemed to be temporary things, rafts that would quickly be torn apart by the forces of unchecked nature.

I wonder if they have whales, or anything comparable, Lon thought after the shuttle had dropped well down into the atmosphere. They were traveling almost due north, at less than forty thousand feet. *With all this water, there could be unbelievably large creatures.* Whales. Monsters. Lon smiled, alone with his thoughts. *Fire-breathing dragons and mile-long sea serpents and who knows what all.* A child's nightmares, a romantic's yearnings. *Why is reality always so ho-hum?*

Too many adventure vids, Lon decided after the shuttle passed into the massive cloud bank of an organized low-pressure system in the tropics. *Maybe I should be writing them instead of trying to be a soldier.* It was a rare bit of whimsy, and he almost chuckled aloud at the image of Lon Nolan, fantasy *auteur.*

For a time the images on the video monitors were all infrared. Even though it was night over the ocean, there had been some illumination from the stars. But visibility was nil in the storm system. There was a certain amount of turbulence, but the pilots did not take the easy path of climbing above the storm—a category three hurricane, the pilot informed his passengers. It gave them an additional measure of concealment.

Lon let his thoughts drift to more comfortable territory. *Sara, will I have things to tell you when I get home.* He closed his eyes and leaned back. Sara. Lon Nolan, young married man. That was almost as fantastic a notion as the other, but more satisfying despite the brief sensation of nerves in his stomach. The idea still needed getting used to. *Maybe it's a good thing this contract came up,* Lon told himself. *It gives us both more time to think. We were rushing hell-bent for leather before, letting emotion dictate everything.* His stomach gave him another nervous jab, sharper. *God, I hope she doesn't change her mind.* That possibility was scary, worse than going into combat. At least now, when there was no immediate prospect of battle.

I don't think of her all the time now, the way I did before we left Dirigent, or on the first part of the trip. Maybe some of the glow is *wearing off.* Lon could still picture Sara in his mind, but her image was not quite as crisp and clearly defined as it had been before. *I still love her. I still want to marry her,* he assured himself, and he felt relieved when no dissenting opinion arose within his head.

"We're about twenty minutes from Landfall," the pilot announced shortly after the shuttle emerged from the storm. They were now at twenty thousand feet. "I'll start braking maneuvers in two minutes."

We'll need to be subsonic before we get near the coast and the settled areas of East, Lon thought. The braking maneuvers were noticeable. Lon felt himself being pressed forward against his restraining harness. He had to hold his head back, stiffen neck muscles. The engine noises increased dramatically as thrust was reversed, momentarily, several times, bringing the shuttle's speed down in steps without losing a lot of altitude.

When there were only five minutes left, the braking maneuvers became even stronger as the pilot forced the craft's airspeed below five hundred miles per hour. The shuttle went into a long glide, losing altitude steadily, and going through a series of turns to line it up with the runway at Landfall's spaceport. Finally the pilot cut all thrust from the engines. They would be switched back on only when the shuttle was on the ground, braking to a stop.

Lon did not notice that he had gripped the armrests of his seat so tightly that his knuckles were white. This was the part of flying he enjoyed the least, the landings, even when it was not a "hot" combat landing. The shuttle's skids touched the plascrete runway, sending almost steady vibrations through the body of the shuttle, and a high-pitched whine. The jets came back on, reverse thrust, straining to stop the lander as quickly as possible. The landing was not as . . . violent as it would have been going into combat, but it was enough to make Lon nervous. He looked toward Major Esterling and noted that he also looked anxious about the maneuver, even though Colonel Flowers was talking to him, apparently attempting to reassure him.

The shuttle came to a halt. They were on the ground in the enemy capital.

19

The shuttle was towed into a hangar before its passengers disembarked. The government of Aldrin East was doing everything it could to assure the secrecy that Colonel Flowers had requested. Inside the hangar there was an honor guard waiting, four soldiers in dress uniforms, carrying flags or chromed antique rifles—ornamental rather than practical.

When the shuttle doors opened, the honor guard came to attention. A group of civilians also was present. At the center of this group was a man identified as the minister of defense, Desmond Lanch. There were several other dignitaries with him.

"The prime minister will greet you at his office, Colonel," Lanch told Flowers. "We have cars waiting to take you and your people there." Except for the shuttle's crew.

The cars were limousines, their dark blue exteriors polished as brightly as any military dress-uniform brass, their windows darkly tinted to give total privacy. The chauffeurs wore fancy uniforms—clearly not military. The vehicles had been parked inside the hangar, waiting. Five were needed to transport the dignitaries and the new arrivals.

The car bearing the minister of defense, the two colonels, and Major Esterling led the procession. Lon was in the second vehicle with Captain Orlis and two of the lesser officials who had been present to meet them.

"It will take about fifteen minutes to get to Government House," one of the civilians told Lon and Orlis. "There is scarcely any traffic at this time of day."

Lon nodded politely, while Captain Orlis made small talk with the civilians. Lon was more interested in looking out the side window. He knew from his study of the file on Aldrin that Landfall had more than two million inhabitants—one of the three or four largest cities anywhere off Earth. It had been built to showcase the government buildings at its center. Around that hub, marked by a circular avenue fifty yards wide, six main thoroughfares radiated out through commercial and residential districts. Broad greenbelts gave Landfall almost the feel of a collection of small towns, separate from their neighbors.

Traveling the nearly deserted streets an hour before dawn, Lon saw how the residents kept their city clean. There appeared to be a considerable fleet of small street-cleaning automatons collecting refuse along the way, adroitly maneuvering around obstructions too large for their collector vacuums.

"We're coming up on Government Center now," one of the civilians announced about eight minutes after the motorcade had left the airport. "There in front of us."

Lon dutifully looked out the front, and he was impressed. Although he had read about this, and seen photographs, the reality was startling. The government district was a mile in diameter, and the architects had subscribed wholeheartedly to the monumental style of public buildings. A low stone wall, three feet high, was the only visible "security" around the district. There were no serious barricades, no visible guardians patrolling the perimeter. A series of winding drives worked their way through the district, offering carefully staged views of the buildings and the landscaping that separated them.

Almost makes Corps Headquarters look like a lean-to, Lon thought. *This would stand up to comparison with any of the old national capitals on Earth.*

"Landfall was a planned city," one of the civilians said with obvious pride. "Our original settlement was a dozen miles north of here. We built the new capital on the site of the first landings. Of course, it was not built all at once. What you see represents the fulfilling of the original blueprint over more than two hundred years, as finances and other needs permitted. Just across Colony Boulevard from Government Center we have our opera house, national theater, and three museums, one dedicated to works of art that were brought from Earth."

"A remarkable achievement," Captain Orlis said. "A work of art as much as anything else."

Both civilians seemed to beam at that.

The motorcade slowed down severely when it entered the governmental district. It was not, Lon thought, solely because the streets were narrow and winding. Their hosts wanted to make sure that the visitors had time to be suitably impressed.

Government House stood in the exact center of the district. It was three stories high, built of some lustrous white stone that glinted as the headlights of the limousines caught it. The cavalcade came to a halt on a circular drive at the front of the building, below a flight of stairs that was twenty yards across and rose thirty feet to the ceremonial entrance.

But the Dirigenters were not taken up those stairs. *The secrecy again,* Lon thought as they were led around to the left side of the stairway. Double doors opened into an anteroom below the stone stairs. There the prime minister of Aldrin East, Edmund McGrath, waited to greet his visitors.

The formalities were brief, introductions and McGrath's statement that he hoped their discussions would be fruitful. "I know you must be tired, Colonel," he said then. "And while I am eager to start our talks, I would not impose so heavily on you. Guest quarters have been arranged for you and your people, and you will have whatever time you need to rest and refresh yourselves. If you and your officers would do me the honor of sharing breakfast first . . . ?"

There was, of course, no chance that Colonel Flowers would decline that invitation.

• • •

By the time Lon reached the guest room that had been assigned to him, he was so bleary that he was almost ready to fall asleep on his feet. He had not slept in twenty-four hours. *I've got six hours now. Let's not waste any of it,* he told himself, heading directly for the large and comfortable-looking bed. *Five and a half to sleep, thirty minutes to get presentable afterward.* Breakfast had been, thankfully, brief. Prime Minister McGrath had contented himself with a minimum of talk. Lon accepted that the food had been excellent, though he had been in no condition to appreciate the niceties. Stifling yawns had been his primary focus; shoveling food in as quickly as he could without appearing to have the table manners of a hog came second. And his mind had been unable to cope with three demands on it.

Lon stripped to his underwear after checking to make sure that the duffel bag with his two changes of clothing had actually been delivered to the room. Everything had been unpacked and put in drawers or hung in the closet. *Better than they deserve,* Lon thought, staring at the battledress uniforms hung in perfect order. Battledress was disposable, recycled rather than cleaned . . . when possible. Not knowing how long the visit to Landfall might be, Lon folded the uniform he took off. He might need to wear it again before they returned to fresh stocks. He set the folded uniform on a chair next to the dresser. Perhaps someone would collect it and clean it while he slept.

The bed was so soft that it seemed to swallow Lon. He felt an instant of subconscious panic as he sank into the mattress, but he was asleep before he could even fully recognize the sensation. Exhaustion brought the void, sleep so profound that no dream had a chance.

Lon's time sense did not fail him. He woke almost precisely at the time he had set for himself. He was still tired, but bearably so. He allowed himself a few minutes to lie in bed, warm and comfortable. But duty would not let him remain abed too long. *I need time to shower and shave,* he reminded himself, wasting a few more seconds with that. Eventually, and still with time enough so he would not have to rush, he stretched and sat up, yawning to help clear the sleep from his brain.

Standing next to the bed, he did a few very quick and sloppy exercises, still cranking himself up toward full alertness. He stopped when he noticed that the dirty uniform had been removed. He had not heard anyone come into the room. *I guess I was really dead,* he thought. Normally, even the slightest noise was enough to wake him. Especially on contract, when noise might mean that danger was too close to avoid.

The bathroom attached to his bedroom was larger than his combined office and bedroom in the barracks on Dirigent. It was fully furnished with everything he might possibly want, including a few items that he wasn't certain how they were meant to be used. There was a variety of scents, colognes and perfumes. After his shower, Lon sniffed at each and finally chose the least intrusive, and even then dabbed it on very sparingly. *Wouldn't be proper to smell like I'd just come from one of the private rooms at the Dragon Lady,* he thought with a smile. He shook his head. *I guess my visits there are over anyway.*

That led to thoughts of Sara, and Lon was whistling under his breath by the time he finished dressing. He was ready to face the world when a soft knock sounded on the door.

"Come in," Lon called, his voice almost cheerful.

A servant dressed in what would have passed for formal wear on Dirigent came in. "Excuse me, sir. I was sent to tell you that your commander and the others are gathering."

"Thank you," Lon said. "I'm ready."

"Very good, sir. I shall show you the way." The servant bowed Lon out of the room ahead of him, then closed the door behind them and started down the corridor—which was fifteen feet wide. They entered a lift tube, went down one floor, then walked back in the direction from which they had come. Office space had been found for the Dirigenters. Everyone but Colonel Black and Captain

Orlis had arrived. Several of the enlisted men were seated at complinks, working at something or other.

"You look rested, Nolan," Colonel Flowers said while the servant who had led Lon to the room bowed his way back out.

"A little sleep does wonders, Colonel. I could get used to this soft life."

"Don't get used to it too quickly. With any luck at all, we won't be here long. To get this thing settled, we'll have to go back west, and convince the other side to go along with whatever arrangements we can come up with here."

I doubt West will give us this level of VIP treatment, Lon thought.

"We'll be meeting with the prime minister and several other members of the government in twenty minutes," Flowers said. "I'll listen to Prime Minister McGrath's position statement, then probably offer a few ideas of my own. Then we'll see where we go from there. I may have work for you later, but for now, I just want you to pay attention. If you have any insights, give them to me afterward."

"Yes, sir. Listen hard and keep my mouth shut."

Flowers grinned. "We'll all be doing a fair share of that, lad. The idea is to find out just where East stands."

Prime Minister Edmund McGrath and his defense minister, Desmond Lanch, each had a deputy with him—mostly to serve as surrogate memories, Lon guessed. Major Esterling sat at the end of the table, symbolically a middleman between his government and the mercenaries. There were two other Eastmen present, but sitting back from the table in the cabinet's meeting room. For the Corps, the four officers sat at the table. The two colonels were in the center, with Lon at Colonel Flowers' left and Captain Orlis at Colonel Black's right. Lead Sergeant Osier hovered behind them, ready to go back and forth from the cabinet room to the office below if necessary, and one clerk was present with a complink ready for anything he might be called on to do.

Prime Minister McGrath's opening statement was everything that Lon expected. McGrath spoke of deploring the fighting, and pointing out that Aldrin East had been ready, eager, to accept the Corps' offer of mediation and peacekeeping in months past. He pointed out that his government had not ordered the steps leading toward their abortive invasion of West until after West had refused that offer. "It was the counsel of desperation that ruled. Since West declined any peaceful settlement, we felt that we were left with no viable alternative." He spoke briefly of the population pressures that both colonies were feeling, but went to some pains to stress that West had never indicated any plans to use the disputed territory in the south and that East had stepped into a vacuum. "That territory had never been occupied or even—so far as we can determine—visited by anyone from Aldrin West. They had no valid claim to it."

For Lon, there was nothing at all new in what Colonel Flowers said in response. The Dirigent Mercenary Corps preferred to see a peaceful solution to the dispute between the two governments on Aldrin and offered itself as mediator and guarantor of the peace during the interim. A world that was not unified was at a distinct disadvantage, subject to pressures and dangers that could be alleviated, if not eliminated, by unification. The Corps was willing to put pressure on Aldrin West to accept a just settlement of the current disputes, if suitable agreement with East was found. And so forth.

McGrath spoke again then of the population pressures. "If there were peace between the two governments, and perhaps—hopefully—talks directed toward planetary government, then there would be no reason why both sides could not avail themselves of the land in the south. And both sides would be able to more effectively utilize the land on either side of the continental divide that separates us—if we were free of the threat of military intervention by West, for example. Aldrin could conceivably support a population three times as great as it does today, without any serious decline in the quality of life, if we could all use all of the available and acceptable lands.''

Lon received his only surprise of the day when Colonel Flowers spoke again. "We know that a world can support many times the population that some think possible. Lieutenant Nolan here was born and raised on Earth, which has managed to support as many as six billion people. True, Earth has several times the available land that Aldrin does, but by analogy one must suspect that Aldrin could support a population of a billion without running into the debilitating stresses that Earth has encountered over the past several centuries. Lon, perhaps you could explain some of the ways that Earth has successfully dealt with the intense population pressures she has felt?''

"Yes, sir," Lon said, thinking, *It's time to put the freak, the outsider, on display again.* He took a few seconds to try to sort out where he could begin, what he could say. He had been given absolutely no warning about this. *The colonel is playing things by ear,* Lon realized. *He probably didn't guess himself that this might come up.*

"I do have a rough idea of the populations here on Aldrin, and the available land areas," Lon started, speaking slowly, trying to feel his way into the topic. "Earth has long since been forced to utilize every available bit of land, even areas that you on Aldrin would consider submarginal. For instance, humans on Earth have always heavily used tropical zones. The evidence is that humanity arose in tropical savanna, very like the area where the settlement of Hope is. That is, most likely, mankind's 'natural' habitat. On Earth, only the most extreme parts of the polar zones do not have permanent civilian inhabitants, and even those areas have often been utilized for long-term research projects. The mountainous regions of Europe and the Americas have been intensely settled for centuries, in some cases dating back to before the intense population pressures forced people to live anywhere that they could produce any agricultural products to feed themselves. The development of molecular replicators, nanotechnology, in the twenty-first century in large measure reduced our dependence on arable land. Of course, Earth did not move toward dealing scientifically with population pressure until that pressure was almost overwhelming, until the planet was crowded almost to a Malthusian limit. On Aldrin, as on all colony worlds, those questions either do not arise or are dealt with early enough that the more extreme measures of . . . adjustment need never arise.''

It was not an elegant speech. Forced to talk extemporaneously, Lon often slowed down, searching for words, for direction, wondering how long Colonel Flowers expected him to divert the people from Aldrin East—and what the colonel expected his rambling discourse to produce. Other than boredom. ''There are some rather extreme theories, mostly dating back several centuries and only modestly supported by available evidence, that claim that all war can be traced directly to population pressures, ignoring the clear facts that religion and differing political systems have caused some of the bloodiest and most bitter conflicts. It took Earth a long time to escape the destruction of war, but there has not been a major conflict on the world in centuries, despite the continuing stresses of intense population. Emigration to other worlds has never managed to alleviate, even temporarily, those stresses. It simply is not possible to move enough people off-world fast enough for that.''

Eventually, after nearly forty-five minutes, Lon wore to a stop. He glanced at Colonel Flowers, who nodded his satisfaction.

''A very impressive tale, Lieutenant,'' Prime Minister McGrath said. ''We have had very little direct contact with Earth in generations, though, naturally, we attempt to follow what happens there with some interest. You have given us much to think about. Colonel Flowers, if you would care to submit specific proposals for our consideration . . . ?''

''Of course, Prime Minister. I can have them for you in an hour, perhaps less.''

McGrath nodded. ''I think we've made a good beginning today, gentlemen. If there is no objection, we might consider adjourning until tomorrow morning. That will give us time to go over the proposals of the Dirigent Mercenary Corps in detail.''

20

In less than twenty-four hours, the government of
Aldrin East and Colonel Flowers came to agreement on a
set of proposals. Prime Minister McGrath asked for only
two minor, cosmetic, changes in the language of Flowers'
written suggestions. It took even less time to agree on how
they would attempt to persuade Aldrin West to go along.

"We'll return to Hope tonight," Colonel Black said.
"I'll return to my headquarters in the north. I'll transmit
the peace proposals to the government in Syracuse as
coming from the government of Aldrin East, and put the
Dirigent Mercenary Corps on record as favoring this solution as it stands. We'll do everything humanly possible
to persuade West to accept the proposals as not only the
best that can be obtained but also as the best prospect for
the world as a whole and its people. If everything else
fails, I'll threaten to void our contract with West and accept employment with East."

No one at the table in McGrath's cabinet room showed
any emotion at Flowers' statements, but Lon virtually held
his breath. Voiding a contract and switching sides was
almost unprecedented in the annals of the DMC. The
honor of the Corps demanded that such a step be taken
only in the most extraordinary conditions, and with the
fullest contractual delicacy. It was something that other
potential clients would remark on for decades, a question
mark standing against offering a contract.

There was a formal banquet held in honor of the Dirigenters. The affair was small, a measure dictated by the
continuing desire for secrecy. The mercenaries were sup-

posedly not in East, they were still—as far as West was to know—where they had been. Eight members of McGrath's cabinet attended, along with Major Esterling. Security officers were posted around the banquet room and in the kitchen. Every care was taken.

At the spaceport, everyone boarded the shuttle inside the hangar. The limousines left. The hangar doors were opened and the shuttle towed out to the main runway—after runway lights had been extinguished.

"It appears that my government takes seriously the possibility that West may have planted agents among us," Major Esterling said. He appeared disheartened by that realization. "It seems impossible, just from a practical standpoint. We have had so little to do with each other. But, still, all of this . . ." He could do no more than shake his head.

"That very feeling that it would be impossible is the biggest advantage an agent would have," Colonel Flowers said. "But you can take some comfort. It is almost equally likely that your government has agents in West."

"Almost?" Esterling asked.

"An open society is always more vulnerable than a closed or tightly regulated one," Flowers said.

"One of the prices a people must pay for individual freedom," Colonel Black added.

They're taking a lot for granted, aren't they? Lon asked himself. *It seems they're accepting that East is open and that West isn't, and we have only their word for that . . . or do we?* Lon recalled that the colonel had been going to investigate, as best he could. Had he learned something to confirm the claims that Esterling had made in Hope? West had not given them much opportunity to see living conditions among their citizenry, and contacts with West's military units had been minimal, mostly conducted by radio, at a distance.

Lon worried at that until he fell asleep. It was not a comfortable slumber, but it was, as he told himself later, better than sleeping in a wet foxhole.

•   •   •

"Stick around a bit longer, Nolan," Colonel Black told him after they reached the 2nd Battalion CP. Major Esterling and his driver had started back to Hope. Colonel Flowers had remained aboard the shuttle. It would be heading back to the rest of the regiment within minutes. "I'm going to set up an officers' call as quickly as everyone can make the trek, so there's no point in you and Captain Orlis going back to Alpha first."

"Yes, sir," Lon said. Orlis was already back in his battle helmet, using the radio to call all the battalion's officers to headquarters. With the companies spread out around Hope, it would take an hour for them all to arrive.

"We've only finished the easy part of our job," Black said then. "East always looked to be the easy part. Now Colonel Flowers has to tackle West, and that's going to be a lot touchier. I don't expect them to agree quickly or easily, and there's a chance that they will react violently when Colonel Flowers has to give them the final ultimatum."

"You're that sure it will go that far, sir?" Lon asked. "That they won't agree short of us threatening to change sides?"

"Let's say that I'm not optimistic. As of today, we go on full alert status, and I want effort put into preparing the strongest possible defenses. Major Esterling is going to put his people on similar alert."

"Without weapons?"

There was no humor in Black's smile. "They were brought back down while we were gone. Before today is out, Major Esterling's men will have their weapons and ammunition."

"I assume that plans have been laid so that West's representatives here won't know about that?"

"We'll do our best."

"They'll see that we're beefing up our defenses though, won't they, sir?" Lon asked.

Black shrugged. "That can't be avoided."

• • •

The meeting of the battalion's officers allowed Black to flesh out the synopsis he had given Lon. He detailed the preparations he wanted, and offered a full slate of contingency proposals. "The ultimate risk," Black said, "is that West will attempt a preemptive strike against the regiment when Colonel Flowers tells them to accept the proposals or we switch sides. That is what we have to guard against."

"They can't really manage a *sneak* attack against us here," Captain Orlis told his lieutenants and Cadet O'Fallon as they walked back to Alpha's camp. "That's the biggest advantage 2nd Battalion has. West doesn't have forces close enough. They would have to move them in by shuttle, and the fleet would spot that sort of movement as quickly as they got off the ground. That would give us at least forty-five minutes' warning."

"Long enough to worry but not long enough to do anything useful," Carl Hoper suggested.

"They won't catch us with our pants down," Orlis said. "And it gives CIC time to launch Shrikes to hit the shuttles coming in. That makes it enough time to be useful."

"I meant on the ground," Hoper said. "We'll know they're coming but won't be able to do more than wait and worry."

Orlis shrugged. "It's more likely that any strike—if there is one—will be directed at the other battalions. West has troops close enough to them that they might try to move in undetected. If they're smart about it, and lucky, they could get close enough to do damage. Remember, we're talking about highly trained soldiers here, not a ragtag militia. We've seen how good they are. That's one of the reasons I want us to be at maximum readiness even though I don't expect a strike here. If I'm wrong about where they hit, I want every other advantage going for us."

Captain Orlis and his lieutenants made the rounds of the company perimeter, with Esau O'Fallon tagging along, listening, not offering opinions. The officers discussed what preparations to make, and where. "It's not just the perimeter," Orlis said after they had negotiated half of it. "I want dirt buttresses around the tents, at least three feet high. There are bags to fill in one of the shuttles. It's a lot of extra work, but it's either that or take the tents down and go primitive, and I don't want to do that, at least not now. In this heat, the cover of tents is important. I don't want any more trouble from dehydration than we already have."

"Stockpile water in case the lines coming out from Hope are hit?" Hoper suggested.

"Good idea. Round up whatever tanks we can, and tell your men to keep their canteens as near full as possible."

"What about switching schedules around and doing most of the work at night, Captain?" Lon asked. "That would be easier on the men. They can get more done when it's cooler. And it would make it harder for the team from West to see what we're doing."

Orlis hesitated, then shook his head. "I don't want to waste the eight hours of daylight we've got left today. We need to get started. But don't push the men hard right off the bat. Keep the work periods short and rotate jobs. Maybe a third of the men working, a third on watch, and the other third resting. We'll keep going after sunset, pick up the pace, get switched around gradually. There's no way of telling how much time we have, how long the talks will remain diplomatic."

"As least we've got good fire zones," Hoper said. "If the people of Hope get their harvest in before anything happens, it'll be better. Any force coming in will have a lot of open ground to cover, and only a little dry grass to hide in."

"Which reminds me," Orlis said, not quite interrupting. "I want more snoops planted, out as far as a thousand yards. We don't need dense coverage, but more than we've got." He lowered his voice then. "This next bit is, uh, unofficial, but I want particular attention paid to laying snoops between us and the Westers. If they come nosing about, I want to know early.''

''I guess it's too much to hope that they might head back to Syracuse in a snit,'' Hoper said.

''I wouldn't hold my breath,'' Orlis said.

Lon gave his platoon sergeants directions for the work parties. He talked to the men of each platoon separately, telling them as much as he could about the situation. And the potential danger. ''With a lot of luck, maybe none of this will be needed,'' he said, ''but if we do need it, I want to have it all done. We don't want our butts hanging out later.''

There was some grumbling—there was always grumbling over fatigue duty—but it was low-keyed, natural grousing about the work and the heat. And there were bright spots.

''We get dirt piled up around the tents, and maybe scoop out a foot or so from the ground inside,'' Phip Steesen suggested, ''it'll be that little bit cooler inside.''

Squad leaders and their assistants bossed the work—while doing their own share. Lon and the platoon sergeants circulated. Lon and Carl met to pitch in with the work on their tent, scooping out dirt from under the floor and helping fill the sandbags that were piled up around the outer walls. Esau O'Fallon was with the squad from first platoon that he was assigned to, working along with the others in the squad.

''It's good for morale,'' Hoper told Lon. ''The men won't grouse as much if they see us sweating right along with them.''

I know, I know, Lon thought, saving his energy for work.

The two officers did not attempt to do all the work around their tent, but they made a good start, and men from all of their platoons chipped in to finish the job.

Breaks were frequent, along with reminders to drink plenty of water. The mess tent provided chilled fruit drinks. There was a cold lunch, which was all the men wanted while they were out in the heat, with the promise of a hot supper after dark, when the temperature started to drop. Lon gave his men an hour off, starting just before sunset, to rest, get cleaned up, and eat. Cold showers were popular. Squad leaders had to remind their men to get in and out and let others have a turn.

"How long do you think we'll have before things turn ugly, if they do?" Lon asked Carl Hoper when they met for supper.

Carl shrugged. "No damn way to know. That's the sad truth. Colonel Flowers can be awfully persuasive when he wants to. I've seen him sweet-talking people. If it wasn't for the language barrier, he could talk a bluecat into becoming a vegetarian." The bluecat was one of Dirigent's major predators. Similar to large terran felines, but not exactly, bluecats had been a menace in the early years of the colony. "But I don't think he'll be able to talk West around without leaving a lot of hard feelings that could complicate the later talks between East and West."

"You think we're going to end up fighting West." Lon did not attempt to make it a question.

"Maybe I'm a pessimist by nature," Carl said, "but, yes, I think we're going to have to fight them. They might not pull a sneak attack, but there's no guarantee. Right now my best hope is that the Council of Regiments already has reinforcements on the way. Another regiment shows up, maybe with another fighter carrier or a brigade of armor, that might sway West."

"That would be nice," Lon said.

"We've been here long enough that reinforcements *could* be on the way if the Council acted quickly," Carl said.

"Sounds as if you're trying to convince yourself."

Hoper shrugged. "I think I'll see if they've got any more of that fruit juice."

Just before dawn, as Lon was telling his men to knock off and get breakfast, the shuttle of the Aldrin West contingent took off and headed north. The craft made no attempt at stealth. It went supersonic low, sending a shock wave along the ground.

"I think maybe they're pissed, Lieutenant," Sergeant Girana commented.

Lon shrugged. "I guess there was no way we could hide what we were doing, and maybe they put two and two together. Or maybe they've had information from other sources."

"If they were smart, they'd have left their people here to watch what we're doing," Girana said.

"Half and half watches, Tebba, three-hour shifts," Lon said. "Unless I get different orders, we won't get back to our construction work until sundown tonight." That had been the last word from battalion headquarters. "Tell the men to get as much rest as they can. We've still got a lot to do."

"Yes, sir. But we've made a good start."

"Very good, Tebba. I hope it isn't necessary, but I think we'll be ready if West decides to play it hard. But the watches stay. Even for breakfast. Two shifts."

"Yes, sir."

"Lieutenant Hoper and I will be taking turns as well. One or the other of us will always be up and available. I don't know what the captain's schedule is going to be."

Tebba saluted and went off to see to his platoon. Weil Jorgen had already checked in by radio and received his orders. Lon took another tour of his platoons' area, looking at the work that had been accomplished. The tents were already bunkered, and a good start had been made on the interconnected trenches that would give the company camp a solid outer perimeter and avenues across it.

Lon stifled a yawn. He had three hours until he could lie down and get some sleep. Carl Hoper had the first sleep shift of the day, while it was relatively cool. Hoper was eating breakfast now. When he finished, he would hold the duty for the fifteen or twenty minutes that Lon would need to eat. *That's the way it goes,* Lon told himself. *Carl's senior lieutenant in the company. My day will come when he replaces Orlis and O'Fallon gets his commission.* Soon, whenever they got back to Dirigent from this contract.

21

After a week of work, Captain Orlis decided that there was nothing left to be done to improve the defenses of Alpha's camp. The first forty-eight hours had been almost frantic, getting everything to an acceptable minimum. Beyond that, the work had been slower, tweaking everything. To a cursory examination from a distance, it looked almost as if the camp had disappeared. Tents had been recessed into the ground, dirt buttresses extending to the peaks. They worked hard to camouflage the site. The perimeter trenches were linked to secondary defensive positions within. It was possible to get anywhere within the camp without going aboveground. The linked trenches were six feet deep, with platforms along the side at every firing position.

"Like the First World War back on Earth," Lon commented during a meal break after the work was finished. "They had vast systems of trenches between the two sides. The trench lines went for hundreds of miles, I think. Millions of men faced each other across narrow no-man's-lands for nearly four years."

"As long as they don't ask us to dig trenches to connect with the other companies and Hope," Carl Hoper said. "Even if we had power equipment that would take weeks."

"We don't have the men to cover that much perimeter, even counting Major Esterling's men and Hope's militia," Orlis said. For the past several days he had made a point of eating supper with his lieutenants each evening, an informal officers' call. But, so far, there had been little to discuss. There was no substantial news from regiment, no word of progress in the talks between Colonel Flowers and Aldrin West. And intelligence about West troop movements had proved to be spotty.

"Trench warfare was a disaster on Earth," Lon said. "All that it led to was millions of casualties, without either side being able to gain much ground. That's why mobility was the key word for both sides in the next major conflict."

"Things start popping here and I imagine we'll be mobile again," Orlis said. "All this work is just to keep us in one piece in case our employers turn against us. We've got to stay in one place as long as there's no overt aggression against us. We can't be seen as starting hostilities against West."

Second Battalion had been in place around Hope for a month before there was any change. Colonel Black had moved his headquarters into Alpha's camp. It had been too isolated where it was. Colonel Flowers sent a message to all of the regiment's officers. "The government of Aldrin West has stated formally, in writing, that 7th Regiment has fulfilled its contract, that they see no purpose in our remaining any longer to prevent new settlers from coming in from Aldrin East, and requesting—demanding—that we leave Aldrin as soon as practical, and in no case are we to remain longer than seventy-two hours from the time of receipt of the message. My reply was to thank them for acknowledging our successful completion of the contract but I informed them that we would be unable to leave Aldrin within the time frame they 'suggested,' that I am required to wait for clearance from Dirigent and the Council of Regiments. I renewed our proposals, and my support for those made directly to Aldrin West by Aldrin East. 'Since we are now recognized as neutrals here,' I told the government of West, 'we are even more suitable for the role of mediation during any extended negotiations between the two governments toward resolution of their long-standing differences.' So far I have had no reply. The watchword remains *vigilance*."

"They've pulled in the welcome mat and told us to go away," Orlis commented to his lieutenants.

"How long do you thing Colonel Flowers can stall before things get ugly?" Hoper asked.

Orlis shook his head. "I imagine he's used up everything already, or West wouldn't have told us to get out so bluntly."

"But we're not going," Lon observed.

"There's nothing about packing our bags in the colonel's message," Orlis said.

"We could go east. We're welcome there, it seems," Carl suggested.

"Or bring the rest of the regiment down here," Lon said. "That gets us out of the way but doesn't abandon Hope."

A smile crossed Orlis's face. "I imagine that would be considered extremely provocative. Any move that wasn't up to the fleet would be. My guess is that the rest of the regiment will just have to hunker down where they are and take their chances."

"Makes the tropics seem almost welcome," Carl said. "At least we can count on some warning if West attacks."

There had been occasional message rockets from Dirigent—about one MR every three or four days. Lon had received two letters from Sara, long but with little real substance. Lon had also sent several letters to her, but neither of her letters mentioned any word from him, so he assumed that she had not received them when she wrote. Two days after the ultimatum from Aldrin West, an MR from Dirigent brought news that was even more welcome to Lon than Sara's third letter—the first to mention one of his notes. Twelfth Regiment was coming.

"They should be overhead in about fifty-six hours," Captain Orlis said after telling his lieutenants and his lead sergeant. "They're already in system. Apparently they popped out of Q-space little more than six hours after the MR.''

"West must know that they're in-system as well," Lon noted.

"Probably," Orlis said with a shrug. "It's not quite so important now. Colonel Flowers said he will be delivering his ultimatum to the government of West this morning. 'Negotiate in good faith with East or else.' West refused to extend their deadline for us to leave the planet yesterday afternoon.''

"Captain, there's no way we can enforce any peace between the governments here unless we're prepared to keep troops on Aldrin indefinitely," Carl said. "That's the weak point. Sure, we can go home and say we'll be back if there are any breaches, but the month it would take for us to respond could be too much to make any difference.''

"That's always been the case," Orlis said. "We have the reputation of the Corps, and the threat to return. Maybe we'll have to, even if there's no profit in it. But if we get them working together, making contacts instead of using those mountains as a wall between them, time ought to do the rest.''

"They fight for long," Lon said, "the Confederation of Human Worlds might take an interest, see them as easy pickings. They won't have any independence at all left then. I'm surprised CHW hasn't tried to enforce sovereignty already.''

"Captain, if it's going to be two and a half days before 12th Regiment is available, and Colonel Flowers is going to hit West over the head with his demands this morning, that's going to leave us particularly vulnerable for the next couple of days," Carl said. "They might well try to strike first.''

"They might," Orlis agreed.

Lon sat in the trench with third platoon's second squad. He spent much of his days going from one group of men to the next, talking, sharing the latest news, answering the inevitable questions. Second squad had rigged a camouflage tarp over the trench to shade them from the sun, but the tarp also cut down on the circulation of air. It was still hot, but bearable.

"It's coming, isn't it, Lieutenant?" Lance Corporal Gen Radnor, the assistant squad leader, asked. "We're finally going to have us a real fight here."

"I don't know about us, personally," Lon said. "We may be far enough away for now. But I think the rest of the regiment is likely to catch hell before 12th lands. After that, who knows?" He shrugged. "Even with two regiments and all of East's armed forces, West could put up a hell of a fight. It depends on how determined they are. If there's only one government on Aldrin, they want it to be theirs, not some hybrid that forces them to share authority with East. That's the only possible reason they could have for refusing to negotiate."

"This sure is nothing like any contract I've been on before," Phip Steesen said.

"I don't think it's like anything anyone in the Corps has been on," Dav Grott said. "It's peculiar, that's what it is. I know what we're trying to do, Lieutenant, and maybe it's all well and good, but it's still peculiar."

"I won't argue with you, Dav," Lon said. "All we can do is follow orders and do everything we can to minimize the cost if fighting comes." Everyone knew he was not talking about money, but lives. The veterans had been with Lon on two expensive contracts, the kind no soldier liked to experience.

Dean Ericks started to say something, but Lon held up a hand to cut him off. Lon was receiving a call from Captain Orlis. He listened for a moment, said, "Yes, sir," then spoke to the squad.

"Got to go. I've got to accompany the captain on a run into Hope. Be back in a couple of hours. No slacking off. I don't *think* we're apt to get hit here, but I could be wrong. It wouldn't be the first time."

•   •   •

They drove to Hope, just Lon and Matt Orlis. The captain drove, and he looked unusually somber. "It could get grim, Lon," Orlis said, shaking his head. "If we have a fight here, it's going to be something like the Corps hasn't faced in a couple of generations, a large-scale war with both sides up to the minute in weapons and tactics. It could go on for months, if not years."

"Years?" Lon asked, a little surprised.

"Like the big nationalist wars of Earth," Orlis said. "The Corps might have to bring in more regiments, and . . ." He stopped, shaking his head again. "It would be costly in people and money. If we get dragged in as a full participant, no one's going to be paying our way, and that's bad for business."

"You think it could really come to that, Captain?" Lon was as much surprised by Orlis's glum mood as by what he said.

Orlis took a deep breath and sighed. "Maybe I'm just not myself this morning, Lon, and we've been here so long that I had about convinced myself we wouldn't have any more fighting. Yes, it could get that bad, but it probably won't. West might put up some sort of a fight, but I can't see them pushing it to the ultimate. Once they see that the result is going to go against them, I would think they would want to avoid weakening themselves any farther, keep whatever leverage they can for later. For all the posturing, they have to think about the future."

"That didn't always happen on Earth, Captain," Lon said—with some reluctance because he didn't want to contribute to Orlis's apparent depression. "We had wars where one or both sides insisted on an all-or-nothing result."

"This isn't Earth," Orlis said with force. "We've learned those lessons, over and over. It can't go that far here. It just can't." His vehemence seemed to help. While he did not end the drive with a smile and a whistle, at least his face looked normal—quietly confident.

• • •

Hope also had been preparing for the possibility of more fighting. The town's defenses had been bolstered considerably. Strong points had been established at key points along the perimeter. Key buildings inside the town also had been strengthened. Trenches had been dug.

"Of course we helped them," Orlis said when Lon made a comment about it. "If things go bad, Hope is our fallback. That would give us a shorter perimeter to worry about, let us consolidate. Between 2nd Battalion and Hope's own defenders, we would present quite a formidable obstacle. Especially since we can count on air support."

Most of the grain in the fields had been harvested, the automatic machinery working overtime. If Hope faced a siege, its people would not worry about starving. Direct stores of food and the raw materials to keep food replicators working ensured that. Starvation, long the chief threat of a siege, had been negated by nanotechnology. Ammunition was far more likely to run short.

Major Esterling was waiting for the two officers. He had put aside dress uniforms. Now he wore camouflage battledress, like his men. Work was still going on in the town, with most of the civilian population helping.

"If trouble does come, we'll be as ready for it as humanly possible," Esterling said after an exchange of casual salutes.

"I'm sure you will," Captain Orlis said. "And if it is going to come, it might well be within the next two days, maybe even as early as tonight."

"You have news?"

"Colonel Flowers has delivered his ultimatum to West," Orlis said. "And our reinforcements are still two days out."

Esterling nodded thoughtfully. "Let's go inside, out of the sun. We can be comfortable while we worry." He worked up a modest smile, but Lon could see that the major *was* worried—seriously worried.

The building they entered housed Hope's only pub. There were no customers in it. The woman behind the bar—she appeared to be in her early thirties but could easily have been much older—seemed glad to have company. Esterling ordered beer for himself and his guests.

"If West strikes," Esterling said after their beers arrived, "they'll strike here."

"That's not the way our intelligence sees it," Orlis said. "Our other battalions are far more likely targets. They're closer to West's army, accessible. If West tried to strike here, we'd have plenty of warning, time to do serious damage to their transports before they could put men on the ground."

Esterling shook his head. "I hate to disagree, Captain, but I must. Certainly, the purely logical move would be for West to strike your other battalions, but this has never been an exercise in pure logic. Hope is a thorn in the side of Syracuse. As long as we're here they will insist on feeling violated. If they see trouble coming, such as your reinforcements, they will want—above everything else— to remove the thorn while they have a chance. No, if they attack anywhere, it will be here, with everything they can bring to bear."

Lon sipped his beer, watching the other two. For the first time Lon began to feel some doubt about the careful analysis provided by regiment and CIC, that the odds were overwhelming that West would strike at the nearer target, the battalions of 7th Regiment in the mountains between the colonies. *The major lives here. He might have a better handle on what West will do than we do. Maybe our preparations weren't a futile exercise.*

"West doesn't have a town or a military base within seven hundred miles," Orlis said. "The only ground route goes through a bottleneck along the seacoast, and it would take a convoy twelve hours to get here that way. And if we see unusual air activity, we can have interceptors in before they can get here."

"I hope you're right, Captain, but I'll wager two bottles of my best wine against your canteen of water that right at this minute West has troops within three hundred miles, out of sight, ready to strike. From that distance they could have shuttles up and down before your fighters could arrive.''

Matt Orlis did hesitate—for about five seconds—before he took the bet.

He lost.

CIC did come up with a logical explanation—in hindsight. The nearest concentration of Wester soldiers was actually only 250 miles from Hope. Most had been there since before 7th Regiment reached Aldrin, and they had been reinforced and resupplied by sea. CIC admitted to having seen several small ships within a hundred miles of the rendezvous, but had written them off as fishing trawlers or pleasure craft. Both colonies had taken to the sea, over generations. With a world that was more than 80 percent water, that was natural.

West's troops moved after sunset, using ground effect trucks concealed from the spy-eyes by extensive thermal shielding. The convoy spread out over a front that was several dozen miles across at one point, gradually narrowing as it approached Hope.

The trucks unloaded their troops two miles from the outermost electronic snoops. With four hours until first light, the Westers had plenty of time to move in on foot. Seven hundred miles to the north, several civilian air shuttles suddenly changed course, turning south. They were on their new headings for several minutes before fleet CIC sounded an alarm. The squadron of Shrike fighters was put on alert but was not immediately dispatched. It was possible, if not likely, that there was no sinister intent behind the sudden course changes. The shuttles were, after all, civilian. Seven minutes passed between the time of the course change and the time when the order was given for a pair of Shrikes to investigate each of the shuttles. Those seven minutes made the difference.

West launched two squadrons of air defense fighters as soon as the mercenary craft started in. Coming from a series of unsuspected small landing strips no more than five hundred miles from Hope, West's fighters forced the Shrikes to divert. Military fighters were more important than civilian shuttles.

Five civilian shuttles landed and unloaded three hundred soldiers within four miles of Hope. A hundred miles north, the two groups of fighter aircraft moved toward engagement. West launched military shuttles then, from farther away, burning on the most efficient trajectory to get through the danger zone before the Dirigentan fleet could launch more Shrikes.

Far to the northeast, West's army initiated a series of small firefights against the other battalions of 7th Regiment. More fighters rose from air bases within Aldrin West, heading into the mountains. Fleet CIC later determined that West had put every fighter it possessed into the air, striving for maximum effect . . . and for maximum confusion among their enemies.

In the latter, at least, they succeeded.

An alert whistle sounded in every battle helmet in 2nd Battalion before the first rockets were fired between aircraft. Lon had been asleep. His last watch had ended little more than an hour earlier. He had dropped off to sleep almost at once, near exhaustion, but the shrill call of the whistle coming from the speakers in the helmet next to his head was enough to shock him awake instantly. The few seconds of mental confusion that came with the rude awakening ended with something approaching total alertness. He pulled the helmet on before he reached for his boots.

Reports on what was happening, and orders for the response, started coming through. The clerk in battalion headquarters kept his voice calm, showing no agitation or emotion. Captain Orlis checked in with Lon as soon as there was a break in the action reports. Lon had his boots on by then and was getting up. He had the tent to himself. Carl Hoper had been out, on duty.

Lon passed orders to his platoon sergeants. The men of Alpha Company who had been asleep were already awake and moving to their posts. By the time Lon got to his station on the perimeter, every firing position was manned.

"It hits the fan now, right, Lieutenant?" Tebba Girana asked, sounding relieved that the waiting had ended.

"That's what it looks like," Lon said. "West pulled a good move. They've got at least two full battalions almost within spitting distance, and we didn't know they were coming until it was too late to intercept them." *Esterling knew his enemy better than we did,* he thought.

The fighting in the air started. There were exchanges of missiles, countered by defensive maneuvering and other measures. Fighters on both sides went down, often in shreds. Few aircraft got close enough to each other to use cannons. The additional West shuttles made it south without casualty.

Lon moved along the section of perimeter that his platoons were responsible for, talking with each squad. The enemy was still not close enough for the early-warning detectors to signal their approach. "If they take the straightest line to Hope, they'll either hit Charlie Company or go between us," Lon told his platoon sergeants. "If they're so damned intent on taking the town, they might try to move through without engaging us."

"We gonna sit still and let them do that?" Jorgen asked.

"No, Weil. If they try to go through we hit them from both sides, force them to stop and take notice." Those orders had just come from battalion headquarters. "We stop them, and the companies on the far side move to reinforce us."

The orders had come through quickly enough that Lon guessed that Colonel Black had been prepared for the contingency. Captain Orlis had passed along Major Esterling's fears about what West might do. Lon recalled the bet Orlis had made. *Too bad. I would have liked another taste of Esterling's best wine,* Lon thought. He could not work up a smile to go with it.

Reports came of engagements in the mountains. West's attacks on the rest of 7th Regiment were clearly meant as a diversion. They were not being pressed in force. Four Shrikes that had been started on a vector to support Colonel Flowers' main force were diverted south to help defend Hope.

On the ground, West's soldiers moved toward Hope. They aimed for the center of the gap between Alpha and Charlie. But flanking units—platoon-strength, according to the first estimate—were sent against each of those mercenary companies.

"They want to keep us pinned down while the bulk of their troops move by," Lon told his sergeants after new orders came from Captain Orlis. "We stay put. First and second platoons are going out to try to slow down the penetration."

Electronic snoops sounded their warnings and transmitted video. Lon sampled those, looking at the skirmish line of West soldiers moving toward the company. "Get ready," he told his noncoms. "They're five hundred yards out. Have your beamers ready. Start sniping as soon as you've got clear targets." Each squad had one man armed with an energy weapon. Silent, those weapons could fell an enemy before he knew he was being targeted. The most reliable marksman in each squad drew the long-distance killer.

Lon settled into firing position, with third platoon's second squad. For the moment it would not be necessary to have his men spread out to cover the half of the company perimeter that Carl Hoper's men were vacating to attack the enemy thrust. *As long as we know where the enemy is and they don't try sliding around, we can stay put,* Lon thought. He would keep a close eye on the enemy's movements, ready to order men to new positions if there seemed any possibility that West would try to flank them.

The platoon moving toward the camp stopped three

hundred yards from the perimeter. They had started taking casualties and were ready to start returning fire. "They just want to keep us pinned down," Lon reminded his sergeants. "If they don't know that we've already got half our force out, so much the better. Let's keep them from moving any closer."

Lon started firing his own rifle, an occasional short burst, generally when he had a decent target. *Put up enough fire that they don't suspect we've cut our numbers in half until the others hit their main force. Then we'll see what happens.*

Another five minutes passed before a firefight opened in the gap between Alpha and Charlie. Two platoons from each of those companies caught the point of the West main force, and hammered it from both sides as it moved into the vee of the ambush. Delta Company, whose camp was near the southwestern corner of Hope, was sending two platoons around to flank the attackers.

In the air, the combat drifted closer. West had all of its fighter aircraft up, and most were targeted against Hope. There were not enough Shrikes to match the enemy one for one, but the Shrike pilots were mostly combat veterans. Their opposition was not. Lon saw a couple of explosions in the air but had no way to determine whether the losses were friends or foes.

West's riflemen got additional help. Mortars started a systematic bombardment of the defensive emplacements of Alpha and Charlie companies. Those did little damage, and not only because there seemed to be only two mortars directed against each company. The mortar fire was not efficiently directed, and the mercenaries had had time to prepare. Their trenches were narrow targets, and the lines were staggered enough to prevent a hit from being overly disastrous.

"That's too far out for us to do anything about it from here," Lon reported to Captain Orlis. "It looks as if the nearest mortar is twelve hundred yards out."

"We can't get a Shrike in yet," Orlis replied. "And I don't want to deplete our numbers by sending a squad out to try to get close. Just disperse your men as much as possible. Have your beamers looking for targets out there. That's a long shot even for them, but maybe someone will get lucky.''

Lon spread his men out along more of the perimeter, and moved a few back into the linking trenches toward the center of camp to minimize the number of casualties that one explosion could cause. He worked toward the west himself, trying to get to a vantage point where he could see how the fight in the gap between Alpha and Charlie's positions was going. That fighting was fierce, and had been going at full tilt for more than a quarter hour. He had only been able to monitor Carl Hoper's reports sporadically, catching a shout now, a few tense words then.

"Captain!" Lon blinked at the intensity of Carl's shout. "We need help fast. We're facing two full companies here, and we can't hold much longer."

"Delta's people are almost in place on your left," Orlis said. "Pull back if you have to, toward our positions. Let—''

There was a loud explosion then, undoubtedly only a grenade, but amplified by someone's radio, cutting off whatever Orlis said. Lon blinked against the almost physical pain of the noise over his earphones. He shook his head, trying to get rid of the ringing in his ears. Thirty or forty seconds passed before he was able to hear anything but the aftereffects of the blast.

"Carl, are you there?" It was Orlis, shouting. "Hoper?"

"Captain, this is Sergeant Grawley. I think the lieutenant's dead. The cadet, too. I haven't been able to get anyone to them, but a grenade went off within four or five feet of them."

Lon felt his breath catch in his throat. Ernst Grawley was first platoon's sergeant.

"Grawley, you and McCoy"—Roy McCoy, second platoon sergeant—"start pulling your men back toward our position. Charlie's platoons will try to give you cover before they start pulling back, too. We're going to let West through, give them a chance to run into the next line.''

"Roger, Captain," Grawley said. "I've got Roy on our channel and he's listening in. We'll start back quick as we can. We've got at least twenty wounded between us."

"Nolan, send one squad to help them get their wounded back in," Orlis ordered.

"Right, Captain." Lon signaled to Dav Grott. His squad was closest. Lon felt an urge to go out and help himself, but he restrained the impulse. His place was with the bulk of his men, especially now that it appeared that Carl Hoper was dead. Lon had to put Carl's fate out of mind. He had more urgent work. Grieving for a friend would have to wait until there was time.

The rest of Lon's men increased their rate of fire to cover the squad going out and the platoons coming in. Lon used his helmet's electronics to separate friend from foe in the gap west of his position, directing his fire at the enemy who were closest to first and second platoons. It was nearly dawn. The sky was lightening, but there was a low, light haze of smoke in the air.

One Shrike got free of entanglements in the air and swooped down out of the north, loosing two rockets at the nearest enemy mortar positions, then banking slightly to bring the enemy force penetrating between Alpha and Charlie under Gatling cannon fire—for the second he could without endangering the withdrawing DMC units. The pilot went into a tight bank, turning before he reached Hope to come back for a second pass down the center. By the time he was in position again, the withdrawing platoons from Alpha and Charlie had given him more freedom. He launched rockets and started his cannon firing, coming in low over the heads of the enemy before pulling into a steep climb and accelerating as rapidly as the Shrike could to get away from two antiaircraft missiles. Lon's attention was drawn to that race. For several seconds it appeared as if both missiles would hit the Shrike before it could climb above their operational limit.

The pilot deked from side to side, unloading chaff to confuse the missiles, and undoubtedly using electronic jamming as well.

One enemy missile suddenly veered left and dove for the ground, exploding a thousand feet from anyone. The Shrike's pilot banked hard right, east, gradually increasing his lead over the remaining missile. The fighter climbed out of sight, and the missile was marked only by the bright spot of its rocket. Lon watched for a few more seconds, but there was no explosion.

The Shrike did not return. Lon assumed it had burned for orbit and rendezvous with its carrier. It would take at least an hour to rearm and return. Lon scanned the northern horizon, looking for any trace of other aircraft. Friend or foe. He saw nothing, but could only spare that search a few seconds. He had men at hazard. They needed his attention. It was only then that Lon realized that one of the mortars had been silenced.

The fight to Lon's west picked up in intensity again, but only for two minutes as Grott's squad joined in and all of the mercenaries worked to disengage and return to the trenches. Medics were waiting for the wounded. Captain Orlis came over to see the damage for himself. It was bad. The two platoons had lost nine men killed, and a fourth of the survivors were wounded.

"Keep as much fire on the enemy as possible while they're going through," Orlis told Lon. "I'll handle first and second platoons myself until we've got time to get better organized."

Delta's two platoons had been redirected. Instead of going around Charlie Company, they moved between the two northern camps and Hope. They would strike as soon as the enemy came within reach, then pull back to avoid being caught in a crossfire between West's force and the defenders inside Hope. The sun was up now, more than half its diameter above the horizon, banishing the last of the morning twilight. Delta's men would not have the benefit of night's cover. They would have to pull out before the enemy got too close.

It was then that the next wave of West's soldiers arrived, landing south and east of Hope. Their passage had been unhampered by DMC Shrikes. All of the mercenary fighters had been forced to return to their ship to rearm.

23

Even without Shrikes, the mercenaries were not *completely* without air support. The three shuttles that had been kept on the ground near 2nd Battalion got into the air before the second wave of Wester ground forces landed. With two Gatling gun cannon mounts and a rack of HE missiles, the shuttles were far from being just cattle carriers. Shuttles were less maneuverable than Shrikes, though, and more vulnerable to ground fire. The three DMC craft dared not expose themselves for long to the enemy. They made quick strikes, expending as much of their munitions as they could, then burned for orbit. But in the few seconds they were on hand, the DMC shuttles made their presence felt. One of the incoming enemy shuttles exploded as it touched down, another as it was unloading its passengers.

"It helps," Captain Orlis told Lon. "Battalion figures that West must have a thousand men on the ground here, maybe more. And it looks as if there's another wave of them coming."

"Even if there are a thousand here now, that still gives us the edge in numbers, adding the garrison of Hope in," Lon said. "Will our Shrikes get back before this next wave arrives?"

"It's going to be close," Orlis said. "And West is attacking the rest of the regiment again, forcing CIC to divert some of the fighters up that way."

There was time for no more. Lon and the captain were still trying to get Alpha Company reorganized. Medics were treating the wounded. Several men had been moved into one of the squad tents in the center of the camp and put into portable trauma tubes. Dav Grott had one man slightly wounded in his squad. The wound was treated and the man back with his mates.

In both Alpha and Charlie Companies' camps, the mercenaries received only passing attention from the troops moving between them. In a variant of fire-and-maneuver tactics, part of the West force stopped to take the mercenaries under fire while the rest continued to press toward Hope.

Unless they've got a lot more men coming in soon, that's suicidal, Lon thought, astounded at the tactic. *They'll be in the middle, with a superior foe in position to encircle them.*

After a hiatus of twenty minutes, mortar rounds started hitting the camp again. The frequency was less than before, and the aim unimproved, as if West was merely scattering mortar bombs over the entire area to make the defenders keep their heads down.

"I think they moved the mortars," Lon told Weil Jorgen.

"Off behind their troops in the middle now," Jorgen said, nodding. "Looks like they didn't leave more'n about a squad of rifles to protect the tubes."

"You think you could get to them and back with a couple of squads?" Lon asked.

"At night, sure, Lieutenant," Jorgen said. "Now, in the daylight? It wouldn't be fast, and it might not work at all. They'll probably move the guns faster than we could get close."

Lon hesitated. It would be difficult to sell the idea to Captain Orlis in any case. "I suppose you're right. Oh, well, it was a thought." He shrugged.

Jorgen laughed, a short bark devoid of humor. "I know, Lieutenant. I've been having the same thought myself, every time one of those damn bombs goes off anywhere close."

"Keep your beamers looking over that way once in a

while. Maybe we can knock off one or two of the gunners.''

"We've already had one or two of them," Weil said quietly. Then he was off again, moving toward his fourth squad.

Another half dozen Wester shuttles landed, this time east of Hope, between Alpha and Bravo Companies' camps. The landers came in fast and low, and their passengers disembarked as if the fires of hell were no more than a step behind them. In a way, they were. The returning Shrikes were coming in hot. They had accelerated into Aldrin's gravity well, pushing men and machines to the limit, braking at the last possible second. Sonic booms and the roar of engines suddenly switched to maximum reverse thrust muted the sounds of combat on the ground. The Shrikes launched their first missiles at the grounded shuttles and the troops leaving them at long range. The cannons could not be fired until the fighters' airspeed was reduced, or the Shrikes would run into their own rounds.

On the ground, the shuttles were easy targets. All six were hit. But their soldiers had already moved out and away. The only casualties would have been among the lander crews—if they, too, had not abandoned their craft immediately.

Eight Shrikes came in, two waves of four fighters, twenty seconds apart. They separated while they were above ten thousand feet, giving each other room to maneuver when surface-to-air missiles started coming at them.

Lon pulled his head down and watched. For a moment the Shrikes had slowed the pace of combat for Alpha Company. West's soldiers were more concerned about the threat from the air. Even the mortars stopped firing at the camps, though they were no threat at all to aircraft.

Lon used the lull to check with his squad leaders and to get the latest updates from Captain Orlis and battalion, including the most recent news of the other battalions, now under more serious attack. Although it was not spec-

ified, Lon assumed that 2nd Battalion would get no reinforcements on the ground until 12th Regiment landed.
West now had at least fifteen hundred men around Hope,
possibly two thousand. The combined defenders—mercenaries, Eastman garrison, and Hope's civilian militia—
were at least matched in numbers and might already be
outnumbered.

Do we start moving into Hope? Lon wondered. Under
the circumstances, he thought, consolidating within one
defensible perimeter might be the best move, despite the
mercenary doctrine of remaining mobile as much as possible. *We're not very mobile hunkered down in four
camps, and there isn't enough cover on this savanna to
let us operate the way we do best. At least inside the town
we'd have all of our forces together until 12th gets in and
helps out.* But unless the move was made before West's
soldiers could fully establish a siege of Hope, it might be
difficult—and costly.

If we stay out, Lon thought, still trying to reason his
way through the situation—the way Colonel Black and
his staff must also have been doing, *we force West to split
their forces several ways as well. They can't ignore us.
We'd be like four massive knives at their backs.*

An explosion in the air brought Lon's mind back from
his tactical exercise. *Every plane we lose is one less we
have to keep us out of trouble later,* Lon thought. *How
many so far?* It was a question he could not begin to
answer. There had been no way for him to keep track of
what was going on in the sky.

"Nolan!"

"Yes, sir," Lon said, responding instantly to Captain
Orlis's call.

"Start shifting your platoons around to the south and
southwest in the trenches. I'm going to leave first and
second platoons to cover the rest of our perimeter. We've
got to start putting pressure on the troops who made it
through. As soon as CIC gets the situation sorted out,
we're going to counterattack. Things are so damned confused now, nobody knows who's where. West has their

forces split up even more than we do. We've got to find out what's going on before we can do anything effective.''

"I'll start sliding my men around, Captain. I take it we're going out after them, not just sniping from long distance?"

"That's the plan, once we know where we can hurt them. Just get moved and stand by. I'm going to be busy for a while, getting the other platoons organized and setting up a little better cover for our medtechs."

West had finished its penetration between Alpha and Charlie. The northern part of the battlefield had grown almost quiet. Even the mortar teams had moved through the gap, perhaps to target Hope. Lon relayed the orders to his noncoms, then stayed with Grott's squad until squads from the other two platoons could move into place—in case West had left a few troops behind to exploit any holes in Alpha's defenses.

The trench system proved its value. Lon's men were able to move without giving away the fact of the move, or exposing themselves to the few enemy snipers who were still operating against them—from maximum range. As soon as the first squads from second platoon came around from the east, Lon passed the codes for the mines and snoops to the squad leaders, then started moving to his own new position with his last squad.

"Make sure everyone is carrying a full load of ammo and water," Lon told his squad leaders while he moved. "When we go out, I don't want anyone running short. No telling how long we'll have to operate on our own." It was almost an afterthought when he added, "Tell them to grab a meal as they can, too."

Once they were in position near the southwestern corner of the camp, Dav Grott handed Lon a meal pack. Lon nodded, but set the pack aside. Before he could eat, he had to have a good look at what lay in front of the platoons' new positions. He switched his faceplate to maximum magnification and did a slow, careful scan of the entire front. If there was confusion in CIC and at battalion,

Lon wanted to get as much information firsthand as possible.

Virtually all of the grain had been harvested, leaving wide tracts of ground with no cover at all. Some of the savanna grasses had burned during the fighting. There were areas with a haze obscuring vision—heat and smoke, slow to disperse.

Hope's outer perimeter was slightly more than two miles from Lon's position. He could see grenade and mortar explosions, occasionally the flash of a rifle muzzle. The sounds of battle were muted by the distance and the heavy tropical air—background to death and pain. Only rarely did a single event provide enough noise to override the background.

It appeared that the ring around Hope was not complete. West had—so far—not chosen that route but had grouped its forces at a number of positions that gave them fire zones covering the entire northern flank of the town. *Probably the same all the way around,* Lon thought. *And they might still be hitting Bravo Company over on the southeast.* That was where the latest West force had landed. Lon thought they probably had not had time yet to get everyone through to throw against Hope.

"I hope Major Esterling and his men are coping," Lon said under his breath. *They've got civilians to contend with as well, and hard telling how they're reacting to being under fire again.*

There was little especially heartening about Lon's scan of the fighting. It would be brutal out there in daylight, with no darkness to give even a semblance of safety, and virtually no cover. In the dark, the mercenaries could snake their way along the ground, silent, and presenting little in the way of thermal signature to give them away to infrared night-vision systems. In the daylight . . . *This is one time I wish we had heavy weapons with us,* Lon thought. *Artillery, even a half dozen tanks pounding the enemy into the ground. Or a lot more Shrikes.*

Lon shook his head and looked into the sky. The air fight was moving north again. West's fighters had to go back to their bases to rearm. The DMC's Shrikes that were still on station were pursuing. CIC had not sent all its Shrikes at once this time, but was staggering the missions to keep some air cover around most of the time.

A brilliant explosion on the ground brought Lon's attention back down. The blast was inside Hope. *Must have been a secondary explosion,* Lon thought. *Ammunition or explosives going up.* For perhaps three minutes, flames rose sharply, but the blaze died down quickly, leaving only thick smoke to mark the location. Lon went back to scanning the enemy positions, trying to decide what sort of tactics might work best in the situation—as if the decision might fall to him.

"Nolan?" This time Orlis's voice was softer, less stressed than before. He sounded almost tired.

"Yes, Captain?"

"We're about ready. Maybe ten minutes. I'm going to leave first platoon inside the firebase to guard the medics and wounded. First because they got chewed up before." That choice was unremarkable. First platoon was the most shorthanded. "The colonel's headquarters staff will remain in the firebase as well. Charlie is going to leave one platoon in their digs. The rest of us will act in concert, heading toward Hope. We are not, repeat *not*, planning on going *into* the town. We stay outside and work to keep West in a crossfire. I'll be with second platoon. This is still pretty much by ear. How West reacts determines our next moves. For the time being, Bravo and Delta will remain in their firebases and do what they can from there."

"Ten minutes. We'll be ready, Captain," Lon said.

"Travel light. Field packs stay behind," Orlis said. "We plan to come back here." He did not have to add, *if we can.*

"Are we going forward in a straight skirmish line, Captain?"

"Not all the way. Unless West makes significant changes in their deployment before we jump off, we'll head toward that concentration about ten degrees to your left. We start out moving as quickly as we can, until West reacts and we get too close to stay on our feet. Then it'll be down on stomachs, working closer as we can. I don't expect us to get closer than three hundred yards, maybe two-fifty. That's subject to change.''

"Yes, sir.''

Lon passed along the orders and stripped off his own field pack. That lightened the load he had to carry by twenty-five pounds. *I can carry a couple of extra magazines for my rifle,* Lon decided, although he had already added several above the "standard load."

"Pick up some extra magazines," he told the squad leaders. "But let's not get so loaded down we can't move."

Then it was time to wait. Again.

24

When the advance started, the skirmish line was not a straight rank, as if the men were drawn up on parade. The lines were staggered, the distances between individuals irregular. Each platoon put three squads in front, forming the primary skirmish line, and one squad forty yards back. Lon took his position with the trailing squads, the proper place for a platoon leader in this type of maneuver. He looked to right and left, checking everything, a routine and almost unconscious series of actions. Captain Orlis was with second platoon, on the left. Third platoon was in the center, fourth on the right. Much farther right, Lon could see Charlie Company moving as well.

The men moved forward in a semicrouch, rifles at the ready, safeties off, fingers over trigger guards. Eyes squinted, trying to see the enemy, as if squinting would bring them into clearer focus at such a distance.

Although he was sweating freely, Lon no longer thought about the hundred-plus-degree temperature, or the sun that seemed to be baking his head in his helmet. He was too tightly focused on what he and his men had to do. His eyes scanned the distant enemy and, more infrequently, the ground directly in front of him. He was not overly concerned about the chance that the enemy had planted land mines or booby traps. They had been under constant observation. There was the crackle of dry grain stalks underfoot, a faint aroma of new mown hay, a smell that tried to trigger memories of childhood on Earth for Lon. He fought it by trying to calculate the distances ahead and behind. *We've come fifty yards. Hope is two miles off. The enemy only four hundred yards less than that.*

Until the skirmish line had covered more than half the distance, the danger from enemy rifles would be minimal. West had shown no use of beamers. A marksman might, with considerable luck, bring down a moving target at a mile or more, but most ammunition expended at that range would be wasted. The danger from rifles would not be appreciable until they were within six hundred yards, even in such completely open terrain as this.

There was no running, just a methodical, slow walk. Time seemed suspended. The sounds of fighting ahead were constant, the volume increasing too gradually to notice. Lon could not tell when the enemy spotted their advance. They did not rush into any panicked redeployment or start taking wild shots at the mercenaries. West's troops were also professionals, though few could be veterans of combat aside from the fighting that had taken place since the Dirigenters had come to Aldrin.

They've got to move one way or the other, Lon thought, insisted. *They have to see us, have to do something to avoid getting trapped between us and Hope.*

It would be difficult to arrange positions so there was no risk of friendly fire between the allies. The mercenaries would stay low, and the garrison of Hope had physical barriers for cover. But there was no guarantee that only the enemy would be hit by gunfire.

A mile. Half the distance. The Dirigenters had taken eighteen minutes to cover it. Almost unconsciously, the pace slowed. There were occasional shots coming toward them. Most hit well in front, raising tiny clouds of dust at impact.

"Let's spread the line out more," Captain Orlis said. "We could come under mortar fire any second."

Lon passed along the order, and used his arms to indicate when he thought the greater separation between men was sufficient to minimize the casualties a mortar bomb might cause. His rangefinder showed the skirmish line fifteen hundred yards from the enemy when he heard the whine of a mortar round.

"Incoming! Take cover!" Almost as one, the men of Alpha Company dropped to the ground, landing in firing position, even though they were still well out of effective rifle range. The first mortar round hit fifty yards behind the trailing squad. Shrapnel and debris flew up and arced over, falling harmlessly.

"Up and move!" Captain Orlis ordered.

The three platoons traveled another thirty yards before the next mortar round arrived. Again Alpha went to cover. This time the round fell short, but within thirty yards.

After the two ranging rounds, the Wester mortarmen found their rhythm, sending out their bombs quickly. The Dirigenters ran forward to close the range, forcing the enemy to adjust for each round, slowing the cadence, diving to the ground only when an incoming bomb was near, getting up as soon as the debris settled. There were only two mortars targeted against the mercenaries, and they could not put up enough volume of fire to saturate a front spread across three hundred yards. Several Dirigenters were wounded, but in the first minutes of the mortar assault no one was hit so badly that he could not continue moving forward.

A thousand yards from the enemy, Captain Orlis finally told his company to get down and crawl forward. The men with the energy rifles were put to work sniping, pausing in their advance to take several shots at the enemy before doing a hurried crab crawl to regain their places in the skirmish line. The best marksmen with slug throwers took occasional shots now, but with less hope of hitting anything but dirt. They fired single shots, not bursts, just enough to perhaps interfere with the enemy's aim . . . and peace of mind.

"Enemy fighters coming in from the north," Dav Grott screamed into his radio.

"Get the SAMs out!" Lon ordered. Two men in each platoon carried surface-to-air missile launchers. Those men turned and brought the antiaircraft weapons to their shoulders.

"Careful with those," Captain Orlis said, breaking into the channel. "There are Shrikes coming from the west to intercept. Make sure of your targets."

Lon turned, looking for the aircraft. There was little chance of a mistake immediately. West's two fighters were almost close enough to begin their rocket and strafing runs. The Shrikes were considerably farther out and much higher.

"Quickly," Lon said, "before our fly-guys get close."

Six missiles streaked into the sky, three aimed at each enemy fighter—which launched rockets of their own before taking evasive action. Lon almost cheered when one fighter exploded. The other pilot evaded the missiles aimed at him, but his gyrations ended with him climbing directly toward the Shrikes.

The three high-explosive rockets launched by the Wester fighters exploded well short of the Dirigenters. The remaining enemy aircraft ran into a missile from one of the Shrikes and exploded in a blinding orange and gray fireball.

It was while Lon was distracted by the fight in the air that the enemy infantry started to move from their precarious position between two opposing forces. Most headed east, across the front. Only the westernmost detachment moved in the other direction.

"Pivot around second platoon," Orlis told Lon. "We keep going straight for them."

Lon gave the orders, and the skirmishers changed directions. With the enemy mortars silent again, the mercenaries were on their feet, moving at a walking pace. The enemy was trotting.

"Looks like they've decided to merge with their troops over on that side," Orlis said. "Bravo's too heavily engaged to head them off, but the troops inside Hope are going to try a sortie to slow them down. We've got to let the ones on the other end get away for now. We don't have anyone close enough to get to them."

For the moment the danger had lifted, but not far enough for the flow of adrenaline to stop. The enemy might turn and fight at any minute. There might be more enemy fighters coming in. Lon did not let his focus slip.

"Captain, we need to take a minute to patch up the few wounded we've got," Lon said. "No one's hurt bad enough to need medics, but we've got bleeding wounds that need med patches."

"Right, Nolan. Good thinking. We're not in a race here," Orlis said. "I've got two men who need patching as well."

The pause was not much longer than a minute. Alpha started to move again, adjusting its vector to keep the skirmish line moving toward the withdrawing enemy troops. The Westers were nearly opposite the northeastern corner of Hope, four hundred yards from the town's outer defensives—close enough to take casualties from riflemen on the barricades. The Westers increased their pace rather than take cover, hurrying to get out of range, pulling farther away from Alpha in the process.

"You'd think they were late for a hot date," Sergeant Girana suggested on his link to Lon.

"Maybe they are, Tebba, but keep your eyes peeled. They could turn to face us anytime at all."

"They've got to be getting awfully hot moving like that, Lieutenant," Tebba said. "It's got to weaken them eventually. They'll have to stop, or get strung out all over the place."

"Maybe not all that soon, Tebba. Even if they're not used to the climate, they've got a lot of reasons to keep moving until they drop. Us and the people in Hope. They've got to have a little fear pushing them along, no matter what. And they don't have a lot farther to go to get to friends."

"At least we're not running after them. Time enough for fighting when we get there, and best after dark at that."

Lon smiled. Darkness, still the friend of the infantryman, in spite of centuries of night-vision systems. There was more than fancy to the feeling of being cloaked that the night gave. Even the best night-vision systems did not give sight quite equal to daylight.

After another five minutes Alpha was still losing ground to the fleeing Wester force. "Hold the advance," Captain Orlis ordered, and Lon repeated the order for his noncoms. "Battalion says to call off the chase," Orlis added once all of his men were on the ground.

"Back to camp?" Lon asked.

"No," Orlis said. "Have your men dig in, a full defensive perimeter. We let the Wester forces rendezvous, then plan our next measures. My guess is that we're not likely to do much before sundown, but that's all it is, a guess. Get 'em dug in and a chance to rest. I'll have a squad from first platoon bring out food."

We might as well have stayed where we were, Lon thought at about midafternoon. He was lying in a slit trench, face down, resting his head on his arms. *Been more comfortable and saved energy.* He had eaten a meal and drunk enough water to keep his body hydrated. But the sun beat down relentlessly, and there was nothing to keep it off, nothing to do but sweat. And think.

The fight on the ground had ended, except for occasional sniping on both sides—too far away to affect Alpha Company. Of the mercenary units on the ground, only Bravo was still directly engaged with the enemy, and that fighting was minimal. Hope was still under attack on the south, but that was also little more than sniping. Even the fight in the air had ended. There hadn't been a fighter in the air near Hope in three hours. Nor had West attempted to bring any additional troops in. The latest estimate, agreed on by Colonel Black's staff and fleet CIC, was that West had perhaps two thousand men on the ground around Hope, giving them a three-to-two advantage over the combined forces of 2nd Battalion, Hope's army garrison, and the civilian militia.

Time to think. Too much time. No one from third or fourth platoons had been killed in this fighting, but Lon remembered that Carl Hoper and Esau O'Fallon were both dead. Carl had become a close friend over the past three years. And O'Fallon . . . he had shown promise, even if he tended to be too combative in his arguments. *Kept me on my toes,* Lon thought, smiling over some of their more intense discussions. Death was a routine occupational hazard for a mercenary who needed warfare to earn his living. The Corps never tried to pretend otherwise. "Death is our business, both the giving and receiving," read a carved scroll just inside the entrance to the cemetery at the Corps' main base. The dead, those who could be retrieved, and the wounded were always the first to return home from a contract, carried in style at the head of the returning parade, past a formation of the regiments.

Lon's thoughts moved to Sara, although he could not take his usual joy in them. There was a certain pain to memories of Sara, and his love—longing—for her. Death was too much on his mind, and how desperately he wanted to get home to Dirigent, to Sara. Her image was blurred in his mind, as if behind a curtain of tears. Lon felt a catch in his chest, a subliminal pull toward tears of his own. He lifted his head enough to open the visor of his helmet and rub at his eyes. He would not cry, perhaps could not. Not now.

Distractions were few in the afternoon heat. From time to time Lon checked with his platoon sergeants and squad leaders, or listened for an update from Captain Orlis or battalion. There was little news, though, and no decision on what the mercenaries would do next, or when. Only in the mountains, a thousand miles to the northeast, was any significant fighting taking place. Colonel Flowers was pressing the fight against the battalions of West's army that remained there, trying to force a decision—or disengagement sufficient to permit him to reinforce 2nd Battalion. The sun slid toward the western horizon with agonizing slowness through the hottest hours of the day. It beat at Lon's mind, a numbing impulse that did not numb the right things. It left his memory operating at full speed.

Lon tried to concentrate on a series of stretching exercises, but his trench did not give him room to reach full extension. The effort simply reinforced the feeling of confinement. He lifted up to scan the horizon, another way to occupy a minute or so occasionally.

It was, by Lon's helmet timeline, 1652 hours when Captain Orlis called again. "I guess we're waiting for dark," Orlis said, his voice heavy, tired. "That might be what the enemy is waiting for as well. If they're going to get anything done, it has to happen tonight. Tomorrow night we'll have 12th Regiment coming in, and that should be that. At least around Hope."

"Maybe we should do something before they get started, Captain," Lon said. "Disrupt their plans rather than wait to react to whatever they cook up." He closed his eyes at the reference to cooking, a reminder of how hot he felt.

"I know, but after dark our Shrikes can operate a lot more safely than in the light. They'll be damned near invisible to the enemy. CIC says we've lost five so far. They don't want to risk all of them. Colonel Flowers will want them to cover any movement of troops from the mountains down here, if they get enough clearance to bring in shuttles."

"It gets dark about an hour earlier there than here, doesn't it, Captain?" Lon asked.

"About that. By the time the sun sets here, it should be full dark in the mountains."

25

Aldrin's sun became a darker orange as it settled toward the horizon. There were none of the angry reds that Lon recalled of sunsets on Earth. Aldrin was nearly free of man-made pollution. With nothing more productive to occupy his time, Lon watched this sunset with an intensity he had rarely displayed for any natural phenomenon. He remembered staring at his last sunset, and last sunrise, on Earth with this sort of intensity, knowing they would be his last there and not wanting to forget the slightest detail.

Now he had seen to his men's needs, and his own. Everyone had eaten. Canteens had been refilled. The squad from first platoon had brought both water and food, making a couple of round-trips. The main order had been to get as much rest as possible; the night might be long and busy. No one moved from the slit trenches. Each man remained alone, separated from his nearest squadmates by as much as twenty-five feet. There had been no idle chatter over the squad radio channels either.

Not much chance the Westers will forget we're here, Lon thought, *but no need to remind them where we are in case they're scoping our electronic emissions.* There had been no formal order for electronic silence, but the squad leaders had clamped down on loose talk early on, without any prodding from above.

The hours of waiting had exhausted Lon's memory, something of a blessing. There was a numbing quality to lying inactive under a blazing sun, sweating constantly but gaining little cooling from its almost immediate evaporation. Even the deep worries that might otherwise have

blossomed into fear had been put to sleep, bored coma-
tose. The afternoon had given new vigor to the ancient
military maxim of *Hurry up and wait*.

There seemed little difference between wakefulness and
sleep except when there was talk on the radio. Lon had
drifted in and out of a restless slumber. In other circumstances such a lazy afternoon might have been welcome,
even with the swelter—perhaps with flies buzzing around,
adding a pleasant drone to somnolence. But there were no
flies, nor anything resembling them.

Tropical heat had apparently spread its lassitude over
Hope and its environs. Lon had heard no gunfire in three
hours, on the ground or in the air. Reports from the other
companies of 2nd Battalion supported his conclusion. No
fighting was going on. West's army had dug hurried positions as well and showed every inclination to wait for
the dark and cool of night.

Sunset came at last, the sun touching the horizon and
easing itself below it. A slight breeze, the first of the day,
seemed to start when Aldrin's sun was about a third of
the way below the almost flat western horizon.

"We've got Shrikes coming down to strike the Westers
in the mountains," a voice—one of the battalion headquarters staff—said on a channel that connected all of the
officers in 2nd Battalion. "Shuttles will be waiting to
come in on ten minutes' notice if it's safe."

I hope it works, Lon thought. It would be nice to have
another battalion on hand for the night's action against
the troops West had brought south. Or more. But Lon did
not expect miracles. The rest of 7th Regiment was engaged. They would be lucky to spring one battalion safely.
*Enough to hold us until 12th Regiment comes in tomor-
row,* Lon decided.

"Weil, Tebba," Lon said, switching to his platoon sergeants' channel. "Get with your squad leaders. We'd best
do some limbering up. If things go right, we might be
moving before long. I don't want anyone staggering along
like they're a hundred years old and drunk. And make

sure everyone's getting plenty of fluids. We don't want a lot of leg cramps.''

Both sergeants acknowledged the orders. Lon lifted his faceplate to rub at his cheeks and eyes, the first step toward forcing full alertness. He took his helmet off long enough to scratch at his scalp and let a breath of air circulate around his head. Once his helmet was back in place—he dared not leave it off long—he started a more thorough set of limbering-up exercises, stretching arms and legs as well as he could in the shelter of his shallow hole. When he had finished the routine, ten minutes of methodical work, he took several small sips of water, rolling the liquid around in his mouth each time before swallowing, taking maximum benefit from minimal moisture.

The approach of twilight seemed to drop the temperature more than the six degrees that Lon's helmet sensor indicated. The setting of the sun helped, psychologically as well as physically.

An hour, maybe more, Lon thought, considering how long it might be before orders would come to start moving. With all the heat, he had taken less time than usual at the junior officer exercise of war-gaming, trying to guess what his superiors might order and why. But he had done some. There did not seem to be many alternatives. The primary variable was whether 2nd Battalion had to operate alone or had reinforcements from one of the other battalions. The latter would make things easier. Land the reinforcements beyond the Westers and drive them against Hope. Move 2nd Battalion the same way, try to force the enemy between two forces, make them fight in unfavorable circumstances or surrender. Hammer-and-anvil tactics.

If West started something sooner, it would throw his calculations out of whack. He waited for word on the progress of the fight in the mountains to the northeast. But for quite some time there was nothing, not even routine updates.

The tropical dusk seemed truncated to Lon. The sky went from twilight to dark too quickly. The first stars were visible in the east within minutes of sunset, and the celestial carpet unrolled rapidly.

"Any minute now," Lon mumbled to himself. It was dark enough that Shrikes would be visible only as they occulted stars, and that would not give a man with a SAM launcher time to get a preliminary target fix. And the Wester commander might start moving his men against Hope just as quickly, now that night had been draped across the area.

"Captain?" Lon whispered after clicking his radio to the channel that connected him to Orlis. "Anything happening yet?"

"I was just about to call you," Orlis replied, also speaking in a whisper. "We're going to start moving, but slowly. We stay low and close the distance between us and the Westers. I mean *low*, on stomachs. The idea is not to let the enemy know that we're moving. When something starts, that might give us a little extra advantage. The compass heading is one hundred degrees. On my mark. We move in about three minutes."

"Right, Captain," Lon replied. While Lon passed the orders to his noncoms, he thought about the course. The right end of the line would get closer to the outskirts of Hope on the move, but never near enough to come within easy rifle range of the garrison there. *I wonder if the others are going to be moving closer to the enemy as well.* Lon shrugged. If it had been important, Captain Orlis would have told him.

Moving stealthily was basic drill for Dirigenters— taught a mercenary's first week in recruit training, and every unit practiced the techniques regularly. The boast that a veteran Dirigenter could sneak within twenty feet of an enemy, across open ground, without being spotted was not far from the truth. "Ghost-in-the-night stuff," another cadet had suggested to Lon when they went through training. It had seemed spooky to Lon, even when the cadre had demonstrated just how good they were— even when their trainees *knew* they were coming.

It was something like a ballet played out in ultraslow

motion, the crablike scuttling forward, with frequent pauses, no one ever getting his stomach more than an inch or two off the ground, propelling himself forward with arms and legs, rifle balanced on forearms. Breathing was controlled, slow and kept in rhythm with motion. Men glanced to either side to make certain they remained at proper distances from their neighbors.

In some ways it was more taxing than running. Muscles cramped. Knees and elbows ached from scrapes and the constant pressure on them. Frequent stops helped, often after no more than twenty or thirty yards of crawling. But it was all done in almost perfect silence. Slow movement helped squelch the crackle of dry grain stubble .the men crawled over. Radio traffic was kept to an absolute minimum; any talking that was required was conducted sub-vocally. The insulation of DMC battle helmets kept any hint of sound from escaping.

News filtered in slowly from regiment. The fight in the mountains was continuing. Lon had been crawling for thirty minutes before word arrived that the other battalions had secured an area large enough—and far enough from the enemy—for shuttles to come in. Third Battalion was boarding now, and would be arriving within a half hour.

"We're all going to open up on the enemy just before the shuttles arrive," Captain Orlis explained to Lon and the platoon sergeants. "Keep the enemy distracted, make sure they don't have a chance to interfere with the landings. Those are going to be spaced around Hope to let 3rd Battalion close with the enemy as quickly as possible. We push the Westers against the town and press until they have to surrender to avoid destruction. Our role will be to cut off escape on this end of the pocket."

We could end up with a lot of panicky enemy soldiers charging straight through us to get away from a worse situation, Lon thought. The tactic was not unexpected, but if the main enemy force east of Hope tried to escape northward, through Alpha, the Westers might have immediate tactical odds of four to one in their favor. It would be a question of just how discipline and desperation balanced in the stampede. And, so far, the Westers had shown themselves to be very highly disciplined troops.

One flight of Shrikes was to the north, making certain that Wester interceptors could not contest 3rd Battalion's landings. A second flight of Shrikes would be coming in to cover the landings directly, to add their fury to the assault against the Wester troops. Major Esterling had been notified of the schedule so his garrison could take part in the diversionary strike. Hope's soldiers would be at extreme range from the enemy concentrations, but they could add to the sound and fury, and compound the enemy's confusion . . . and fear.

Lon and his men moved forward one slow yard at a time. The more ground they covered before the attack, the less they would have to cover under fire. The ache in elbows and knees, the protest of cramping muscles, all started to fade, partly a response of a body's natural and nano-boosted defenses, but more from mental accommodation. They were almost "normal" sensations now, and the men focused on what was coming. The only remaining question was whether the Westers would remain in place for the next twenty-odd minutes, or start to execute whatever plans their commander had cooked up for the night before the Shrikes and 3rd Battalion arrived.

They have to have heard about the shuttles taking off by now, Lon decided. *They'll either start moving or dig in deeper and try to hold out.* After only a few seconds of thought he decided that the most likely course would be for West to attack Hope now, from all sides, hoping to break through the defenses before more mercenaries arrived. If the Westers were successful at that, it would limit the response the Dirigenters could make. They would have to take care to minimize civilian casualties in Hope, try to get in before the enemy could do too much damage or establish themselves in the defensive positions Esterling's garrison had created. *We don't want to have to destroy Hope to free it,* Lon told himself.

•   •   •

When the Westers east and south of Lon started to move, ten minutes remained before the scheduled start of the diversionary attack on them. The timetable had to be thrown out. Lon was not surprised when the order came.

"Hit them before they get too far from their positions. Start the beamers firing now," Captain Orlis said.

Lon's men were too far from the enemy for slug throwers to be useful, but the men with beamers could find targets, linking their helmets' night-vision systems to the sights of their weapons. The Dirigenters did not wait for the enemy to notice that they had come under fire. Thirty seconds after Captain Orlis passed along the command to start the beamers, he was back on line. "Up and at 'em. We move full out until we get to within four hundred yards, then down and slow." Orlis gave Lon time to relay those orders, then gave the final "Go!"

As Lon scrambled to his feet, he felt a moment of instability. Both knees started to buckle. He had been flat on the ground for so long, lying in a trench through much of the day, then crawling, that his body resisted getting vertical. He used his rifle as a crutch to get up. Looking ahead and around, he saw that more than a few of the men in his platoons were having the same kind of trouble.

"Captain?"

"I know," Orlis replied before Lon could explain why he was calling. "We're going to have to take ten seconds to get the kinks out. Just do it quickly."

It was a nervous ten seconds. Standing exposed, even far enough away that most rifle fire would be only minimally hazardous, made everyone want to move forward as soon as legs would support them. Many men limped as they started forward, a slow walk building only slowly to an awkward jog. Neither Lon nor Orlis tried to slow the charge. All they did was call noncoms to keep the skirmish line dressed as best they could.

Alpha Company was eight hundred yards from the nearest enemy positions when they came under heavy rifle fire. The Westers had given up their attempt to move toward Hope and had returned to the minimal defenses they had dug during the day to meet this attack. At eight hundred yards, rifle fire was only minimally accurate. Even with Westers firing short bursts of automatic fire, they caused few casualties.

The run forward was finally reined in. The men moved to a more normal walking pace, crouched over, rifles up and at the ready. Only the men with beamers had permission to fire. The rest held back, not wasting ammunition at long range. Lon felt the temptation, though. He wondered how much a determined volley of automatic rifle fire from the entire company might intimidate the Westers. *Not enough,* he decided. *I guess we do need to wait until we're close enough to do some real good.*

At six hundred yards, Captain Orlis gave the order for a brief response. Men stopped to take the best aim possible and loosed short bursts at the enemy. Then they moved forward, stopping after another fifty yards to fire again.

If those volleys had any effect at all on the Westers, it was too slight for Lon to notice. As Alpha came within five hundred yards of the enemy, it started to suffer casualties. Medtechs moved up to care for the wounded. Lon monitored the radio channel the medics used. Two men were dead in fourth platoon. There were at least half a dozen wounded in each of his platoons; several of those would need trauma tubes as quickly as they could be transported to them.

But the shuttles carrying 3rd Battalion were landing.

Lon had not noticed the first passes by the Shrikes that had come in to cover the landings. He had been too intent on his men and the hazards directly in front of them. Alpha Company reached the five-hundred-yard mark, and Captain Orlis gave the order for the men to get down. They would continue to advance, but it was back to slithering along on stomachs, one squad in each platoon moving while the other three squads laid down covering fire.

As Lon went into a prone firing position, he finally noticed that his lungs were aching with the effort of breathing. He was almost gasping for air. He had to hold off on shooting until his panting would not interfere with his aim.

The first squads had already moved forward. The second squads in each platoon followed. The trailing squads moved closer, getting themselves open fire zones. This, too, was a maneuver they drilled in regularly, basic unit movement.

Alpha did not get significantly closer to the enemy before the Westers started to move. The Westers on the east side of town started moving toward Hope again, across the front presented by Alpha.

"Dress the line and hold it," Captain Orlis ordered, speaking to the three platoon sergeants as well as to Lon. "We're still here to hold the flank. Bravo will chase this lot in." A second later he added, "Our turn will come."

26

Across open savanna and harvested fields, Lon had a good view of what was happening. The Wester force between Hope and Bravo Company moved toward the town in a shallow wedge, using fire and maneuver tactics. Its mortars were moved after every few rounds, brought closer until the trajectory of their bombs was almost straight up and down and any additional movement would put the near side of Hope's defenses out of their reach. It was a highly disciplined attack, squads and platoons leap-frogging each other with practiced precision. Lon shivered at the idea of a frontal assault, the most deadly type of combat for attacking soldiers. Even the cover of darkness was not enough to make it a decent proposition. *Unless the alternatives are worse,* Lon conceded. He was not sure whether that was the case this time, or if West's determination to take Hope from the Eastmen was simply too strong for logic to be part of the calculation.

Firing from carefully constructed defenses, the garrison and militia of Hope met the attack with equal discipline. Lon wished that they were on the same communications net so he could listen to the talk inside the town. News did come over the battalion's information circuit that the other Wester forces were also attacking Hope, and the Dirigenters were in position to start attacking the Westers from behind and the flanks.

Bravo Company moved forward, rifles and beamers striking the Westers from behind, forcing them to take notice. The attack against Hope did not stop, but part of the attacking force had to turn to try to fend off the mercenaries while their comrades continued to move forward.

"If they get inside the town, it's a whole 'nother kettle of fish," Tebba Girana whispered to Lon over their private circuit.

"They're not inside yet," Lon whispered back. "Here come the Shrikes again."

Two Shrikes made another pass at the Westers, with rockets and cannons, raking the soldiers from north to south, then returning to repeat the maneuver south to north. The Westers launched missiles at the Shrikes. Lon closed his eyes against the glare as one found its target.

"Maybe we should be hitting them, too," Tebba suggested. "Hit 'em from every side at once. They'd have to surrender."

"Maybe," Lon said. *And maybe not.* It seemed possible that nothing would make this enemy surrender. They might have to be destroyed. "The orders are for us to wait," he reminded Girana. "We're to keep them contained if they try a breakout."

The Wester advance against Hope slowed, then stopped with the leading line nearly two hundred yards from the outer defenses. A series of land mines, planted days before, was detonated, one or two at a time, catching the attackers. The Westers turned then and concentrated their fire on Bravo Company behind them, forcing the mercenaries to stop moving in.

"Okay, we're going to slide in a little closer," Captain Orlis announced. "We want to get within two hundred yards of their flank, put more pressure on them."

Lon acknowledged the change of orders with something approaching relief. Sitting on the sidelines was hard on the nerves. Maybe they could help end the fight quickly.

The move was done slowly, on stomachs. No one wanted to alert the Westers prematurely. Lon kept an eye on the range-finder on his helmet's head-up display. If they got within two hundred yards undetected, the gunfire they would be able to add to the fray would be devastating. With bullets coming in from three sides, the Westers would have to surrender or die.

They were spotted eighty yards short of their goal. The Westers turned mortars and rifles against Alpha Company. For a few minutes the enemy seemed to concentrate exclusively on them, until Alpha had to stop. The men started to scrape out dirt to give themselves a little cover, while returning the enemy's fire.

"There's been a breakout on the other side of Hope," Captain Orlis informed Lon and Alpha's noncoms. "A battalion of the enemy broke through the line Charlie and Delta had around them. It looks like they're coming our way."

"We'd best take care of this batch in a hurry then, hadn't we?" Lon asked. "So we can get ready for the others?"

"It would be nice," Orlis agreed, "but Bravo makes the push. We just lie here and do what we can."

The range was long but not impossible. Lon had his men improve their cover. All anyone could do was scrape out a little dirt and pile it in front for a few inches of protection. Most of the enemy fire was high anyway. But enough came in at the proper height to cause casualties. The medics stayed busy.

It was the garrison of Hope that had the best vantage. Behind barricades and makeshift walls, they had a few feet of altitude, letting them fire down into the enemy. Lon looked toward Hope, then to the east, where Bravo and the new arrivals from 3rd Battalion were again trying to edge closer. *They'll have to stop eventually,* Lon thought, *before they get close enough to start taking friendly fire.*

Lon opened his mapboard and looked over the area, trying to make sense of the scattered deployments of Westers and mercenaries. Both were fragmented, dispersed on all four sides of Hope. Only the garrison of Hope presented a unified body, and they were in the center, at the focus of the battle. The militia did not have helmets with electronics that could be traced by CIC and displayed on the mapboard. But the rest of the troops could be tracked. Different-colored blips represented mercenaries, Esterling's troops, and the Westers. With the scale on the mapboard set so Lon could see the entire battlefield at once, some of the different-colored blips were so close together that they appeared to be in the same location.

"A hell of a way to run a war," Lon mumbled as he adjusted the map scale to focus on the nearest threats. If the Westers just south of Alpha turned and came toward them, it might be rough. Alpha would be outnumbered five to one—not counting the mercenaries from Bravo and 3rd Battalion who would, Lon hoped, be hot on the tail of the Westers. He scrolled the view on his mapboard around Hope slowly, looking for movement by the other contingents of the Wester army. There was one force on the south, another on the west. Both were moving around the fixed barricades of Hope, looking for either a weak point in the town's defenses or a chance to consolidate.

That's new, Lon thought. The last time he had looked, the Westers had been trying to force their way straight into Hope. Now everyone was moving. And Dirigenters were moving with the enemy, chasing, for the most part, held back by barrages of mortar fire. Lon's perusal was interrupted by soft words from Captain Orlis over the company's all-hands channel.

"Mind your front. They're moving our way."

Lon flipped his mapboard shut and slid it into the pocket designed for it on the leg of his battledress as he searched the front. The Westers were definitely coming toward Alpha, but they were moving slowly, still a disciplined unit even though they were facing enemy fire on three sides. They stayed low, crawling, fire and maneuver tactics as practiced as anything the mercenaries were capable of.

"Get the grenadiers ready as soon as the Westers come in range," Lon told his platoon sergeants. "We might not have mortars, but RPGs ought to slow them down." *And thin them out,* he thought. Weil and Tebba gave terse acknowledgments. *They probably had the men alerted already,* Lon realized. It was rare when he thought of something before his senior noncoms, both of whom had more than five times his length of service in the DMC.

"There's about a battalion right in front of us," Lon said, still on the channel that connected him to the sergeants. "We can't expect them to just fall apart because it's us they come up against. They're good, maybe as good as we are."

Neither sergeant replied to that. Captain Orlis came on-line again, to tell Lon that 3rd Battalion was the only reinforcement they could expect until 12th Regiment landed. "And that won't be until sunset tomorrow, it looks like," Orlis added. "Until then we're on our own."

I already anticipated that, Lon thought. Colonel Flowers had to keep enough troops with him. Unless they could break everyone out, he had to retain the firepower to hold off the enemy in the mountains.

Lon wiggled his body side to side a little, squirming into the dirt, looking for even a fraction of an inch of additional cover. The Westers had closed to within two hundred yards, and they had skirmishers concentrating on Alpha's positions. *They know where we are,* Lon thought. He started listening for the whine of mortar bombs, expecting them. Dreading them.

When they came, it was a sudden storm, three or four mortars working in concert, launching bombs as quickly as the gunners could load the tubes. The aim was still poor. The mortarmen were setting up, lobbing a few rounds, then moving, operating without spotters to correct their aim. The bombs went off over a wide area, many of them far enough behind Alpha's positions that they could do no harm. But a few did strike closer.

Two mortar bombs exploded almost simultaneously, eighty yards left of Lon and not more than ten yards apart. Some of the debris showered down on him. He kept his face in the dirt until the rain stopped. As soon as clods of dirt and pebbles stopped hitting around him, Lon was up and shooting again. The enemy was still moving closer.

"Lieutenant Nolan?" The voice was Lead Sergeant Ziegler's.

"What is it, Jim?" Lon asked.

"It's the captain, sir. He was hit by one of those mortar rounds. He's alive, but in pretty bad shape. The medics are with him. I guess you've got the company until he comes back. I've already informed the noncoms in second platoon."

"Right. How is second doing?" Lon used the head-up display on his faceplate to find the blip representing Ziegler.

"We're holding, sir. Taking casualties, but holding."

"Good. Same here. I'll notify battalion that the captain has been wounded. I want you to get first platoon moving toward us. Right now we need them more here than guarding our tents."

"Yes, sir. I think that's a good idea. Don't know if they'll make it in time, though." Ziegler did not mention that he had suggested that course to Captain Orlis and been turned down.

Lon made his call to battalion and spoke directly to Colonel Black. Lon told the colonel that he was bringing up the company's last platoon. "Hold as best you can there, Nolan," Black said. "I'm trying to get a couple more Shrikes in, but I don't know if they'll get here in time to help you much."

Lon switched back to the channel that connected him with the company's lead sergeant. "Jim, I want your advice. What if we pull in the men on either end of the line, give ourselves something approaching a full perimeter?"

"Might help, sir, if we can do it fast enough," Ziegler said. "The way we're laying now, all they've got to do is run right over us and pick us off as they go. We've got no depth but the one squad in each platoon we've had trailing, and no flanks."

"Do it. You start second platoon around on your side, three squads at least. I'll do the same with fourth on this side."

Alpha's grenadiers launched their first salvo of grenades just then, as the enemy came to within 120 yards. Lon called Weil Jorgen and told him to start pulling his men around—the three squads that were on the front.

"We can't stop the Westers in a line, but maybe we can put up enough fire that they'll flow around us," Lon said. He switched back to his channel to Jim Ziegler. "It looks as if first platoon is too far back to reach us before the Westers do. I'm going to redirect first east. Maybe they can hook up with Bravo if they can't reach us. If we can't hold, first would be hung out to dry if they're on their own."

"Can I make a suggestion, Lieutenant?" Ziegler asked.

"Anytime."

"Let first platoon set up behind us, maybe a little to one side or the other. If we're overrun, they can stay put as an ambush. Even if we go down, we're going to slow the Westers. That and an ambush from first platoon ought to give the rest of our people time to close in on the Westers."

It might mean sacrificing first platoon as well as the rest of the company, Lon thought, but he realized that Ziegler would have taken that into consideration. Lon hesitated for only an instant before he said, "Okay, set it up."

I get command of a company for the first time, and it looks as if maybe the only thing I can do is watch it be destroyed, Lon thought, in grim appreciation of the situation.

"Pull the lines in tighter," he ordered, connecting to all of the platoon sergeants. "Let's give them the nearest thing to a solid wall we can." It was a trade-off. Bringing the men closer would leave them more vulnerable to mortars and grenades, but they would present a tougher surface. *If we're going to make them break around us, this is the only thing that can help.*

The company's grenadiers were firing as quickly as possible, expending five-round clips in seconds, then reloading. There was no sense in trying to conserve ammunition—not to leave it for the enemy. Lon was slow to notice that the enemy's mortars had stopped. The mortarmen were moving forward with the rest of their troops and were too close to Alpha. They could not elevate their weapons enough to drop the rounds that close.

Lon loaded a fresh magazine into his rifle and set another full one on the ground within easy reach. He reached along his side and unsnapped the flap on his pistol holster. Before long the fight would get close enough for that.

"Fix bayonets," Lon ordered when the leading Westers were within a hundred yards. He let off several short bursts of rifle fire before he obeyed his own order.

Second and fourth platoons had finished pivoting to the sides. Lon directed the rearmost squad of each closer in, toward the center. Everyone was still facing south, but the men on the flanks could turn quickly enough if the enemy went around the human blockade. And the squads that had originally been trailing the skirmish line could turn to face north, or either flank, wherever their fire might be most useful.

As the distance between Alpha and the enemy continued to decrease—with extreme slowness now—the number of casualties on both sides increased. Inside one hundred yards, even prone men were highly vulnerable. There was nowhere to go, no way to escape, for either side. Behind and to the right of the Westers, other mercenaries were moving closer, trying to take pressure off of Alpha, but it was not clear to Lon that they could arrive soon enough to do anything but count bodies and administer first aid to anyone who survived.

"Sara, I love you," Lon whispered after switching off his transmitter, just for that instant.

The enemy was ninety yards away when their skirmish line got up and started running forward, abandoning the illusion of safety on the ground to close quickly, firing as they came, rifles on full automatic, profligate with ammunition. Lon's men were equally abandoned, firing entire clips at once, panning back and forth across narrow kill zones directly in front of them. The enemy was too close for many misses, but no matter how many Westers fell, there seemed to be as many ready to take their places.

"They're not going around," Lon said on the circuit that connected him to Alpha's noncoms. "They're going to try to run right over us."

"Nolan, there are two Shrikes coming in, but it's going to be five minutes before they arrive," Colonel Black said, breaking into Lon's words to his noncoms. "Can you hold that long?"

"They'll be all over us in five minutes, Colonel, maybe past us," Lon said.

"Hang tough. Bravo and a company from 3rd Battalion will hit them from the east in thirty seconds."

Thirty seconds or thirty years. It won't make much difference to us, Lon thought. *Nolan's Last Stand.* A man could run eighty yards in fifteen seconds, even burdened by a full load of combat gear and firing a rifle. Lon raised up to give himself a better angle of fire, holding down the trigger of his rifle until the bolt stayed back over an empty magazine. By the time he had a new magazine fitted, and the bolt run to put the first round in the chamber, the enemy was forty yards away, close enough to be in range of hand grenades. Except for the men who carried RPG launchers, every enlisted man carried two hand grenades. Those were used freely now, and they did slow the enemy down . . . but only momentarily. Westers fell. More moved forward into the front line and came on.

If a battalion of Westers had started the assault on Alpha Company, fewer than half were still able to fight when they closed with Lon and his men. Alpha's men stayed on the ground until the enemy was fifteen yards away. Then Lon gave the order to get up and close with the enemy. It was time for bayonets and fists.

Lon stood with his men, rifle in his right hand, pistol in the left, firing both. He dropped the pistol when the magazine was empty and moved toward the nearest Wester with his bayonet. He parried the Wester's initial thrust with the butt of his rifle, then pivoted left and slashed with the blade of his own bayonet. The Wester countered and the two men came face to face, their weapons pressing against each other. Lon pushed forward and brought a knee up into his opponent's groin. As the man doubled over, Lon kneed him again, in the head, knocking the man's helmet off. As the Wester fell backward, Lon brought his rifle around and fired a three-shot burst into him—the muzzle no more than eighteen inches from the Wester's chest.

Another Wester was coming. Lon had no time to get turned and set to meet him. He dove to the ground and rolled, coming back to his feet behind this new Wester, who had turned and started at Lon again. A bullet from the side dropped the Wester, but Lon had no idea who had fired the shot.

Lon moved toward the nearest of his own men, and the enemy. There were scores of individual fights going on, a tangle that confused the sides. Only the pattern of battle-dress camouflage and the shape of helmets allowed any-one to tell friend from foe.

At first Lon did not notice the additional DMC uni-forms coming from the left, behind the Westers. Three or four minutes passed before the remaining Westers in this section of the greater battle realized that they were in a hopeless position and started to surrender—one or two at a time.

Lon stood as he had been, his rifle at port arms, numb, almost as if he were waiting for another enemy. He was conscious only of the heaving of his own breath, and the exertion and fear he had been unable to feel during the fight.

"Lieutenant?" Lon did not respond, did not really hear the voice or notice the Dirigenter standing right next to him.

"Lon?" He blinked, turning his head slowly. He still needed time to realize that he was being addressed, and to recognize the voice of the man next to him.

"What is it, Phip?" he asked.

"You're bleeding." Steesen gestured toward Lon's left arm.

Lon looked down. There was a gash across his upper arm. He reached across with his other arm to touch the wound. His hand came away bloody. "I guess I am," he said, dully. He felt no pain, nothing. "Is it over?"

"It is here. Bravo and the lads from 3rd got to us. I guess the rest are still fighting."

How many men do I have left? Lon wondered, but what he asked was, "Dean?" Phip and Dean were the two closest friends he had left among the enlisted personnel of the company.

"He's cut up a little, but he'll be okay," Phip said.

"We got hurt bad tonight, Phip," Lon said, knowing he should start checking with his sergeants, Ziegler and the platoon sergeants, to find out how badly. But he had to concentrate on this first. Phip was right in front of him.

"We did," Phip agreed, "but we did ourselves proud. Let me put a patch on that arm, Lieutenant, before you lose more blood."

Lon started to wave off Phip's offer of help. There were undoubtedly others who needed attention more. But the wave did not get completed. Vision closed in on Lon and he passed out, almost hitting the ground before Phip could catch him.

27

There had been a dream, but it fled too rapidly for Lon to grasp even the vaguest sense of what it had been about when he woke. He blinked several times before he realized he didn't know where he was. What had happened was slow to present its fractured memories. Then there was surprise. Lon had not wakened in a trauma tube, ready to be released from treatment. He was on a cot. There was light around him, but not bright enough to hurt his eyes. Lon was not surprised to see Lead Sergeant Jim Ziegler standing at the foot of his bed, but the presence next to Ziegler of Major Esterling was unexpected.

"Welcome back, Lieutenant," Esterling said.

Lon blinked several times. Words were slow to form in his mind, slower to reach his mouth. "What happened?"

"They had too many people waiting for trauma tubes, Lieutenant," Ziegler said. "The way the medtech explained it, they kept you in the bare minimum necessary, then sedated you and moved you to a bed. You had a bad gash on your arm, and some smaller cuts from shrapnel. They said you lost a lot of blood." The medtech had been more emphatic than that, but Ziegler was not ready to tell Lon just how close his call had been. "But you'll be all right now, sir. Good as new."

"The company?" Lon asked.

"Bad enough, Lieutenant, but not as bad as we thought it was going to be. Twelve dead, sixty-seven wounded, forty-two bad enough to need time in a tube, and twelve will need regen and rehab time before they return to duty."

Lon blinked once. "Captain Orlis?"

"Back aboard *Long Snake*. Lost part of an arm and leg. He's one of the people needing double-R."

Finally Lon shifted his gaze back to Esterling. "Sorry to ignore you like that, Major, but I had to know about my people."

"Of course you did," Esterling said. "I'd have done the same if it were the prime minister wanting my attention. You and your lads did a bang-up job. One of the most remarkable feats of soldiering I ever hope to see."

"Is it over?" Lon asked.

Esterling shrugged. "Our piece of it—for now, at least. There are a few small bands of Westers running loose, but not close. Your people are chasing them down, last I heard. And your reinforcements will be on the ground in another three hours or so, so maybe the rest of it will end soon as well."

"Three hours?" Lon asked. "Just what time is it?"

"After eighteen hundred hours, Lieutenant," Ziegler said.

"I've been out, what, about fifteen hours?"

"Something like that. Like I said, sir, they could only give you the minimum time in a tube. The rest you've been in bed here with the medbugs building new blood for you and finishing the patch job on your wounds."

"The medtech should be along to check you out any minute now, Lieutenant," Major Esterling said. Your people and mine have been working together—rather well, I must say. It's only been in the past hour or so that some of them have been able to get off their feet for a few minutes."

"How did you make out in Hope?" Lon asked. He glanced to either side. Since he was in a building and not a tent, he assumed he was in the town.

Esterling chuckled in anticipation of the pun he could not resist. "We never lost Hope. Not one of the Westers got through . . . not until he was a prisoner and the battle was over. I've no fault to find with my own men or with the civilian militia, but our safety was, in large measure, due to your people. Without your lads we'd have been overrun for sure.''

"Casualties?'' Lon asked.

"Not as many as there might have been were we fighting alone, or if your people had been less . . . valiant, Lieutenant.''

"I do want to thank you for coming to see me, Major,'' Lon said. "And I don't want to sound ungracious, but right now my greatest desire is to find a medtech to let me out of here. I've got men to see to.''

The major grinned. "I'll see if I can't scare one up. I hope we get to talk again before you leave Aldrin.''

"I do also. When I can set duty aside a little better.''

Esterling left the room. Lon started to sit up, waving Ziegler around to the side of the bed as he moved. "Who has the company now?'' Lon asked.

"Well, sir, I've been minding the store until you get back. Since we're out of the fighting, Colonel Black said he couldn't spare an officer to baby-sit us while you napped.''

Lon shrugged. If Alpha Company was out of the fighting, they might actually leave him in charge until the regiment returned to Dirigent and permanent changes could be made. "Are the men here in town, or back out at our previous luxury retreat?''

"In town, sir. Still in tents, but we're right in the plaza now, in the middle of everything.''

"It can wait until we get out of here, but I'm going to want the casualty lists first off. Then talk to the platoon sergeants and squad leaders. Have I got anything to wear but this hospital throwaway?'' Lon asked, looking at the disposable gown he was in.

"Yes, sir. On the chair, t'other side of the bed. I'll get them,'' Ziegler said. "But don't you think you should wait until the medtech makes it official?''

"Probably, but if he's not here pretty damned fast, I'm going to start without him. Him?'' He looked at Ziegler.

"All I've seen in here were men, Lieutenant. Dispensary in the military compound.'' Ziegler grinned. "I've had complaints from a few of the men about that. Seems getting fixed up isn't enough for some of them. They want pretty nurses, too.''

The medtech insisted that Lon drink a tall glass of orange juice before he would release him. "It helps, sir," the medtech said. "Really it does." Lon was not certain about that. He still felt weak when he left the dispensary with Sergeant Ziegler at his side. It would not have been like that if he had spent a full four hours in the trauma tube. He would have wakened about ready for anything if that had been the case.

On the walk to the company's new bivouac, two hundred yards from the garrison's compound, Ziegler named the company's dead. He did not have to consult his portable complink. Lon listened to the slow roster. "They've already been transported up to *Long Snake*," Ziegler concluded, "along with the others the battalion lost." Both men were carrying their helmets rather than wearing them. Lon had not asked where his weapons were. He assumed they were being looked after.

"If trouble comes, how prepared are we to meet it?" Lon asked when they reached the tent that was the company command post. It had been Captain Orlis's tent. Now it was Lon's.

"We've got ammunition. We can muster four platoons, though they're all shorthanded," Ziegler said. "By morning we'll be in better shape, with the last of the wounded back from treatment, those not shipped up for double-R. And everyone will have a little more sleep by then. That puts the last fight farther back in the head, if you know what I mean."

"I know," Lon said quietly. Like a nightmare after waking, the horror of the battle would fade . . . but never completely.

Lon sat at the folding table in the front half of the tent. Ziegler slid a complink in front of him, keyed to the casualty lists. While Lon was looking through those, Ziegler took out a meal pack, opened it to start it self-heating, and set in on the table next to the complink.

"The medtech said to make sure you get plenty to eat tonight and in the morning," Ziegler explained when Lon glanced up. "He said whether you want it or not." He pulled a canteen from a box on the floor and set it on the table as well. "Filled fresh this afternoon, here in town."

"As soon as I finish these lists," Lon said quietly. *I don't want to eat while I'm reading about our dead and wounded.*

He had not finished eating when a call came from Colonel Black. "Come on over to my HQ if you're feeling fit," Black said. "Your lead sergeant can tell you where to find it."

Lon asked Ziegler after the colonel had disconnected. "Yes, sir. The colonel's got himself fixed up real good. The locals here let him use the back room at the pub. Swear to God, Lieutenant," Ziegler added when he saw the look of disbelief on Lon's face. "Got its own door, over on the side, just about due east from where we are now."

Lon nodded slowly. "I remember where it is. I'll want to talk to the platoon sergeants when I get back, and the squad leaders, too, if it isn't too late. Has battalion said whether we're supposed to mount sentries or anything?"

"Nothing was said, Lieutenant. I figured on two men at a time, plus a corporal here to keep us posted if anything happens. It's just us and Delta in town. Bravo and Charlie are still outside, along with 3rd Battalion, but 3rd is ready to move north, set to land just behind the shuttles from 12th Regiment."

Lon found his way to the side door of the pub without difficulty. A tent had been set up just outside. Battalion Lead Sergeant Zal Osier was in the doorway of the tent, talking to one of his clerks.

"Glad to see you up again, Lieutenant," Osier said. "The colonel is expecting you, sir. Just go right on in."

Lon said thanks, then turned the doorknob and went into the pub's back room—now battalion headquarters.

"Come on in, Nolan," Colonel Black said, looking up from the table he was working on. "You fit?"

"Yes, sir, good as new," Lon said.

"Good, good," Black said, nodding his acceptance of the lie. "Have a seat. If you feel up to it, I'll ring for the landlord and see if we can't get a beer or something."

"A beer would go down nicely, Colonel," Lon said, grinning in spite of himself. "Very nicely."

Black ordered the beers. "Orlis is going to be out of action for at least two months," the colonel said while they were waiting for their drinks. "Damned inconvenient, especially after Alpha lost Hoper and O'Fallon, but there's nothing to do but make the best of it." He shook his head. "Hard luck all around for your lads," he said, more softly.

Black postponed the official talk until they had sampled their drinks and expressed approval of the beer, brewed right on the premises. "Brewed, not replicated," Black said. "That gives it high marks indeed to come out this well," Black told the landlord before he left.

"I don't like to do any unnecessary shuffling around of personnel," Black said when he and Lon were alone again. "Shift people around here, then have to shift again when we get back to Dirigent and do more permanent reorganization. Bad for morale if men get to thinking they've got their officer for a week or what. So, for now, I'm leaving Alpha in your hands. You assumed command in battle when your captain became a casualty, all good and proper. I see no reason to change that before we get back to Dirigent. Orlis will still be taking up his position as my full-time adjutant when he returns to duty. I can't give you two platoon leaders, though, just one lieutenant from Charlie Company, Jeb Rogers. He's junior to you by a year or so."

"I know Jeb fairly well, Colonel. I'm sure we can work together without difficulty."

"I don't know how much longer the mess here is going to last. We hurt West badly last night. They're out three battalions of good soldiers, killed, captured, or broken into small units on the run. The rest of the regiment has hurt West as well, up in the mountains. With any luck, we've had our bit of fighting for this contract, but I can't give any guarantees. You'll have to keep your men ready for whatever comes.''

''Alpha has good men, Colonel.''

Black's harrumph seemed so predictable that Lon almost laughed when it came. ''There is one other thing, Nolan,'' the colonel said, not meeting Lon's eyes. ''In the dispatches and so forth that 12th brought out there was one item that might interest you. Corps finally vetted your marriage application. You can go ahead with the wedding as soon as we get home, whenever that is.''

Lon blinked once, absorbing the news. ''Thank you, sir.''

Now all we have to do is get home, Lon thought as he walked back to Alpha's command post—*his* CP. But the prospect of an early return followed by a quick marriage left him with mixed feelings. He was still eager for the wedding, but . . . *As soon as we get back to Dirigent, they'll bring in a new commander for the company.* A captain or a senior lieutenant who was due promotion. The odds were strongly against a lieutenant with only three years in rank being left in command of a company.

Lead Sergeant Ziegler was waiting when Lon got back. ''The colonel has decided to leave me in command of Alpha until we get home,'' Lon said. ''Captain Orlis still moves to battalion when he's fit again.''

Ziegler nodded. ''It's the only way he can make major.''

''There is that,'' Lon agreed, nodding back. ''Lieutenant Rogers is coming over from Charlie. He'll have first and second platoons. I'll double as leader for third and fourth. That keeps the disruptions to a minimum.'' *And paves the way for whoever they bring over to take over when we get home,* he thought. He could go quietly back to simply being the leader of his same two platoons.

''Lieutenant Rogers should be here almost any minute,

sir," Ziegler said. "I had a call from the lead sergeant over to Charlie to let me know he was on his way."

"Is there a tent set up for him?"

"In the works now, Lieutenant. I put three men on it soon as I got the word. Over with first and second platoons."

Lon smiled. "Someday I'm going to have to find out how sergeants get to be psychics, Jim."

Ziegler grinned. "Trade secret, sir. You have to *be* a sergeant to find out."

Jeb Rogers arrived fifteen minutes later. "They couldn't find transportation, so I walked," he told Lon as soon as he had "officially" reported. Rogers was several inches taller than Lon and just as lanky. He looked like, and was, a distance runner. That was how Lon had met him, on the track at camp on Dirigent. He was two years younger than Lon.

"We *are* foot soldiers, Jeb. Take a load off." The two men sat in the tent, Lon on the edge of his bunk, Jeb on the chair. Lon explained the situation and the chain of command. "You're getting good men, but we've all had a rough fight."

"I know. My old CO gave me a complete briefing on the spot you were in last night; then he gave me the news to pack my kit and move."

"Your platoon sergeants will be along in a couple of minutes. I'll introduce you, and you can go off and get acquainted with your men. With 12th Regiment about to land and our 3rd Battalion going north, maybe West will come to its senses and we won't have any more fighting of our own on this contract."

"We can hope," Jeb said.

It was barely twenty-four hours later when that hope was dashed.

28

Second Battalion's shuttles landed south of Hope just after sunset. Colonel Black had just completed his officers' call for the battalion, and given the officers time to get back to their company with the news.

"Our job is to neutralize their number two air base," Lon told the men of Alpha Company. "It's just outside Port Orca, eighty miles west of their capital. If fleet intelligence is anywhere near correct, they have only minimal ground assets to guard the aircraft and support facilities. The troops normally stationed there are in the east, involved in the fighting in the mountains. Our opposition should be, at most, one company of regular infantry, perhaps a company of the air wing's ground support crews, and a few odds and ends." *I hope it's not more than that,* Lon thought. *We're not up to handling much more.*

Colonel Black had skirted the same thought in his briefing. "It may be too soon for an offensive landing like this, but the Westers seem to be settling in for a fight, and our regimental commanders decided that the more pressure we put on rapidly, the better the odds of changing their minds. We go in tonight. If necessary, East will bring a battalion of troops across the mountains in Corps shuttles tomorrow evening for a landing near the Wester capital. The idea is still to force negotiations, but it now looks as if the Westers may need a lot of persuasion."

"You've got forty-five minutes to eat and get ready to leave," Lon told the company. "Don't forget the meal. Hard telling when breakfast will be."

Then he went over the plan of attack on mapboards with Jeb Rogers, Jim Ziegler, and the platoon sergeants. The latter would brief their squad leaders, who were getting their men ready. "We come in northeast of the air base, deploy our initial perimeter, then move against the hangars and barracks." Lon indicated each of the salient points on his mapboard, a cursor on each of the other mapboards slaved to his so there could be no mistakes.

"There's only one bridge across this river that runs between Port Orca and the air base," Lon noted, his cursor lingering on the bridge. "We can't count on Shrike support for the landing, though Colonel Black said we might have two to cover us against air attack. That means we've got to take care of the bridge ourselves." Lon shrugged. "The last shuttle in, from Delta, will launch rockets at the bridge before it lands. The way the timing goes, those rockets should be hitting as we're landing."

"A wake-up call for the locals," Jeb Rogers said. "If they don't see us coming, they'll know we're there when the bridge blows."

"It may cause enough confusion to give us a break-through," Lon said. "We'll be coming in on the far side of the base, two miles in the opposite direction. If they think the explosions mark where the attack is coming, it could give us a few minutes unhindered to deploy. And the rest of the shuttles will hit the buildings inside the air base after they drop us off, unless they're running from enemy fighters."

After the platoon sergeants went back to their platoons, Lon ate his own supper with Jeb and Jim.

"You'd have thought that the colonels would have given West more time to digest their situation before ordering us in," Rogers said. "Hell, it's politicians who need to figure out that they can't win. They need more than one day to jawbone themselves into realizing what they're up against."

Lon shrugged. He had no real argument with what Jeb said. "Maybe the colonels don't want to give the enemy time to regroup, not after the fight they've been putting up,'' he said.

''Cuts both ways, sir,'' Jim Ziegler said. ''We wait, and maybe the Westers have time to convince themselves that maybe they hurt us so bad we'll be extra careful, and maybe they can talk their way into a better deal.''

Lon boarded a shuttle as company commander for the first time. The knot in his stomach felt the size of his battle helmet. *Don't let me fail my men,* Lon thought, his eyes held closed for an instant behind the tinted faceplate of his helmet. It was as close to a prayer as he could come. There was a final check from Colonel Black before the shuttles were buttoned up, ready for takeoff. Lon checked with Rogers and Ziegler. The platoon sergeants and squad leaders were tending to their men. Lon stayed out of that. He had already given his own brief pep talk.

When the shuttle pilot gave Lon a warning that takeoff would be in thirty seconds, Lon passed it along and gave a final tug to his safety harness to make certain it was as snug as possible. The entire flight would be atmospheric, hopping hedges and wavetops. The plan was for the flight to head southwest until the shuttles were well out to sea, then curve around to come in on Port Orca from the northwest, low and hot. Riding at low altitudes, fast, in a shuttle could be bumpy. It was not what they were designed for, and atmospheric turbulence could buffet passengers around badly.

There were too many empty seats in the shuttle. Each of the craft was designed to hold two platoons and part of the headquarters detachment. Neither of Alpha's shuttles would be full for this trip. As his lander made its short takeoff run, Lon tried not to look at the empty places, but could not keep his eyes from them. And he could not stop the thought *How many more will be empty when we finish this fight tonight?* He did not wonder if his seat would be one of the empty ones. It never occurred to him to worry about his own survival. Going from being the junior lieutenant in Alpha Company to being its commander had happened too fast, and in the worst way.

As soon as the shuttle was up and on its way, Lon pulled out his mapboard and started going over the terrain at the other end of the flight. There had been too little time to study the charts. Lon liked to go in knowing the land as if he had been there before. But he had never heard the name Port Orca until Colonel Black had said they were going in. Tonight.

The town was not right on the ocean, but several miles up a small river. Port Orca was on high ground, with the wharves for its fishing fleet fifty feet lower, at the base of a fifty-degree rock slope. The river ran through a gorge. There was a fifty-foot cliff on the north side. *That means they can't easily use floaters*—ground effect vehicles—*to get across if the bridge is blown,* Lon thought, nodding in minor satisfaction. *They'll have to go ten miles up-stream to find a slope gentle enough to get floaters down and back up.* For a time, at least, the battalion would have to face only whatever opposition might already be north of the river.

Most of the area on that side was forested. From the views he could find through his mapboard, Lon saw that there were no more than half a dozen farms there, and a small cluster of buildings near the base that might be the local equivalent of Camo Town—bars and so forth to service the garrison.

The clearing where the battalion's attack shuttles would set down was the only one of any size—except for the runway inside the base. *It's a wonder we don't set down right there,* Lon thought. *Right in the middle. Establish our perimeter and just push them out or run them over.* It was not, Lon realized with little more thought, really a good idea. No commander likes the idea of being surrounded, and starting out that way, in the center of an enemy base, would be right only under very restricted circumstances.

Lon had plenty of time to study the charts, cranking the mapboard to its maximum magnification, going over the ground where the battalion would land and the routes to the air base almost yard by yard. He made preliminary plans for the deployment of his men—subject to the vagaries of whatever opposition they met. For an infantryman, the terrain was much less intimidating than the open savanna around Hope. North of Port Orca the ground was rolling and forested, with plenty of cover once they got away from that one large clearing. *If we move fast, we could be on them before they know we're coming. If they're not expecting trouble, we might be able to roll them over before they can get their rifles from the armory.* Assuming they were stored the way they might be in garrison, under lock and key, unloaded. There might be no more than a dozen men on guard duty with loaded rifles, a few officers with pistols.

Maybe, but don't count on it, Lon reminded himself. *They know they're at war.*

The journey was more than half over before Lon glanced at one of the bulkhead monitors showing the terrain below the shuttles. They were over the ocean, in the dark, only highlights showing up even with infrared. Lon looked around the compartment then. Few of his men were watching the monitors. *I don't know if that's good or bad,* he thought. He hadn't noticed any particular signs of poor morale before leaving. No one had seemed quite as "up" as they had been at the start of the contract, but that was normal. They had been through a lot.

Coastline. Waves breaking against the shore. Lon received a warning from the pilot, then relayed the news to the men with him. "We're three minutes out," Lon said. "Lock and load. Let's do this by the numbers, as quickly as we can."

The monitors showed the scene directly in front of the shuttles now. There was little sky visible. The shuttles were coming in below the crest of the bluffs overlooking the sea. Lon felt his stomach lurch when the lander climbed sharply to get over the bluffs. The view of sea and rock changed abruptly to a forest of green flashing by far too rapidly—vastly inflating the feeling of speed.

Lon closed his eyes for an instant, and did not look directly at the monitor when he opened them again.

The shuttle's crew chief provided a countdown of the last sixty seconds before landing. Lon wished his noncoms a routine "Good luck."

Then the shuttle was on the ground, skidding to a quick stop with its engines at full reverse, shaking the craft so much that Lon felt his cheeks vibrating. He did not hear the explosions he assumed were taking out the bridge to Port Orca, but any blast would have to be almost on top of the shuttle to be heard over the engine and other noises of landing.

Lon slapped the release on his safety harness as soon as he had rebounded from the last lurch against it as the shuttle ground to a halt. "Up and out!" he called on the all-hands channel, the way he had often enough as platoon leader. "We've got a perimeter to establish."

Even with so many men missing from the company's ranks, this deployment went as smoothly as a drill. It was a task they practiced often, getting out of the box and into position to defend themselves. "The box" could be a deadly place to get caught, with men unable to do anything to defend themselves or escape if the lander was hit.

Ninety seconds after Lon released his safety harness, Alpha Company's section of the perimeter was complete, the men facing out, lying on the ground, weapons protruding, leaving room for the shuttles to make their hasty exit. The crews of the landers wanted to get to safety as quickly as they could, out of the reach first of enemy surface-to-air missiles and away from any fighters that might come hunting them.

"Hold fast while the shuttles take off," Lon reminded his men. Like many of them, he lowered his head until his faceplate was in the dirt as the sound of so many shuttle jets revved up to maximum and they took off. Not one of them had been on the ground for three full minutes.

Nothing about enemy fighters coming in, Lon thought as the din faded. *That means they should be able to make their pass at the buildings on the base before they burn for orbit.*

Spreading confusion would be almost as much help as the destruction and casualties the rockets might create. The order came through to get the battalion up and moving.

Alpha and Bravo moved on the left flank. The other two companies were on the right, two hundred yards away. Within the columns the companies moved in well-dispersed fashion, men four abreast. Skirmish lines would not be formed until they reached the air base or came under fire. The pace was rapid at the start. The leading elements of Alpha were only eight hundred yards from the air base's perimeter fence when they started.

The explosions, ahead and to the right, started before the battalion had fully formed for the short march. Pillars of flame and illuminated smoke were visible through and above the trees. At least two buildings continued to burn, adding a flickering illumination to the night.

Lon moved at the side of his company, watching his men as much as he watched the forest off to the side, occasionally talking to a platoon sergeant or squad leader. A squad from second platoon was alerted to move ahead as scouts, to cut holes in the base's perimeter fence if it was undefended, and the fence could not be *closely* defended unless there were far more troops present than they had been led to believe. "Probably no more than sentries every fifty or a hundred yards, if that," Lon told the squad leader. "But don't take that for granted."

Cut through the perimeter if it's not tightly defended. Cut loose platoons to roll over any sentry posts while most of the battalion tackles the barracks and whatever defense they manage. Destroy any aircraft on the ground, and as much of the support facilities as possible. Colonel Black's directions had been brief if somewhat vague. Each platoon carried a few extra charges of explosives for the destruction of enemy assets.

For Lon, the first few minutes were the worst. Then his tension eased instead of increasing. He felt, if not relaxed, at least comfortably in command of himself. He even noticed the smells of the forest, something quite familiar, like the pine forests of the Great Smoky Mountains near his childhood home, a resinous fragrance in the damp. Damp. And cool. The temperature was just under sixty degrees, a decided relief after the tropical savanna.

"Send your scouts out and slow the advance to give them a chance," Colonel Black instructed by radio. "There's no sign of any significant force along the base's perimeter. A couple of guard towers in our path. One directly in front of you. Have your scouts take that out if they can get to it."

Lon acknowledged the orders. "Send a man with a rocket launcher along with the scouts," he told Jeb Rogers. "Let's get that tower fast."

Except for the scouts, the battalion took a four-minute rest, men dropping to the ground behind the nearest cover, waiting almost motionless. Keyed up. Ready for action.

Four minutes. Lon started his men forward again. They moved more slowly, segueing into skirmish lines. Lon shifted into his own proper position behind third and fourth platoons, near the center of the formation now that he had the entire company. Three squads up front, one behind. That was the formation for each platoon except the one that had the scouts out. They were two and one.

Lon heard the explosion of the rocket in front of his company, then the quick report from the squad leader that the tower was down and the fence was being cut to drop a fifty-yard-wide section. "We're using little boomers to drop the fence posts," the corporal said.

Three minutes later, all of Alpha was at the fence line, inside the base. Bravo sent two platoons to the left to chase any sentries or guard posts along the way, and the other two platoons moved straight across toward the far side of the base, ready to string its own sentries along that line, cutting the base in half.

The forest ended fifty yards outside the fence line. Lon noted that the locals had not cut down the cover far enough. They had never made contingency plans for a ground attack against the base. If they had, there would have been at least three hundred yards of ground cleared around it.

There were no trees inside the fence line. It was an *air* base. There was only one paved runway—Aldrinian shuttles and fighters had wheels rather than skids—with two parallel taxiways. The buildings were all at the south end of the base, along the sides of the compound, hangars and maintenance sheds to the south, barracks and offices on the north.

"Okay, Nolan, start bringing your people west, angle about thirty degrees to the left, toward the hangars," Colonel Black ordered. "We're just starting to hit opposition."

Lon could hear rifle fire in the direction of the barracks and offices. "We're on our way, Colonel," he said.

As soon as the skirmish lines could be turned, the company started along the new heading, across ground that was flat and offered no cover. *Hell of a place to get caught in a firefight,* Lon thought before they had covered fifty yards. *Not even a tall blade of grass to hide behind.*

Alpha Company moved at a slow jog. No one needed to be told to hurry. Their goal was the cluster of hangars and maintenance sheds another three hundred yards away. One of those buildings was smoking from a rocket hit, but from this distance Lon saw no sign that any of the other buildings in the group had even been hit.

He could see muzzle flashes at the other corner of the base, rifles flickering on full automatic, and he could hear the gunfire. "Keep low," he warned on his all-hands channel. "Some of that stuff is liable to reach us." They would be moving into the angle of fire from Charlie and Delta Companies before they reached their own target.

The skirmish line was within two hundred yards of the nearest hangar when Lon noticed a few scattered muzzle flashes coming from just in front of it. *A single squad, if that,* he realized almost faster than his mind could reason through the data. "Take them under fire but keep going," he ordered. "Not more than a handful, probably mechanics who couldn't hit the broad side of one of those hangars from the inside.''

As soon as Alpha started to return fire, the shooting from the hangar stopped. Lon saw a couple of figures start to run, but neither got very far.

"Jeb, take your platoons around to the left. We'll go the other way. I want a quick look inside each building before we start planting the charges."

"I always did like blowing things up," Rogers replied.

Lon was within fifty yards of the first hangar when gunfire started coming from inside it, through the open aircraft door in the center of the near wall. This was more than just a handful of men, and they were close enough that even mechanics could not avoid hitting some of the available targets.

Suckered! Lon thought as he dove to the ground. "Put a couple of rockets in there. See if there's anything flammable left," he told Weil Jorgen. "Jeb, get your men down. We're going to blow this sucker now." First and second platoons were moving around behind the building. They had to be warned.

It took only a few seconds for men with rocket launchers to set up and do their work. Lon watched the rocket trails head inside, saw the blast of their warheads . . . and then the subsequent eruption of a fuel tank blew the hangar apart.

Flame and debris rained down on Alpha Company. All anyone could do was lie flat, pulled in as tight as possible, and hope that nothing large or particularly hot hit. There were casualties, but—luckily—no fatalities in the company. The same could not be said for however many men had been inside. Little would ever be found of them, certainly not enough for a definitive body count.

"Jeb, how much of that crap hit you?" Lon asked as soon as he had a chance to think of anything but what he could see.

"Too much, but I think we're okay. I'll let you know as soon as we can check our wounded."

"Move out farther. We'll take out the rest of these

buildings the same way. Get it done fast.'' *The hell with looking inside*, he thought. *It's not worth risking lives for.*

"Suits me."

The series of explosions seemed to have an effect on the fighting in the other corner of the base. Each blast muffled the distant rifle fire, but after the last explosion waned, the gunfire slacked off as well. The remaining members of the base's garrison had surrendered.

29

It took three more days for the government of Aldrin West to ask for a truce and agree to binding talks with East, but the fighting was over for 2nd Battalion. No effort was made by the Westers to retake the air base at Port Orca. The early negotiations were not easy. A full month passed before they had progressed far enough for the commanders of the two Dirigenter regiments to decide that 12th Regiment could maintain the truce alone. Seventh Regiment had arrived first and faced the enemy longer. It would go home. A few Shrikes were left from the contingent that had accompanied 7th. They transferred to the fighter carrier that had come with the reinforcements.

There was a parade across Dirigent City from the civilian spaceport to the Corps' main base. It was pure chance that Lon was looking out the window on the proper side of the bus when it turned to go through the main gate. The shock of red hair caught his attention. At first he could not believe his eyes, certain that he must only have imagined that Sara Pine was standing by the gate, looking anxiously at each bus that passed her. Then she saw him in the window and jumped up and down, waving both arms.

Lon's reaction was totally improper, perhaps unprecedented in the annals of the DMC. He jumped to his feet and shouted, "Stop the bus!" The driver, no doubt startled half out of his wits by the outburst, hit the brake before he had a chance to think what he was doing or why. As Lon started toward the exit, he turned to Lead

Sergeant Jim Ziegler. "I'll be along as fast as I can. Get the men settled in."

Ziegler had time to do no more than nod, puzzlement obvious on his face. He did, however, see Sara Pine throw herself into Lon's arms outside the bus before the driver started the vehicle forward again.

Lon hardly noticed the cheer that went up from the men on the bus. His men.

"I just got here yesterday," Sara said as soon as there was time for coherent words. They had moved inside the gate, but no farther. "I came as soon as I found out your regiment was on its way home."

"We can get married as soon as we set things up," Lon said. "They finally got all the red tape tied up."

"Daddy can have everything ready in two days," Sara said.

It was a small wedding, even for Bascombe East. Although quite a few residents of the village were present, Lon was represented by only a handful of people. Phip and Dean were there, as were Janno and his wife. Captain Orlis came, though he was still not back on duty status, using a cane to help him walk on his new leg. The wedding was in the village's only church. The reception was in the pub, but spilled out along the sidewalk and into the street. That did not matter. There was not enough traffic to make it hazardous.

"Thanks for coming, Captain," Lon told Orlis when they finally had a chance to talk alone for a minute, an hour or more into the reception. "It means a lot to me."

Matt Orlis shrugged. "I wouldn't have missed it for anything. Colonel Black asked me to offer his regrets. He wanted to come but couldn't. He asked me to deliver a wedding present."

"A present?" Lon asked.

Orlis nodded. "It's not really a wedding present. That just makes a good excuse. The real reasons can wait until later.'' He reached out to the side, and Phip Steesen handed him a small box.

''The next time you appear in uniform, you'd best have these on,'' Orlis said, opening the box to display a pair of dress insignia—a captain's pips. ''You've earned them at full rate.''